"Frank told you w   g
me a statement, not a question.

"All he said was that Trey Kinsale had been killed, and
Crystal Walker did it."

"Trey was in her shed . . . with at least twenty stab
wounds. Bled everywhere . . . and Crystal's confessing.
I'm appointing you to represent her."

"I'm not practicing law these days, in case you hadn't
noticed. . . . I'll call some friends from the city, see if
they're interested."

"Like hell, Talbot. The way I see it, Crystal Walker's already at the short end of a long rope. No sense in dragging
this mess out any longer than necessary."

Suspicion cut into my foggy brain. The judge wanted
this case swept into the closed case files quickly. Who better to stand beside the condemned, say the necessary pleas,
then keep her mouth shut about it, than the one lawyer in
town who didn't want to practice law.

I wondered what Crystal looked like after all this
time . . .

WISHFUL
Sinful

∾∾∾

Tracy Dunham

BERKLEY PRIME CRIME, NEW YORK

WISHFUL SINFUL

A Berkley Prime Crime book / published by arrangement with the author

PRINTING HISTORY
Berkley Prime Crime mass-market edition / September 2004

For information address: The Berkley Publishing Group, a division of Penguin Group (USA) Inc., 375 Hudson Street, New York, New York 10014.

ISBN: 0-425-19887-1

Berkley Prime Crime Books are published by The Berkley Publishing Group, a division of Penguin Group (USA) Inc., 375 Hudson Street, New York, New York 10014.
The name BERKLEY PRIME CRIME and the BERKLEY PRIME CRIME design are trademarks belonging to Penguin Group (USA) Inc.

PRINTED IN THE UNITED STATES OF AMERICA

10 9 8 7 6 5 4 3 2 1

1

TONIGHT the dream has driven me from my bed to the front porch of the house I inherited from my grandmother, Miss Ena, as the whole town called her. Pulling a bottle of bourbon from the kitchen cabinet as I stumbled by, I snagged a sterling mint julep cup from the drawer with the knives. Miss Ena will rise from the dead one of these days and give me ladylike hell for keeping liquor in her house and her sterling with the stainless.

If she does rise to haunt me, I will explain that I have vaguely managed to keep the Jefferson family values somewhat intact. Never let it be said that the family scion swigged her liquor from a bottle. Such shenanigans are reserved for the good old boys on fall turkey shoots, not such as I. Talbot Jefferson sips her bourbon from a silver cup while she rocks on her front porch.

Sweat cooled at the roots of my hair as I propped my legs on the railing, kicking back in the chair and sliding the bourbon into its antique receptacle. I raised a toast to the dead Miss Ena and hoped she forgave me when some dead friend arrived at the pearly gates and told her what I'd done to her very large, very old, very decrepit house. At least it keeps me busy, and when I'm busy, I try not to drink to excess.

I may as well add my garb to the list of sins for which she'll haunt me. My old T-shirt is hardly proper night wear, and I'll be damned if I'll wear a robe in this heat. But at five in the morning, who the hell cares? No one was awake to ogle my small breasts soaked with sweat and stuck to my shirt. Woolfolk Avenue was lucky I wasn't sleeping in the nude tonight. I usually did.

Trickling more nectar of Kentucky's finest into my silver cup, I drank in a private salute to my dead grandmother. Her, I can see. Hair a shimmering silver, black silk dresses with high collars even in the summer heat, her nails beautifully manicured. I remembered the way her fingers tapped her annoyance at me for some childhood infraction.

She'd raised me to be the family lawyer so I could handle all the family investments. Poor Miss Ena. It went against the grain to educate a woman in a "man's" profession, as she saw it. But she needed someone to untangle the gnarly skein of hundreds of years of legal neglect in a family that had once owned a fair bit of Talmadge County.

I concentrated on memories of Miss Ena. I didn't want those violet eyes I saw in my dream to stay with me when I was awake. If I thought about them, I'd know where I'd seen them before, and I didn't want to do that. Too much pain harbored in their lovely hue. I had enough of my own to handle tonight.

The car startled me. Household lights in Wynnton don't

stay lit much past ten at night. Decent folk are in their homes before that, and the Baptists adjourned Wednesday night supper no later than nine. I stashed the bottle behind the chair and crossed my legs. I wasn't expecting visitors, but with my experience in life, the unexpected was the norm.

Frank Bonnet slowed down the squad car in front of my house. Fear hit my gut like a ball-peen hammer. Frank opened the door slowly, as if trying to keep the noise down. Squeaking as if it needed a caseload of WD-40, the door refused to do its duty quietly.

"Damn," Frank muttered loudly enough for me to hear.

"Morning, Frank." I'd known him since third grade. His family had moved to Wynnton that year. "What brings you out so early?"

I managed to keep my voice calm, only slightly interested. But Frank's appearance on my doorstep, complete with sheriff's uniform, holster, and gun, could only mean trouble. He reached for his hat in the car, changed his mind, and left it where it was.

The gesture reassured me. If Frank had been planning on an official visit, he'd have worn every vestige of his official uniform. Still, I had the feeling the alligator was aiming for my ankles, teeth snapping, antediluvian eyes fixated on my flesh.

"How're you doin', Tal?" Glancing up one side of the street, then the other, he seemed more concerned than I with keeping his visit quiet.

Two years, I told myself. I'd lost the last appeal to save Parnell Moses two years ago. A man had died at the hands of the state because I hadn't been adequately prepared when he went to trial. There was no way Frank could know I'd killed a man, even if the state had shot him full of heart-stopping drugs. I'd been back in Wynnton that long. Frank wasn't at my front porch at five in the morning for no reason, though.

I forced a chuckle. "Frank, you out looking for Wynnton insomniacs? Newest town offense?"

I could have sworn he shushed me, his broad face in the shadows a secret from me.

"Tal, Judge Jordan asked me to bring you over to his house. Got a, well, a situation, you might say."

I thought Frank was slurring his words, as if he'd been hitting the bottle long before I rescued the bourbon from its unnatural kitchen prison.

I kept my bottom in the swing. I couldn't have stood up if Frank had poked me with a cattle prod or promised me salvation for every sin I'd ever committed. Judge Jordan wasn't my biggest fan in Wynnton. In fact, the man had threatened to have me disbarred several times, and I'd never even filed a motion in his court to have him removed. I'd worked hard to offend some big city judges who hadn't been too keen on my attacks on their impartiality, but in those days I'd thought I could keep judges on their toes and a little bit afraid of me. Hah.

Frank's boots scraped on the front steps of the porch. False dawn painted gray hues on his face, he looked older than I, and we were the same age. Frank was growing wider the closer he got to forty, I noted. I hoped age was adding dimension to my spare frame, not the hardened lard packing Frank's gut. I sucked it in, just to be sure.

Frank leaned against a porch column, thumbs hooked in his belt in the time-honored tradition of small-town Southern sheriffs. I half-expected the added weight to send the termite-infested wood cracking.

"So tell me what's up, Frank." I repeated myself often

with Frank, probably because I figured he was too dumb to understand me.

"Judge Jordan told me to haul your sorry ass over right now." Frank was playing this for all he was worth.

"Well, Frank, the way I see it, I'm sitting on my own front porch, minding my own business, enjoying the cool of the morning. Better give me a damned good reason for making me put my britches on."

"Trey Kinsale's turned up dead."

The next sip of bourbon burned my throat.

"Sorry to hear that," I croaked. For the life of me, I couldn't come up with anything more original to say about Trey Kinsale.

"Crystal Walker done it." The edge in Frank's voice set my teeth aching. Frank knew what he was doing to me.

Then I remembered where I'd seen those violet eyes that had haunted my dreams tonight. They belonged to Crystal Walker.

Like Frank, Crystal Walker showed up in the third grade. I stood in line behind her on that first day of school, waiting outside on the walkway for the bell to ring before we could file into our new classroom and face the demon who would torture us for the next nine months. Miss Duncan was to be my lot that year—a large woman with glasses, a limp, and no makeup. For the first time in my short existence, I was made to feel inadequate in my academic life.

The girl in line before me wore a scarf swathed about her head. I thought Crystal was just plain weird. I'd never seen a girl cover her hair before, not so completely that the scarf was folded low on her forehead and wrapped around her throat before being knotted securely at the nape of her neck.

She must have felt my eyes burning a question into the back of her head because she twisted suddenly and stared at me. Rimmed with long, dark lashes, she had the brightest violet eyes I'd ever seen, and they poked holes in my eight-year-old self.

"So whadda ya want?" Crystal snapped at me angrily.

I poked out my hand, as my grandmother had taught me to do when being introduced, and mumbled, "Tal Jefferson."

She unwrapped her arms from around her waist and slid one small hand into mine.

"Crystal Walker." Her eyes dared me to say something about the scarf. I wisely kept my mouth shut.

I didn't know what to do after that, so I mentally stumbled among the platitudes of politeness that had been drilled into me since I could remember. If I never made anything else of my life, I'd be a social success, my grandmother had determined. I finally came up with something to say as Crystal continued to stare at me.

"Pleased to meet you."

Those violet eyes finally blinked and left mine to focus on our hands. I still held her palm in mine. Embarrassed, I dropped hers.

Her nails, I'd noticed at the last second, were bitten to the quick and caked with blood. Hangnails had been ripped halfway to her knuckles. She shoved her fists behind her and dared me, with one defiant look, to say anything. I didn't have any words for her. I'd never seen a girl with such angry, abused hands.

The bell rang, ending my discomfort, and we paraded into our prison for the third grade. Crystal wore that scarf wrapped around her head every day she was in school.

Shaking myself free of the memory, I told Frank I'd

drive myself over to Judge Jordan's house. I considered refusing the summons, but I knew I'd lose. Linwood Jordan had been a protégé of Miss Ena's and knew all her tricks. To him, I was the family disappointment, and whenever he greeted me at Becky's Café, he'd shake his head and mutter something to whomever he was with after I'd replied with my falsely cheery, "Afternoon, Judge." Didn't take too much imagination to figure out he was repeating my grandmother's litany of my sins.

Judge Jordan lived in what was once the country. But the county had paved the road a long while ago, and slowly, bits and pieces of land around his hundreds of acres were sold off to developers. Driving to the judge's house as the sun started cracking the horizon, I found myself wondering if he thought of these small, boxy houses as his sharecroppers' abodes. Probably. Like Miss Ena, Judge Jordan held to a standard of society that had started crumbling at Appomattox Courthouse in 1865. He, at least, had progressed beyond slavery, but not much.

Every light in the large, Georgian brick house blazed. I drove between the classic phalanx of hundred-year-old magnolias, sweet with blossoms, to park in front of the porticoed front door. I'd avoided thinking about what Judge Jordan could want with me at this hour.

I hadn't seen Crystal Walker in seventeen years, and Trey Kinsale and I had never been friends. While I was sorry to see anyone greet his maker before his appointed time, I wasn't going to grieve over him.

I thought of tucking my knit shirt into my jeans, but decided what the hell. Ringing the doorbell, I figured everyone in the house was already wide awake. Still, I was surprised when the judge himself opened the front door. A tall, silver-haired man, he had a firm figure and a tan that said he played a lot of tennis or golf. I'd bet tennis from the size of his forearms.

"Morning, Judge," I started.

"We'll talk out here," he snapped at me, glancing over his shoulder into the house. "Marcy Kinsale's here, my wife's trying to keep her from turning into an hysterical disaster."

I guess the judge didn't believe in impartiality from the bench, but I kept my mouth shut. I did wonder, however, why Marcy Kinsale would come running to the Jordan house. She had people of her own, and they would surely have tolerated her tears with more good grace than Judge Jordan. I'd never realized that he couldn't abide a weeping woman, but I should have guessed. My grandmother didn't hold with displays of emotionalism, either.

I shifted my car keys to my back pocket. I hadn't been invited to sit on one of the wicker porch chairs.

"Yes, sir?" I watched the judge pacing up and down the long veranda. He wore his bedroom slippers with dark trousers and a white shirt, long sleeves neatly buttoned, a tie loose at the collar. I wondered if this outfit was what he wore to bed.

"Frank told you what happened." He was giving me a statement, not a question.

"Sort of. All he said was that Trey Kinsale had been killed, and Crystal Walker did it." I was reserving judgment on the whole thing until the judge confirmed the story. I ran my hand through my short hair, remembering I'd forgotten to comb it. Miss Ena was surely spinning in her grave right now.

"That's the long and short of it. Took a knife to just about every part of him, if you get my meaning. She, Crystal that is, called 9-1-1 about two hours ago. Frank says Trey was in her shed, behind her trailer, with at least twenty stab wounds. Bled everywhere. Frank's got the knife, and Crystal's confessing so fast, he can't shut her up. I want you to get over to the jail, I'm appointing you to represent her."

"Whoa up there, Judge. I'm not practicing law these days, in case you hadn't noticed." My hands felt clammy. I wanted no part of this little scenario.

"You kept your license active. I checked when you took up residence." His eyes glittered in the porch light. I could tell the information had given him no pleasure. "Even if you're wasting your time doing research for the firm, that one that writes briefs for lawyers too stupid to write their own, you're still a lawyer."

"Not for a long time now. It'd be ineffective assistance of counsel and an automatic appeal, and you know it." My mouth was drying out fast.

Linwood Jordan quit pacing and faced me, his back to the front door. I stood with one foot on the top step, one on the next one down, ready to flee. He had no right to ask this of me. My hands were cold.

"You were a hell of a criminal lawyer once, Tal. No one's going to accuse you of flubbing her case. Besides, she's owed a lawyer now, before she sits in that jail a minute longer."

My mind searched for reasons I'd been the lucky lawyer dubbed for this honor. Nothing was this clear and simple, not when it came to the power politics of Judge Linwood Jordan.

"Call up any of the courthouse regulars. They'll get over there faster than I can." I wasn't about to slide into the morass of criminal law ever again without some kicking and screaming. I'd done my stint in the trenches, and like the veterans of World War I, I hid my scars from most folks. The legal community of Wynnton considered me a disgrace. I'd sold out, quit my practice in the big city, and walked away. A lawyer only did that if she was caught doing the naughty, or had become an alcoholic druggie about to lose her license for either offense.

I never told anyone in Wynnton about Parnell Moses.

"She asked for you." The judge glowered at me.

I sat on the top step, invitation or no. "No way. I haven't heard anything about Crystal in years."

"Nonetheless, she says the only lawyer she'll talk to is you. So get your sorry ass over there, Tal, and do what has to be done."

I could have sworn I was hearing Miss Ena all over again, with curse words added, of course. I'd spent half my life telling her 'no.' I could do the same to Judge Jordan.

"Told you, I'm out of that game these days. I'll call some friends from the city, see if they're interested." One so-called friend in particular owed me big time. I'd call in my chit if I had to.

"Take too long. Preliminary hearing's as soon as Henry finishes the autopsy, which should be by Thursday morning. I'm not about to slow the wheels of justice just because you think you don't owe society anything."

I'd heard that ploy, too. "I don't. None of your business, Judge, but I paid my dues."

"Like hell, Talbot. The way I see it, Crystal Walker's already at the short end of a long rope. No sense in dragging this mess out any longer than necessary, she'll say the same, if you get your tail feathers over there and ask her."

Suspicion cut into my foggy brain. The judge wanted this case swept into the closed case files quickly. Who better to stand beside the condemned, say the necessary pleas, then keep her mouth shut about it, than the one lawyer in town who didn't want to practice law? Everyone knew I kept to myself, painting and scraping at Miss Ena's house when the spirit moved me. Working hard clearly wasn't on my agenda. No one, Judge Jordan included, thought I'd dig into Crystal's case with the zeal of someone who wanted her found innocent. My reputation for laziness had preceded me.

Anger clawed away the suspicion, but not all of it, and I stood. The rosy dawn hid the flush on my neck. Judge Jordan's taut chin lifted slightly as I opened my mouth, as if defying me to disobey his order. Something clicked. Those violet eyes again.

"I'll talk to her. No promises." Saying no more, I climbed back into my '66 Mustang and pushed it into gear. I wanted to ask a boatload of questions, find out exactly what Crystal had already told Frank, but I wouldn't get my answers here.

Driving back to town, I wondered why Marcy Kinsale was at the judge's house getting her back patted and her tears dried. I wondered what Crystal Walker looked like after all this time, and why Trey Kinsale had been at her trailer in the first place. I examined my motives in taking on her case, at least for the preliminary stages until I could get her an out-of-town lawyer, and found them to be less than admirable. I wasn't convinced Crystal was innocent. I had no burning desire to see that justice was done. Only one reason stood out as clearly as the arrogance in Judge Jordan's eyes.

I was pissed, pissed as hell that Linwood Jordan saw me as an incompetent boob who would observe the formalities while Crystal Walker was sentenced to die by the state-mandated procedure of lethal injection. I'd been willing to do my little research projects because it kept food on the table and bourbon in the pantry, but I hadn't completely lost my pride when I walked away from the big firm where I'd made partner. My penance for Parnell Moses was my business, and no one else's.

I thought about that scarf Crystal Walker wore in the sixth grade, when she dropped out of school and none of us saw much of her anymore. She'd been sick, Miss Ena explained to me once when I asked if Crystal would come back to school. No, she wouldn't attend school, Miss Ena thought, and I should put her out of my mind. I remembered watching the straight line of Miss Ena's eyebrows, still dark despite her silver crown of glory, getting a little straighter as she admonished me to forget about Crystal Walker. Miss Ena used her tone of voice that brooked no arguments.

Despite my incipient adolescence, I was still fearful of incurring her considerable wrath. I let the subject of Crystal Walker drop. Crystal Walker faded from my memories so rapidly, I was ashamed to remember it.

As furious as I was with Judge Jordan's assumption of my character, I was more angry with myself. If he'd run a con on me, he'd succeeded in hitting me where I.hurt the most. Like all Jeffersons before me, I was possessed of a surfeit of pride. I had dragged only a modicum of it home with me when I'd returned to the big Victorian on Woolfolk Avenue, but what was left was hard and implacable.

I saw, as I drove the blacktop back to town, Miss Duncan ridiculing Crystal because she hadn't brought any homework to school again. Miss Duncan had never bothered to ask why. I knew why. Crystal had no paper or pencils to use when she hauled her books home. I'd kept her supplied in school, but never thought to ask if she needed extra to take home. I'd been furious when I'd realized my own shortcomings and, strangely, angry with Crystal for not asking me for more sheets for homework.

If Crystal had asked Frank Bonnet to fetch me to help her, I couldn't say no. Much as I wanted to stay sequestered in my old house, and I knew that I was stepping into tar pits over my eyebrows, I would do all I could to help her. My pride, my anger, my guilt would have to take a back seat to the Jefferson inability to walk away from a wounded animal.

I felt more a Jefferson than I had in all the time since I'd returned to Wynnton to take up residence in Miss Ena's house once again.

How, I wondered, *had Crystal Walker known I was back in town?*

2

∿∿∿

FRANK gave me a look that said "I knew you'd knuckle under," as he unlocked the security door at the courthouse.

"She's in the holding cell until after the arraignment," he grinned.

"Then let 'er rip." I hadn't been behind the courtroom in years. The small cells there were used to house unruly defendants, those awaiting a jury's verdict, or lawyers like me who shot off their mouths and got thrown in the clink to cool our heels for a few hours. I'd done my time in a few similar holding cells.

I followed Frank down the middle aisle of the courtroom. The maroon velvet curtains clashed with the industrial-strength mustard carpet underfoot. But nothing could hide the magnificence of the carved mahogany bench and jury box. Built before the War of Northern Aggression, the courtroom had been intended for the solemn dignity of upholding the Constitution and dispensing justice. *Too bad,* I thought, *that it seldom happened these days.*

He unlocked the heavy door behind the bench and pointedly stepped through it first. Only Judge Jordan got the doorman act.

Here, aging plaster walls had been covered with cheap vinyl made to look like grained wood. The corridor stank of old cigars and sour spots where the rain had leaked through the tin roof and soaked the acoustic tiling in the ceiling. No air circulated through here when court wasn't in session. As I remembered, a big window air conditioner would hum in the judge's chambers during court days and keep it comfortable. The rest of us poor working stiffs had to sweat it out in the courtroom with its ceiling fans.

"Take your time, counselor." Frank grinned as he unlocked the door to the holding cells. I didn't like it.

I rammed my arm across the door and stared Frank in the face.

"You got her to sign a Miranda waiver?"

I watched the folds of flesh wrinkle into a smile. "Sure enough, Tal. Why, even us backwoods hillbillies done heard of a Miranda waiver."

"I'd like to see it." I didn't move my arm.

"Sure enough," he repeated. The grin was sinking with the rise of his annoyance factor. He shouldered the door under my arm. I weigh about a hundred pounds less than Frank, but I'm about as tall. What I'd once thought of as "willowy grace" had been replaced by angular edges and sharp corners to my bones that matched my temper. I found it hard not to rub, and be rubbed, the wrong way. Frank was doing a good job of both.

I followed him into the narrow corridor running the length of the three small cells. The back walls were brick, the outer wall of the rear of the courthouse. The sides and fronts of the holding cells were made of old iron, welded and inserted back here years before Miss Ena was born. Each cell had a narrow bunk to sit on, a plain ticking mattress, no pillow, no blanket, no toilet. A pot in the corner with a lid took care of personal needs. Wynnton hadn't had the ACLU visit yet.

"Crystal, your lawyer's here."

I couldn't read Frank as he spoke to her. There was something besides officiousness in his voice, but I wasn't sure what. Either way, my attention was stuck like a burr on the figure huddled in the corner. I gestured for Frank to unlock the cell door. He shrugged, opened it, and I stepped in.

She was curled into a ball, her head sunk into the hollow between her knees and her chest. Her arms, locked around her legs, looked like sticks. I couldn't see her face, only the top of her head, glowing strangely under the greenish fluorescent lighting. I tried not to stare, but I'd never seen Crystal's hair before. She didn't have much of it. Her scalp reflected the overhead light, with only thin wisps of dark hair to conceal her face even more.

My gut reaction was to protect her. A good lawyer knows it can't be done—there's no magic garden wall that can provide a safe haven from a bad judge, a rabid prosecutor, or a lying police officer who has the knack of swaying juries.

"Crystal, it's Tal, Tal Jefferson. I came, as you asked." I was surprised at myself. Normally, I went into my "let's get down to business" mode immediately upon finding a client in lockup.

I slid in closer to Crystal, my eyes on her. If I looked away, I was afraid she'd disappear into herself.

Her face bowed deeper into the crevasse between her legs and her chin, but one hand fluttered in my direction. I turned to Frank.

"I'll give you a holler when I'm ready to leave."

He'd leaned against the wall, thick hands in his belt, as if he'd planned to stay awhile. Slowly, as if by taking his time he was showing his disdain for attorney–client privilege, he locked the holding cell door behind me. I hated locked doors of any sort, but I wasn't about to give him the satisfaction of seeing it. I focused on the human ball of misery in the corner.

Frank still hadn't left us alone. I turned, started to remind him I was allowed confidential interviews with my client, but he got the point without my saying a word. *Gee, Frank, swift on the uptake,* I thought.

Disliking my dismissal, he threw me a look that said I was going down the tubes with this one, and he'd love every minute of it. I'd seen that look before. It didn't bother me, but I bet it sure as hell had bothered Crystal.

I waited until I heard the door to the hallway snick shut.

"Crystal, look at me."

I waited for those violet eyes, holding my breath, praying I wouldn't see the little girl in them.

Slowly, she lifted her head, but kept her eyes down. Her jeans had torn knees, and she wore old sneakers, the cheap sort from the discount stores, with holes where her toes had worn through. One toe nail was bright pink. I was, strangely, surprised. I'd expected life to have beaten the shit out of Crystal, as it had me. She had more guts than I, and that pink toe nail proved it.

"Crystal, I need you to talk to me. Frank said you killed Trey Kinsale. Now, I don't want you telling me if you did it or not, it's better that you don't, but I need to hear what happened tonight. Just describe Kinsale when you found him, what you said when you called the cops."

I parked my butt on the edge of the bed, its metal frame cutting into my bony flanks. I didn't have a pen, a piece of paper to take notes, nothing I should have had with me in a well-stocked briefcase. No release forms for medical records, no fee agreement, nothing that I would have had in my old life. The life I had before Wynnton offered me a cell of my own.

"Hey, Tal, how you been?" Her voice was soft as water lilies in a Monet painting. "Long time no see."

I had to swallow hard. She sounded like a girl. I'd listened as my own voice had sunk with the weight of the years and too much liquor.

Clearing my throat loudly, I tried to match her sociability. "Has been a while. Haven't been back too long. You ever leave, Wynnton that is?" I watched the top of her shiny, thin-haired head for any sign that she was ready to look at me, to get down to business.

"No, been here all along. Heard tell you got yourself a fancy job as a lawyer."

In my hard-driving defense counsel days, I'd have ordered her to cut the crap and get down to it. But I wasn't the same woman. I'd learned to listen, if I'd learned nothing else.

"Truth is, you might give some thought to another lawyer. I could recommend someone, if you like. Someone not from Wynnton. Actually, that'd be for the best. You need a lawyer who won't play their game, someone who's not one of the good ole boys." I had an ethical obligation to tell her I was rusty, that she wasn't getting a suit on top of her game. The fact that Judge Jordan hated my guts was irrelevant.

"No!" Her face flew upward and in the eerie lighting, I

saw pain, death, and despair. The colors swirling in her irises were the only signs of life.

"I told Frank I wouldn't talk to anyone but you, and I mean it." The high voice, the breathy quality that had made me think of a child or an older woman playing it younger, was gone. She spoke now like a woman who'd had too many cigarettes and too much whiskey and they'd eaten into her vocal chords like worms into compost. "None of them'll understand, and I sure don't want them muckin' around in my life, diggin' for excuses. My life is no one's fuckin' business, and from what I hear, you're the same."

I listened to her desperation and anger, wondering why the hell she wanted me as her savior. I wasn't anywhere near that status, but if she wasn't buying the truth from me, there was nothing I could do about it right now. I'd work her around to my way of thinking gradually, after we got through the preliminary hearing.

"Okay, you're right, I'm not too thrilled with folks who won't leave me alone. Now how about you tell me what happened, leaving out the parts I don't want to hear, okay?" I was shaken by the face, the voice.

Maybe I'd wanted to see her as the girl I'd known in third grade, and fooled myself from the moment I'd stepped into the cell. She wasn't the helpless child anymore than I was. We were both women who'd blundered into life and made a stupendous mess of it. Only difference was, she was in a holding cell and I wasn't. I should have been.

Resting the side of her cheek on her arms still folded across the top of her knees, she sighed. "Thanks for seeing it my way. Got to keep my daughter out of this, no matter what."

"Daughter?" *Could it get any worse,* I wondered.

"Yeah, got me a kid. Didn't hear that you had any."

My mouth tasted of metal. "No. Not the maternal type. What's her name? Your daughter?"

"Desiree. Pretty name, huh? Heard it in a song." She smiled, a gentle, happy lifting of her pale lips that cut through the anger and despair for half a second. "Is Desiree okay? Frank said he'd see that she got over to Jack Bland's house."

My answering smile froze on my face. "Why Jack?" I'd avoided Jack Bland for the whole two years I'd been back, and it hadn't been easy.

"She's friends with Jack's Donna. They're both nine. Jack'll take good care of her. He'd better." She sounded grim.

She'd given me more information than I wanted. I knew Jack had four children, but I'd never asked any of their names, didn't want to know.

"I'll check with Frank about her." I waited for her to continue.

Silence didn't bother me, and it sure as heck didn't get to Crystal, either. It's been my experience that folks who live alone need silence, like other people need coffee to get going in the morning. I wasn't wearing a watch. It was one of those things I'd put away, along with the briefcase and the expensive suits. But I was getting hungry, and I knew she should be, too.

"I could stand some eggs and biscuits. How about you?" I had a few bucks in my pocket. If I had to, I'd run down the street to Becky's, pick up some take-out, and come on back. I'd sit in that damned cell as long as it took.

"I don't eat breakfast." Her eyes were shut again, and I wondered if she dozed.

"Okay. Well, maybe I can sweet-talk Frank into bringing us something hot to drink."

She snorted her disbelief.

"Frank not one of your favorites, huh?" I chuckled. "Me, neither. Never liked the SOB. Still don't."

She twirled one skinny bit of hair around a finger, and I noticed for the first time her nails were long and manicured. White-tipped and clean, they didn't have smudges from an examiner's powder or dried blood from the dead man. Of course, Judge Jordan had said Kinsale was filled with holes from a knife, and maybe she'd worn rubber gloves. Or maybe she'd had time to wash up before the police showed up. I leaned over and grasped her hand in mine.

It was as small as a girl's, with soft skin and tiny knuckles. I felt as if I were holding a frightened bird, her fingers fluttered so quickly in my palm.

"Don't," she cried, snatching her hand back.

Those hands, I thought, *weren't strong enough to kill.* Even a quick look up close told me the nails were fake. She had an expensive set on there, and from the looks of her clothes, she didn't have money to burn.

"Crystal, did the police do any tests on your hands? Take your clothes? The ones you were wearing when they showed up?"

I thought she nodded yes.

"Did you do anything before the police came, like wash up?"

She hesitated. "There was an awful lot of blood. I touched him, to see if he was breathing. Dialed 9-1-1, then washed my hands, changed shoes. They got out to my place right fast when I said it was Trey Kinsale bleeding like a stuck pig in my shed."

We were making progress. "Why'd you call them, Crystal? Was he still alive?"

A gargoyle of a smile flitted across the side of her face I could see. "No way, Tal. That cocksucker was already on his way to hell."

I tried to control my surprise. "Why did you call the police, Crystal?" In my experience, murders were accidental or unplanned, and the defendant was horrified by what had occurred, or they were deliberate and premeditated. The latter kind usually rabbitted. If Crystal had planned Kinsale's murder, she hadn't planned on running. It didn't fit.

"Wanted him off my property. Too heavy for me to drag down to the river, throw his sorry ass in. Would have, if I coulda." Her voice was froggy now, deep in some knot in her vocal chords.

"How long had he been dead when you called the cops?" Maybe Kinsale had been dying and she just waited him out. That I could buy.

"Hell if I know." Her heart-shaped face lifted, and I saw steel like nothing I'd ever seen in her eyes. "Let's get this over with, huh, Tal? You and me, we go way back, you play this the way I say. Got that?"

I'd never had a client speak to me that way before.

Usually, they were scared and any boasting came from reserves of macho or as a defense mechanism. Crystal wasn't playing any of those games. She thought she was in charge, and I was her hired hand. In my ten years of practice, I'd never had a client act like that. I felt diminished, as if the remnants of the old Tal Jefferson, the one I'd tucked away with the designer suits in my closet, had just taken a kick in the seat of the pants.

I stood. I wasn't going to get anything out of her this morning. I needed food and coffee and to talk to Henry

Rolfe before I tackled Crystal again. Henry would be doing the autopsy quickly, I was sure. Not too many suspicious deaths in Wynnton, he wasn't busy.

"I'll check on you later today, after I find out what Frank's been up to, make sure your daughter's okay." I didn't mean to sound as if I were asking a question, but I did.

"You do that. Just remember what I said. My way, or no way." Crystal stared at her nails, dismissing me. She began to pick at one, jerking off the false nail. I was startled when it came away bloody.

I had to salvage my pride somehow. "We'll see, won't we?" I sounded smug, even to myself.

Hell if I wanted this case. Whatever I owed Crystal Walker was a figment of my imagination. I was already thinking of how I could get my old friend to drive from Atlanta, as I hit the buzzer for Frank to get me out of there.

But before I crawled away with my tail in my hand, if not between my legs, I wanted the answers to a few more questions.

"You married, Crystal?"

The shoulders lifted slightly, as if she wanted to laugh. "Why the hell would I want to go and do some damn fool thing like gettin' hitched?

Question number one bit the dust. "Who's Desiree's father?"

A wall of ice slid between us. "None of your fuckin' business, and don't you go askin' anyone else. You hear?"

I was stunned by her vehemence. "Well, her daddy should have her, by all rights, while you're locked up."

"Forget it." She was back to tired and defeated.

"Everyone in town know but me?" Small Southern towns knew when you got on the can in the morning. "Does it have anything to do with Trey Kinsale?"

"No, and no." Ice was back in her voice, and I didn't find it refreshing in the closed air of the lockup.

I rattled the buzzer once more for Frank. I couldn't think of anything else to ask that she wouldn't shoot down like roadkill. Later, when I had more information, I'd grill her.

I hoped I remembered how.

3

AFTER a day spent trying to find out what Crystal said to Frank, I was exhausted by nightfall. Frank was giving me the old you'll-see-the-report-when-the-prosecutor-provides-it runaround. I wasn't in top shape for fighting the horse-hockey battle, and besides, I wasn't too worried about it. I still hadn't seen the signed Miranda. The judge wasn't returning my phone calls, and I didn't have the luxury of a secretary who could take messages for me and track me down while I hiked around doing legwork I should have had an investigator doing.

I couldn't sleep, again. This insomniac business was getting old. Maybe Henry could help me, but I had a sneaking suspicion he'd tell me to lay off the coffee and the booze. Henry was not only the town pathologist, he was an old friend, one of the few I still liked.

I blamed it on the heat. We'd reached the pit of the summer, that dip into the tar pool when nights were sweaty sheets and hot pillows, no matter how hard the fan overhead batted at the air. One of these days I was going to defy my dead grandmother and put in central air. But for now, I couldn't go quite so far in violating Miss Ena's antipathy for mechanical monsters altering the natural course of a Southern summer. So I sweltered in antiquated splendor.

My supply of bourbon was running low. I'd stock up as soon as I started my morning rounds, when the so-called civilized world was up and about. Tucking my much-diminished supply under one arm, silver julep cup in the other hand, I shouldered open the screen door and headed for the porch swing. I left the light on in the downstairs hallway, its yellow puddle of false hope streaking the gray porch floor through the screen door.

It's a mystery to me how bourbon can cut through the night's crap like the medical examiner's knife through a bloated body. For ten seconds, I didn't want to think about Crystal, Trey, or any of them. I thought of oak barrels stacked in old warehouses, the air thick with the scent of fermentation, cool darkness, no worries.

This case had all the makings of an incipient terror. Parnell Moses was an ancient nightmare that grabbed me by the throat on nights like this. The biggest mistake a lawyer can make is not being prepared, for thinking the courtroom is her oyster. When an innocent man was convicted of a crime he didn't commit, and it was my fault, I found a bottle to be the only answer. Crystal's trial was bringing back all my lawyerly errors in a big way. Pouring myself a healthy dose of Dr. Bourbon, I felt its power plow away some of the phlegm clogging my throat. Now, if only its magical elixir could give me the gift of dreamless sleep, I'd die a happy woman.

The sound of an engine cutting off at my curb hauled me up. The night was too dark, the old street lamp a memory, to see who was upsetting my nocturnal worship at the altar of insomnia. The car had had no headlights. Interesting. Didn't bode well. I decided on a field expedient. I shut my eyes and drank.

"Hey there, Tal. Got another glass? Or you still passin' the bottle around these days?"

The bourbon hurt all the way down my gullet. I opened my eyes, but I didn't need to. I knew that voice. How many nights had Jack Bland and I spent in the back of his pickup, pillows propped behind us, discovering each other?

"Hey yourself, Jack. Sit down, take a load off." I was surprised my voice wasn't shaking. In fact, I sounded surprisingly calm.

I could barely see him. Rising, I flicked on the overhead porch light. He was still long and lean, a man more bone than muscle, with the arms of a working farmer. Taut. Muscles on his forearms bigger than his shoulders, hands tucked into his jeans pockets, they'd be calloused from hard labor. His hair was shorter than when we were kids. Sun creases grew from the corners of his eyes like tattoos. We were both older and probably not better.

I wanted him in the world's worst way.

"Turn that off, please." He sounded pissed. I obeyed.

"Afraid the neighbors will talk?" I had no idea what he was doing at my house after all these years, or if there'd be hell to pay with Alma, his wife, if she found out.

The dim light jutting through the screened front door was a poor magnifier for my tired eyes. His arms were now crossed on his chest as if he were cold. Or he was protecting himself from my thorough appraisal of his current assets.

"They're already talking," he said slowly. "About you taking on Crystal Walker."

"You got a chill?" I didn't want to talk about Crystal.

Jack edged his way to the top step.

"That's not likely. Not this time of year." Stepping one foot closer, he stared at the front of the house as if he'd never seen it before. "Still a pretty place. Even if you are painting it those faggy colors. Why the hell'd you make the shutters purple?"

"I like purple." I was losing it, or I was drunk. We'd been young together once upon a time, hadn't talked since I'd come home, and now he was criticizing my choice of shutter color.

"Hah." He spit out the derision. "We're too old to care about that kind of shit." He seemed to be making up his mind about something. Deciding, he settled beside me on the swing.

The yellow light from the front hall made him seem jaundiced, but his eyes were still dark, his lips reminding me of long, slow, wet kisses on summer nights when he'd sneak out and meet me for a make-out session. He looked tired though, a malaise that hadn't attacked him at seventeen. Four children and a farm could do that, I reckoned.

"Like hell we are." I sipped my bourbon, remembered my manners. "Can I offer you a glass? Got a clean one in there somewhere." I nodded my head at the front door.

"Who needs a glass?" Grabbing the bottle, he tipped it up and did more than sip. I was in awe. A young Jack Bland threw up after one beer. He had gotten older and changed. Not for the better.

I waited for his throat to quit pulsing, watching his skin

as it shimmered in the light. A trace of dark beard prickled his gullet, around his upper lip. I'd loved his jawline, and barely kept my hand from reaching to stroke it. He stared at the darkness outside the porch as he handed the bottle back.

"Whooee, needed that." He turned to me, gave me a prime Jack-grin. "Like great sex, you know? Just the right pick-me-up at the right time."

"Can't say as I know anything about great sex," I chuckled. "Present company excluded, of course." Then my laughter died.

I knew the rumors all too well. Jack alone knew they were untrue. But a woman who didn't stay home and marry her high school sweetheart was automatically under suspicion, especially if she dressed in gray suits and carried a briefcase. I was a condemned woman in the eyes of Wynnton's flowers of womanhood.

Jack must have caught my sudden shift of mood. I'd been as tense as a drowning cat when he'd stepped out of his truck. But old ways had shimmied into place when he sat down. We'd spent too many years together to stay strangers for long, even after so many years apart. I knew now why I'd avoided seeing him when I'd come back in Wynnton.

I longed to reach for his hand, to feel his short, powerful fingers twined in mine. He had tiny hands for a man, but I'd bet they were as strong as any Hindu fakir's feet. I'd known I'd feel this way, and I didn't like it.

"Bet you're wondering what in Sam Hill I'm doing in your neck of the woods." He patted the bottle, knifed between his knees, tapping the porch with his boots as he set us to swaying in the swing. Red clay stained the knees of his jeans, their hem. I wondered why he looked like he'd just come from plowing.

I tried to keep the bitterness out of my voice. "Figured you'd decided it was time to pay a social call."

He snorted. "Not likely."

"Well, I'm here, you're here. So what're we doing?"

He leaned back, bringing the bottle to his lips once more. "Hate nights like this. My house gets so damned quiet, I could scream. The damn dog's not even snoring."

I tried to squelch my impatience, but I've never been good at that. "Things were right quiet here, till you drove up."

Jack lifted one eyebrow, shot me a look that took me back a hundred years. "You shoulda stayed gone, Tal. Look at this house, you're plum ruining it. It'll be like some whore when you get through, and they'll tear it down and build a Wal-Mart or somethin' else ugly, right here, all cause you went and made this house look like a massage parlor."

He made his point with his usual incisiveness. Marriage hadn't dulled Jack Bland's brain one cell.

"After I'm gone, I don't give a shit what happens to this house, or this town, for that fact."

"But you care what happens to Crystal Walker."

His voice was so soft I almost didn't hear him.

"Jack, I can't discuss a case with you. You're smart enough to know that."

"You mean, I'm just some dumb soybean farmer, I don't know diddly-squat? Give me a break, Tal." Anger bit through the soft voice.

"I didn't mean that. I meant, I can't talk about Crystal to you or anyone else. Attorney–client privilege."

"So I'll talk, you listen." Kicking the swing into a creaking swirl, he held onto the chains that suspended it from the ceiling and stared up.

I'd loved him once. Back when all I had to be angry at was my small-town boredom, we'd been golden together. He was the proverbial captain of the football team, the guy who should have dated the girl most likely to. I wasn't the girl his parents would have picked for him, but I was still Miss Ena's granddaughter. I'd have been allowed to take Jack Bland's last name and bear his children.

But I'd been in my rebellion stage, quoting French poetry one minute, Debbie Harry the next, and to hell with a wedding in the Baptist Church, me in a white dress I hated, him looking flushed in a rented tux. We'd found passion and each other with such an intensity I'd never forget him.

He'd married Alma the summer after high school. His oldest girl was about to graduate from high school. There were three more, the youngest still in grade school according to Becky, who'd given me the full scoop the first time I sat down to eat her chili after I'd come home.

He was still silent. I waited for him to tell me what he'd driven into town to spill, but the quiet stretched out like an unspoken agreement. If I didn't ask him now, I figured I never would.

"Why'd you do it?" I hoped I could handle it, after all this time. But doubt was nipping at me like the hounds of hell, and I regretted the question as soon as I asked it. He knew what I was talking about.

"Because she was here, and you weren't. Don't be an idiot, Tal. With your IQ, you should have figured it out long ago." He didn't sound so much annoyed, as tired. "That's not why I'm here.

"Crystal's daughter is in my Donna's class." He paused. "We took her in because she didn't have anywhere else to go. You want to talk to her?"

"I was planning on it." I didn't add I hadn't wanted to see him when I did.

"She understands about Crystal and Kinsale." His voice was low, as if he expected someone to overhear him. "Check it out. Like I said, I know the girl. She's shy, but she'll tell the truth. Crystal taught her that."

He'd use that soft, confiding voice when he wanted us to escape together to the banks of the Wynnton River, where we had a secret place under the low cliffs, hidden from view by ancient oaks and heavy brush. His words had seduced me, led me on, promised me earthly delights. I sighed, wishing I were that girl again, that he could be the boy in my arms. I'd been right to avoid him since coming home. I forced myself to pay attention to what he was telling me.

I pulled myself out of the past with great reluctance. I had the feeling Jack knew a lot more about Crystal and Kinsale than he was going to tell me. "If you know anything, Jack, you have to talk to the police. You know that, don't you?"

"I don't know anything for sure, or I'd tell you. Just check it out."

I retrieved the bourbon, gave myself a healthy dose of it. "Jack, I wasn't pulled out of the pigpen yesterday. Upstanding men in the community don't take in little girls belonging to trailer trash. Not unless there's something goin' on."

His face tightened, his dark eyes growing darker. "You've been gone a long time, Tal. Forget we watch out for each other in Wynnton? Guess the big city must have given you a cynical pill to swallow."

I harrumphed. "You'll never know. I still say, Jack, you're taking a big chance comin' here tonight. If Alma finds out, there'll be hell to pay, and you know it. What's really going on?"

Using Alma's name did the trick. Pushing to his feet, he slipped his hands into the back pocket of his jeans. His T-shirt looked like it could use a washing. I realized he must have been working his fields before dawn, then taken off in his pickup to find me. What would he have done, I wondered, if the lights had been off and I'd been asleep when he drove up? I started to ask him, then didn't.

"You never drank like that, not before." He sounded more puzzled than accusatory. The bottle was still firmly between my fist.

"Lots of things have changed, Jack. You, me, the universe. All those brain cells dying off each nanosecond."

"You didn't used to have such a smart mouth, either."

"Sure I did. You just didn't catch on." I was starting to get royally pissed. "Better get back before Alma comes by lookin' for you."

I could have sworn he looked peeved. Whether at me, or the thought of Alma hunting him down, I didn't know. Old lovers are harder to read than new ones, I was realizing. He twirled his keys in his hands, staring into the darkness, trying to make up his mind. His boots had left red clumps of clay on the porch. I wondered why Crystal Walker's daughter was important, why Crystal had driven him from his fields at this hour of the morning to talk to me.

I wasn't known for my finesse and politic ways. "You more than a friend to Crystal Walker, Jack?"

"I'll be seeing you, Tal. Take care now, hear?" He sounded bone weary.

I could have sworn he tried to tiptoe down my front steps, but it could have been the mud still on his soles that muffled the sound. Jack never listened to me, and I sure as hell hadn't listened to him.

Another night I hadn't slept, and dawn was but minutes away.

4

HENRY Rolfe was as black as North Carolina macadam and as big as a tobacco barn. He'd graduated from Hampton University, gotten his medical degree from the Medical College of Virginia, then shown the poor common sense to return home to Wynnton. Some said he could have played pro football. Henry would laugh at the joke. Why use brawn when he had brains, he'd say.

Henry was both a general practitioner and town medical examiner. We'd been friends since his mother had been Miss Ena's seamstress and my surrogate mother. Those facts of life that Miss Ena found too crass to discuss were all explained with simple clarity by Mrs. Rolfe. Henry and I had had an early and graphic education that had stood us both in good stead.

Today I was in my all-grown-up lawyer mode as I

shouldered open the door to Henry's office. The county paid for a small morgue and examination room in the back. The brick addition had been painted white, and a small sign, stenciled in red, announced it was the official county facility for the unquietly dead. That wasn't what the sign said, actually, but that was how I interpreted it. I preferred to enter through Henry's office, where the living used the front door.

"Been expecting you, now that you're practicing law again." Henry greeted me as grimly as I'd ever seen him. He towered over me, making me feel small at five foot eight. If I hadn't been there on official stuff, I'd have given him a peck on the cheek. As it was, I didn't want to get too close to Henry. He reeked of death.

"That bad, huh?" I'd spent the rest of the morning trying to prepare myself for the pictures of the body in situ. "Morning, Henry. Word travels that fast."

I'd been expecting to convince a skeptical Henry that I was actually Crystal's lawyer and not just fooling around.

"No secrets, you know that, not in Wynnton." Henry's green rubber apron resembled some abstract painting, splatters of brownish-red on kelly.

"You comin' over this Friday?" Henry and his wife Grace had extended a standing invitation that I had so far declined. I loved Henry like a brother, liked Grace a heck of a lot, but I wasn't ready to rehash the past.

"Don't think I can make it. Got a boatload to do, this case and all."

Henry nodded. "Figured as much. How're you going to handle this, seeing as you don't even have a file cabinet, much less a secretary?"

I shrugged. "Good trial lawwyer does her work on her

feet. Don't need much. Got my computer, my law books are in the attic, I'll haul 'em out, if I need 'em."

Henry grinned. "Wrong." He looked strange, his wide smile a grotesque contrast with the bloody apron. "Grace has a cousin, did some paralegal work in Atlanta. Needed a change of scenery, you get my drift." He shrugged.

"Man trouble, huh? Lucky cousin."

"Now don't you go thinkin' she's some sort of loser." He smiled as if he'd just scored a hole-in-one. "You're the proud new employer of June Atkins."

I groaned. "Hell, Henry, I'm making fifty bucks an hour here court-appointed pay. Want to take bets the clerk'll top me out at $500 for a capital murder case? I can't afford Grace's cousin, much less anything else."

I could have afforded her for a while, but I didn't want to get back into all the trappings of the big-shot lawyer. I wanted to see if I could do this by myself.

"You can't *not* afford her. Hit Miss Ena's trust fund." Henry gave me that look that said he'd take no more nonsense from me. He was the only person who knew about the trust fund.

"Send her over this afternoon." I knew when to give up. Plus, Henry was right, I'd need someone at my back, protecting it. Henry and Grace I trusted, and if they vouched for June, she didn't need a personal interview.

I'd tried to avoid Henry when I'd returned to Wynnton, but he'd have none of it. Just as if a white plume of smoke had arisen from Miss Ena's chimney to announce I was in residence, Henry had stormed my front door and crashed his way through to a kitchen chair. Even though we were some twenty plus years down the road from those summers in the seventies, we were both at heart seven years old.

"Glad that's settled. You ready for the report on Trey Kinsale?"

I blinked rapidly, felt my throat tighten. Hoping I could speak, I managed a small croaking "okay." Nothing else worked its way up my vocal cords.

Henry squinted at me. "This your first, Tal? Autopsy?"

I rolled my eyes. "Hardly." I had to clear my throat to get the word out. I'd told no one, especially Henry, of my dreams of autopsy pictures.

"You want some menthol to rub under your nose?" He fished a tube out of one pocket.

"Henry! I thought you'd give me the gory details, maybe show me the film once it's developed!"

"No ma'am. You gotta see this one." I could have sworn Henry was about to drape an arm over my shoulder and swing me into his examining room.

"No thanks. I'll take the facts, sir, just the facts." I tried to lighten it up for my sake, but Henry could see right through me.

"Tal, get a grip. You want to understand why she killed him, you've got to see the body."

"Hey, since when did you start teaching criminal law?" My stomach had tolerated a piece of toast and a ripe peach this morning, but that was it. I didn't have enough bourbon left to settle my stomach for this.

"Damn it, Tal, cut it out." Henry was royally annoyed at me, and I didn't blame him.

"All right." I straightened up, tugged at my paint-spattered shorts. At least I'd thought to haul a pad of paper and a pen with me to take notes. "Let's get this over with."

Henry elbowed his way through the door, holding it open for me to follow. My feet felt like they were made of quicksand, like I'd wobble then spread all over the floor in some silica puddle. I followed him.

The first thing I noticed was the cold. Henry had kept it cool in there to slow decomposition of the body, I was sure, but it felt like the epitome of purgatory to me. Hell had frozen over, and I was there. All business, Henry positioned himself by the corpse of Trey Kinsale so that the body was between us. If he picked up a laser pointer and started lecturing, I was leaving.

I tried to keep my eyes off the naked body on the stainless steel bed, but it was impossible. Like staring at a wart on the end of someone's nose, my eyes wouldn't leave him alone.

My second thought was that the body was a dummy. The pale skin was almost blue. I thought he'd been rolled in that stuff Miss Ena used to rinse her hair. Henry's Y-shaped incision was in progress, but the stab wounds were clearly visible. If Crystal had done this, she was one pissed puppy.

"Most of them are superficial. Just enough to sting but good. But at least two of them did the job. Real professional, up and under the ribs. Blade about seven inches, I'd say."

I knew Henry was watching me like a rodent focusing on cheese in the trap, but I couldn't help myself. I started giggling. Terrible tension does it to me every time, and no matter how hard I try to control it, I can't. The giggles sounded like a maniac was loose in the building.

"Sorry, Henry." I hiccupped as I tried in vain to stifle my sick sounds. "I'll try to behave, promise."

"Tal, get a grip. He's not going to rise from the dead."

Henry had a way of putting things in perspective. I

hadn't liked Kinsale, hadn't found him even a tiny bit charming when I'd known him as the son of one of the town's once wealthier families. Then again, he'd found me as intriguing as a dead frog in the middle of a highway, so we were even. I'd thought him a vain, selfish kid with little to recommend his existence on this earth other than the fact he'd been born into a family with old money, which was long gone. Without it, he was a bottom-feeder with the rest of us.

I held my breath and tried to pay attention. Henry was speaking as slowly as a teacher to a student with an attention deficit disorder.

"This one here," he pointed with his gloved finger, "probably did the trick."

I imagined the force it would take to slide a knife under someone's ribs. "How strong do you have to be to do that?"

Henry shook his head, his smile returning to normal after my show of idiocy. "Good question. Not strong, not strong at all, if you avoid the ribs and cut under the flesh part to the soft tissue. These other ones," he gestured broadly at Kinsale's chest, covered with matted hair and holes, "glanced off ribs. Didn't do much damage, must have hurt like hell. What I'm trying to figure out now is if they occurred before or after the fatal cut."

"Yum. Glad it's your job and not mine." I hated this.

"Pay attention, Tal. If they were done afterward, wouldn't you say the murder was done in a rage? Maybe the knife under the ribs was a lucky blow."

My long-suppressed lessons learned in the hard-knock school of criminal court were kicking in. "If it was a rage, you think this was a sexual killing?"

"Bingo. Knew you were smart. For a lawyer." Henry shot me his shit-eating grin.

"Forgive me for being slow on the uptake here, but my lucrative clients were mainly white collar criminals who never had so much as hangnails." I pouted at him. "But I did practice criminal law once upon a time. So if the superficial wounds occurred first?" I knew there had to be a down side to this what-if scenario.

"Then whoever the killer was, he had a reason for these cuts. They seem odd to me. Almost as if they're in a pattern." Henry began taking pictures of the corpse.

"So we discount the professional killer."

"Not entirely." Henry frowned at the corpse.

"I don't think Crystal falls in that category." I was getting back in the swing of things, already planning the strategy I'd present for her defense.

"Well, if she did, they'll have to come up with some mighty bloody clothes. Kinsale here squirted like a garden hose poked full of holes and turned on too fast."

"Explain." I was starting to make notes and a rough sketch of Kinsale's upper body. Henry had thoughtfully covered the lower portion of Kinsale's anatomy with a sheet. I guessed all the wounds were the ones I could see.

Henry turned, picked up a piece of cardboard from the desk, and shook his fountain pen until it left a wet, dark blob in the middle. Before the ink could soak in, he smacked his hand on one edge of the paper, sending sprays of ink into the air. I got the point.

"Okay, next lesson?"

"Kinsale didn't defend himself. No defensive cuts on the hands, arms. His nails are clean, he didn't scratch or claw. I'll have to wait on the blood tests, but my bet is that he was out cold. Drunk, maybe. Smelled like a vat of Jack Daniels."

"Did he have a reputation as a drinker?" I hadn't seen

him in the liquor stores when I was shopping, but that didn't mean much.

"What good ole Southern boy doesn't?" Henry wiggled his eyebrows at me. "Speaking of which, your purchases of an alcoholic nature are making the gossip circle."

"So what? Tell me more about our boy here." I seldom had a drink when I was working. Seltzer water was more my speed. But life had slowed down a lot, and the bourbon helped it slow down some more. I'd have to make up my mind, and fast, as to which was going to go first, the liquor or my mind.

Trey Kinsale was missing his right ear. Embarrassed by the gaping, ugly wound, I stared at my notepad. As I started to doodle in black, squiggly lines, Henry recovered the body. He'd seen me avert my eyes from the wound.

"The ear was removed post mortem, is my bet. I'll be able to tell you more later."

"Thanks." I tried to keep out of the valley of sarcasm, but it's always been my refuge in time of stress. "Not that I'm guilty of any prurient interests, you understand, but where the heck is it?" I gestured vaguely.

Kinsale had once been what I guess most women would call a handsome man. Personally, I didn't get off on blond-haired men with more testosterone than brains, but I'd watched as the teenagers I'd grown up with had flocked to his minimalist charms. I'd asked Jack once what Trey had that called females to him like some whistle we mere mortals couldn't hear. Jack, I remember, had looked distinctly uncomfortable. Kinsale wasn't so handsome now.

Henry was shrugging. "Police haven't found it yet."

"You know what the Indians did, don't you?" I was

watching Henry to see if he'd be offended. He shook his head in the negative.

"They'd cut 'em off, stuff 'em down the throat of their enemy."

Henry looked mildly interested. "No wild Indian tribes around here that I know of."

"Should you take a look? For the ear, that is. Did they find it in the shed?"

"Not that I've heard, but take my word for it, whoever did this, had another plan for that particular piece of Mr. Kinsale here." *Henry was,* I thought, *looking a bit peaked about the edges.*

The smell of death was beginning to get to me. "Crystal told me the body was in her shed. Where exactly did the police say they found the body?"

Henry checked a manila folder. "Called me out to pick him up from that rat haven behind Crystal's trailer. Funny place, stuffed with old lawn mowers, broken chairs. There was a cot in there, a rusty army thing, and Trey here had soaked the mattress clean through. Not much of his blue blood left in him, after all the holes."

"And how long would you say he'd been dead when you got there?"

Henry turned to look at a piece of paper on the desk behind him. "Don't hold me to this, but I'd say he was killed between midnight and two A.M. That's a rough estimate, I need to do the math on body temp, outside temp, the whole nine yards."

At least I was asleep when Trey had finally met his match. My demons hadn't kicked in until later.

"Anything else I need to know?" I sounded as tired as I felt.

Henry stared me in the eyes. "You up for this case, Tal? You haven't been yourself since you came home."

I knew Henry wanted me to spill my guts, the way Trey would when Henry removed his intestines to examine and weigh them. Henry was an insightful man, but he dealt with life and death too often for me to lay my burden at his feet. He'd peer right through me, and I couldn't bear to see the disappointment in his eyes when he learned what a fraud I was. I tugged on the hem of my T-shirt, slipped my pen behind my ear, and gave him a wink.

"It's the purple shutters. Everyone's sure I'm off my rocker because of those damned shutters."

"You are. Never seen such a piss-poor excuse for paint in my life."

I turned to leave, escaping before Henry pressed me further. "Tell June the front door'll be unlocked. She can set up whatever she needs." I pretended I was calm, cool, a veritable Perry Mason of the Wynnton bar association.

"I'm going out to Crystal's, see the crime scene for myself."

Henry threw me a tight smile, letting me know he wasn't buying the act. "I'll tell her. And Tal?"

"Huh?" I hesitated. Bad move.

"Don't let Linwood Jordan and his Keystone cops give you a load of bull for breakfast. You know why they want you to represent Crystal, don't you?"

"I'm the only lawyer in town stupid enough to take her on?"

"The stupid part is right. You're drinking too much, everyone knows it, and there's talk you aren't much good at the game, girl. They want Crystal to take a short walk to the hot seat so bad they can taste it. Don't prove them right, Tal."

What little self-respect I'd pretended to have had just been confirmed as dead-on-arrival. If Henry was afraid I'd blow it, I was already half-way to my goal of self-oblivion.

"Not too hard to do, old pal." I clutched the door frame.

"That's the ticket. I'm puttin' my money on you, girl."

I hated being the object of pity almost as much as I despised what I'd done to Parnell Moses.

I was so angry, I smacked my face on the door as I flew out of there.

5

∞∞∞

I needed to talk to Crystal's daughter. I tried to tell my-self I didn't need a drink, but I did. What I didn't need was an officious, efficient, busybody woman tearing apart my house. June Atkins didn't see it that way.

"Hello," she greeted me coolly as I trudged up the front steps, my mind fighting images of Kinsale's severed ear and the gaping wound it had left.

"Oh," was the only brilliant opening line I could come up with. "You must be June. I'm Tal."

"I know. Henry called me as soon as you left, told me to get my ass over here and deep six every bottle of booze I could find."

"Henry's an . . ." I managed to stop myself from in-dulging in a childish tirade. But barely. "Henry's an old friend, and how come I never heard of you?"

"I was at their wedding. But then, you weren't there, were you?"

I hadn't done much in a social way with old friends, not when there was money to be made in the legal world.

"No, missed the happy occasion." I was standing on a step that put me about six inches lower than her. I decided it was time to show who was boss. Of course, if Henry had thought I could show anyone who was boss, he wouldn't have sent June over to straighten me out. Henry was as readable as a Dr. Seuss book.

"I was too busy saving some poor soul's ass from the jaws of the legal monster." I thought I sounded cute, but I was actually pathetic.

"Well, let's get to work. I shifted your computer into the front parlor and set up a card table I found in the kitchen in there. Got a list of supplies, you want me to phone in for delivery, or pick them up myself?" She ignored my attempt at superiority. Her shoes were red heels with the pointy toes of a rock star. I stared at them, wondering where the heck she found something like that in Wynnton.

June was pretending to be my secretary/paralegal, but I knew who was boss.

"Whatever you want." I didn't want anyone rearranging my house, my life, or my routine. I shuffled to the porch and got a good look at June.

She was about my height, a tad bit shorter, with a curvy figure that said gyms and careful dressing to emphasize the right angles, but not too much. She had all of Grace's good taste, her pale coffee-colored skin, and a short, tightly curled hairdo that was both chic and in-your-face. She looked like the lawyer. Amber earrings dangled from perfectly shaped ears. Her dress flowed in red and amber swirls around her knees. She was a lady and knew it.

"You need to authorize the Westlaw account, I've switched the modem to the front room, too, and where the hell are your clothes?"

I was surprised. Staring down my front, I saw I was clothed, albeit not half as fashionably as June. "On me," I noted.

"Those aren't clothes, those are covering to keep you from being arrested for indecent exposure." She pressed her perfectly lipsticked lips together. "I'll go through your closet, figure out something for you to wear."

"June," I warned, trying to sound like a boss. "Stay out of my closet. There's nothing in there but jeans and work shirts anyway."

Her mouth did a classic purse of disapproval. "What size do you wear? An eight?"

"Six. But the sleeves are usually too short on a six jacket." I wondered what was coming next.

"Give me your credit card, I'll take care of it."

"Like hell you will. I'll find something to wear to court, but for now, jeans will do me just fine."

June ignored me, gliding efficiently inside and pulling me behind her like a sinking ship. "I'll get the hardware store to install some window air conditioners before the day's out. I can't sit here and concentrate if I'm a pool of butter."

Her tone told me not to try to argue. *Well, Miss Ena,* I thought, *it's all for a good cause.*

"And you'll need a couple more phone lines in here. I want one dedicated to the fax machine."

"Jeez, June, you wanna take the bar exam next month, pass it, take this case, too?" I was getting a mite testy.

June twirled on her unscuffed heels. "Don't you go gettin' snippy with me, Tal Jefferson. Henry said you were in sorry shape to save that woman's life, and he was right. If I have to hold you down in a tub full of ice cubes to wake you up, I'll do it. I told Henry I'd get you ready for this trial, and I'll be damned if I'll disappoint Henry."

I was well and properly put in my place. "No one wants to disappoint Henry," I managed to mumble. "But let's not forget Crystal Walker, she's the one with the most on the line."

The way June stared at me with her large, beautifully mascaraed eyes said more than any of her acerbic words. She was here because Henry said I needed her, and that was the only reason. She didn't want Henry to be disgraced by my losing through simple incompetence. If I lost, she was telling me, it would be because I blew the case up in spite of her best efforts, or because Crystal was well and truly guilty.

"Do whatever you want," I apologized faintly. "I used to wear a Jones New York suit without alterations." Pulling my wallet from my jeans pocket, I tossed it to her. "Should be some credit cards in there without expired dates. Go to it, June."

I'd pay the bill from the trust fund. Miss Ena would have approved of a new wardrobe, I was sure.

I left June on the phone, calling in the troops, to go upstairs and shower. I was suddenly bone weary. Crystal wasn't going to help me much, that much was clear. In fact, she seemed to think I was going to walk beside her as she faced the firing squad. I'd let her know I wasn't any good at that kind of thing, but later. Right now, I had to see her daughter. The thought didn't thrill me.

I had to clean up before I saw Jack again. The rickety shower in the upstairs bathroom was one of my additions. Dropping my jeans on the floor, I stepped in to scrub off the smell of the autopsy. Raining cold water down my naked body restored my addled brains a bit. When I finally dragged myself out of the water I felt almost human. At least I could think clearly as I picked up the phone upstairs and told June, who was talking to a man about getting his tail feathers down to Woolfolk Avenue, that I needed to use the phone. She was right, we needed at least two more lines.

Crystal's child Desiree was staying with Jack's family. I was looking forward to seeing Alma with as much anticipation as menopause. June hung up the phone, and I dialed Jack's home number. I'd memorized it when I got back to town, but never called. The funny thing was, it was the same number his parents had had, and I'd never really forgotten it. But I pretended I had.

I was surprised when a child answered on the third ring.

"Where's your mom or your dad?" I asked without any smoothing of the way into the conversation.

"Dad's around, Mom's not here. Who's calling?" The child was more of a teenager, I thought. Girl.

"Tal Jefferson. Tell your father I'm driving out now to talk to Desiree. He needs to let her know I'm her mother's lawyer."

"Yeah, right." The kid wasn't thrilled. "I don't think that's such a hot idea. She's up in Donna's room and won't come out."

I thought a second. I didn't want the girl to be my enemy, but I needed information before she began to forget details.

"Just tell your father I'm coming." I hung up.

Children weren't my forte, never had been. But I was lawyer enough to know Desiree might hold the key to what happened to Trey Kinsale. If I could get her to talk to me.

I pulled on my peripatetic jeans and a clean shirt. In the back of my wardrobe, on the floor, was the leather brief-case I'd almost tossed in the river when I crossed the bridge into Wynnton. But I hadn't. I threw it on my bed and clicked it open. The old leather datebook, a long-dead PDA, the Mont Blanc pen, a small calculator, some scratch pads, were all where I'd left them.

Making my decision quickly, I tossed it back in the closet. I'd take a pen and pad of paper. I wasn't the hot shot, fearless lion tamer I'd pretended to be once upon a time. I didn't need my leather briefcase to crack at the snarling lions who'd bet on my losing a case.

Throwing June a casual wave and a quick 'I'm heading out to interview Desiree Walker,' I had the feeling I'd be re-turning to a newly renovated house by the time I got back.

Her furniture rearrangement wasn't complete, I'd no-ticed in a quick glance. She'd hauled out chairs and some lamps I'd stored on the winter porch and was still on the phone ordering stuff I'd never use again. She barely looked at me as she made a note on the pad in her hand.

"Wait a sec," she said loudly enough for me to hear. "I'll arrange for a court reporter for the prelim, okay?"

I didn't know why she bothered to ask. I hadn't thought of it, it was a good thing she had. I was even rustier than I'd realized. I nodded my approval.

I tried not to hurry as I hit the road to Jack's farm. But now that I had a legitimate excuse to go out there, I really just wanted to get it over with. No, that was too mild a de-scription. I had to see Desiree, sure, but I didn't have to see Jack. Or his wife. Or his children. Jack's appearance on my front porch had been enough of a reminder of how screwed up my life was, I didn't need to see it in full-bore, living color. If Alma was still a perky little blonde with a tight rump, I'd throw up on her sofa.

Kudzu clung to the pines lining the two-lane blacktop heading out of town. Jack's family had worked the land for generations, pulling cotton, tobacco, and soybeans out of its richness. He'd grown up with an affinity for dirt that some boys felt for a football. I'd been amused by it, but not threatened. Not until I realized I'd never lure him away from where he knew he belonged. Back then, my life had been a book I was dying to read, and I couldn't imagine living the rest of my life within the straitjacket of Wynnton. Jack couldn't see life without it.

I recognized the Bland fields as I got closer. This time of year, they were looking dusty, but still fertile and lush with the latest crop. The morning hadn't yet heated up to its full bore, and the frogs were letting loose in the drainage ditches.

I slowed down at the gate that led to a dirt road lined with old cedars. Their gnarly trunks twisted and spiraled upward, as if saying they'd been there too long and they wanted nothing more of their existence than to shoot into the stars some hot night. I knew how they felt. But stars burn out, I'd learned the hard way.

My hands chilled, my heart did its panic number against my ribs, and I could have sworn I was going to pass out as I turned into the road leading to the Bland farmhouse. *Shit, I told myself, this is ancient history, so quit acting like a teenager.* Besides, Alma Berryman Bland and I had never been friends, let alone best friends. Sucking in deep breaths, I mentally catalogued my assets. I was still thin, I had only a few gray hairs, my hips had never spread in childbearing, and I could talk my way out of a bottle of rotgut if I had to. Not much of a catalog in the plus column, but it gave me enough of a boost to curl my toes against the accelerator. I should have worn Miss Ena's diamond earrings with my jeans, to add the proper amount of élan to my affected-grunge outfit.

The teenager at the other end of the phone must have run for her father to tell him I was on the way. Jack was sitting on the top step of the porch, fooling with a screwdriver and something small and mechanical. I had a hunch whatever it was, wasn't broken, but it sure as heck made a good prop.

I slammed the door to the Mustang and leaned against it. "Morning, Jack. Where's Desiree?"

He barely looked up from the gizmo in his hand. He wore a baseball hat, dirty with finger marks and old sweat stains, low on his forehead. His boots were caked with dust, as if he'd come running from the fields.

"She's not in good shape, Tal." He sounded tired.

"Neither is her mom. I need to talk to her, Jack, before the police." I wondered why he was so protective of this child. Then I thought about his status as the father of many, and for the first time, saw a side to Jack I'd never before seen.

"I won't bite her, Jack. Give me some credit."

He stared at me from under the creased hat brim, his eyes dark on mine. "You been drinking, Tal?"

I could feel my face flush. "No, Jack. In fact, I just saw Henry and he gave me a first class tour of Kinsale's corpse. If I wasn't stone-cold sober before, I sure as hell am now."

"All right, then. She's upstairs. But if she starts gettin' upset, you leave her alone, you hear?"

I wondered what the hell was going on here. By all

rights, Desiree should have been with her father. I started to wonder who her father was.

He was waiting for me to say something. I uncrossed my ankles, and headed for the porch. "Show me up, Jack."

"I'll do that." Alma stood behind the screen door.

I swallowed hard. I'd wonder for the rest of my life what she had that I hadn't.

"That'd be great, Alma. Thanks." I sounded like a teenager.

She held the door open for me, just a few inches, letting me know she was admitting me into her home, but she wasn't going to make it easy for me. I almost wiped my sneakers on the mat, but stopped myself at the last second. She'd inched back inside, just enough to let me get into the hallway.

The tiny yellow flowered wallpaper that had danced everywhere when I was a kid was gone, and in its place was pale blue paint on the old plaster walls. The dark oak trim looked too heavy against the blue, but somehow, I knew it was Alma's favorite color. Glancing at her face, I was surprised by how young she still looked.

She hadn't cut her hair, like most of us had done when we hit thirty. She still had fluffy bangs, wispy curls pulled back in hair clips, and little silver bells hung from her pierced ears. Her blue gingham shirt showed she still had a bustline like a swimsuit model, and even if her waist was thicker than mine, and her hips a tad beyond curvy, she personified mother, wife, and all that was feminine. My old shirt and jeans hung on my spare frame like scarecrow trappings.

Sun and the life of a farmer's wife had given her some dark spots on her naturally fair skin, and her eyes crinkled in the corners without a trace of a smile, but she was still pretty in a way I'd never been. My fire had come from my drive, my self-will, my sure knowledge that I was meant for better things. She had the look of a woman who'd used her youth as God had meant her to use it, providing her man with offspring and a warm cuddle when he needed it. No wonder Jack had married her.

"She's upstairs, first bedroom on the right when you turn." Alma led the way up the stairs as if I were some stranger she'd never seen before. Her back was as stiff as if she'd run a lightning rod up it before I showed up. Her hips swayed neatly in their denims, and I knew she was letting me know she was all the woman I'd never been, would never be. Opening the door to the bedroom, she stepped inside.

I got tired of this shit. "I'd like to speak with Desiree alone," I snapped before she could say a word to the girl sprawled on the bed, an array of Barbie dolls and more clothes than Miss America spread around her.

"But she's so fragile at the moment," Alma explained in a patient, quiet tone of voice, as if she were speaking to the monster of the western world who was planning on eating Desiree for dinner.

"Alma, I must insist. I have to speak with Desiree alone."

I crowded her space, keeping my eyes on her. She didn't like it, not one bit. She wanted me to know she was queen of this castle, and I was admitted to its inner sanctum only because she'd allowed it.

"I don't think this is a good idea." Alma had decided she held all the aces, and she was going to play them.

"Then I'll have to call social services and have Desiree transferred. Maybe a temporary foster home."

Alma had no idea who she was tangling with. She was an amateur in this game of one-upmanship.

She glanced at Desiree, unconcerned by the power struggle going on over her, stuffing one incredibly high-arched Barbie foot into a shoe that would have killed a normal woman.

"Well, all right. But not for long, hear? Desiree will need to eat lunch, it's almost ready."

I noticed I didn't get an invitation. "We'll talk as long as we need, Alma." I wasn't going to let her save face.

She played her last ace, edging to the bed, leaning over and giving Desiree a quick kiss on her forehead. "You just shout, sugar, any time you want this woman to leave you alone. We won't let anyone upset you, you know that, don't you?"

Desiree was either deaf or didn't give a damn. As Alma stroked her long, cornsilk hair, Desiree twisted Barbie's arm to stuff her in a fuchsia dress worthy of a stripper.

"Alma, either you get out of here now or I use my cell phone to call social services." I didn't have a cell phone, but Alma didn't know that.

Alma wasn't easily cowed. Perching on the edge of the bed, she continued to stroke and coo at Desiree, ignoring me. Turning on my heel, I started to clatter down the bare wooden steps to get Jack to talk sense to Alma. I had to talk to the child alone. I didn't want anyone to hear what she said, in case she blurted out that her mother had murdered Trey Kinsale in cold blood.

Jack hung on to the newel post at the bottom of the steps, looking at me as if he'd throw up any second. I wished I understood what was going on between him and Alma, but it wasn't any of my business, and besides, I had enough to deal with on my own.

"Alma, leave the girl alone. You've fussed over her enough for one morning, get down here right now." He sounded tired, his voice raspy, as if he'd talked himself through one set of vocal chords and was in dire need of another.

I waited. If Alma was the kind of wife I thought she was, she'd at least pretend obedience to her husband, especially in front of an old girl friend.

"Yes, dear." Just as I'd predicted, Alma materialized like a very solid ghost at the top of the stairs, her eyes on Jack like magnets to iron. I may as well have been invisible. "Anything you say, dear."

She was putting it on too thickly for anyone to take her seriously. I wanted to lean over to Jack and whisper in his ear, "Let's get outta here before she takes a meat cleaver to our skulls," but he wouldn't have laughed. The old Jack would have grabbed my hand and run.

Alma descended the staircase like an actress, each foot carefully placed on the tread. She was holding a winning hand she wasn't about to give away, if Jack was Desiree's father.

The hunch stuck with me like gum in my hair as I crossed my arms and leaned against the closed door to the bedroom where Desiree continued to torture the Barbie doll. She was small for a nine-year-old, her cutoff jeans revealing legs as skinny as her arms. Nothing in her pale coloring, her sticklike frame, reminded me of a young Jack, and I'd known him at the same age.

I thought about sitting on the edge of the bed next to her, but to be honest, I didn't want to get too close. What if she started to cry and reached for a hug? I wasn't the type to whom children turned for solace. I needed her to help her mother, plain and simple. I settled for a stool tucked under an old dressing table, complete with pink flowered ruffles around the seat. Dragging it closer to the bed, I slipped the pen behind my ear and left my legal pad on the floor beside me.

"Desiree, my name's Tal. Like Alma said, I'm your mother's lawyer. Can you take a sec here and talk to me?"

I wasn't sure how to handle her. Not like my usual, run-of-the-mill witness who knew where the second set of books was hidden, that much I knew.

She ignored me, staring at the garishly dressed doll as if it were a puzzle she must solve. One shoe was black, the other red. Leaning over the bed, I used one finger to flick through a pile of accessories, rescuing the other red shoe.

"Here, now they'll match." I extended my opened palm, the red shoe an offering. It reminded me of June's.

Plucking it from my hand as if she feared I'd close my fingers faster than she could retrieve it, she scooted farther away from me on the bed.

"Desiree, I saw your mother this morning. She sends her love. She wanted me to make sure you were okay. What do you want me to tell her?" I was lying through my teeth, but maybe it would get the conversational ball rolling.

"I'm okay." Her voice was tiny, like her. I hadn't seen her lips move.

"What about staying here? Is it working out for you? I know things must have been kinda crazy last night, maybe there's someone else you want to stay with?" I was grabbing for the proverbial straws here, anything at all to get her talking to me.

"No. I'll stay here." This time I saw her pale pink lips flicker.

"I don't know if they'll let you into the jail to see your mom, but if I can arrange it, do you want to go see her?" I surprised even myself. I tried to tell myself I could use Desiree to get Crystal to open up to me. But I was lying.

"Yeah." The kid was as cool as the slickest professional criminal I'd ever represented. Barbie was now in a lime green knit suit with the red shoes and a purple hat.

"Wanna take a ride, right now? Got my car out front. We can ride down to the Tastee Heaven, get you a chocolate cone." I couldn't have resisted a bribe like that, not at her age.

"Nope. Alma said lunch was almost ready." She'd put me in my place.

"Desiree, I need your help here. Did you see Mr. Kinsale at your mama's place the day he died?"

My expertise in child psychology was zilch and none. But I had to know if she was going to turn into the prosecution's star witness. I was guessing they would be out here as soon as I was gone, so I had to know what she was going to tell them.

"He was a bad man." With that profoundly astute statement, she pursed her skinny lips into a line that promised nothing else. I'll bet she'd been a stubborn baby to feed.

"How do you know that?" I was nothing if not persistent.

"I'm hungry." With that, she flounced off the bed, tugging her shorts down and at the same time tucking Barbie under one arm. Without another look at me, she hurried around the bed and out the door as if I had disappeared.

I followed her down the stairs, careful to keep my distance. Peeking around the newel post, I saw her with Alma's arm draped around her, seating her at a kitchen table filled with children. I didn't take too close a look. I had no desire to see Jack's children with Alma's features.

So far, my investigation was a flop. The star witness was treating me like the prosecutor, and my own assistant made it clear she found me totally incompetent.

I may as well go down on the third strike. I hadn't paid

a courtesy call on the prosecutor as yet. I didn't even know who got the job of turning Crystal Walker into a convicted felon.

Whoever it was, was going to have a cake walk, if I couldn't get my act together.

"I'm leaving now," I called to Alma, her back to me as she bustled around the kitchen table. I wanted to add that I'd be back, that she'd be seeing me as long as Desiree was under her roof. But why stir up more trouble for Jack, I realized before I could open my big mouth.

He was nowhere in sight when I shoved the Mustang into gear. He wouldn't hide from me, I didn't think. But he'd probably make himself scarce while his wife was in a temper.

I was sorry I'd caused the rift between them. Then, remembering that a child usually went to her father when her mother was in jail, I wondered if I'd caused the tension between them, or if it had been a nine-year-old girl.

6

I drove to nowhere the next morning and gave myself a chance to take a deep breath. I'd been running since Frank had hauled me off the porch to attend my audience with Judge Jordan. June had taken one day to rearrange my life, my morals, and my future.

I dreaded going home. Part of my frenetic scurrying about came from a fear that if I stopped for a second to take a closer look, I'd find out that I'd lost it, whatever "it" is. Ditching my briefcase on the floor of the wardrobe hadn't been a gesture of defiance, but an acknowledgment of defeat. I was afraid. I'd lost a case once, a case I should have won with my eyes shut and my hands tied behind my back, and the gods of law had abandoned me. If I sat myself down and gave it a good, hard think, I'd know that

Crystal Walker would be better off with lab monkeys representing her.

I drove without seeing the road, the sky, the cars that passed me, honking as they crossed the broken white line because I was going so slowly. I didn't want to think about failure, about having to explain to Crystal that she lost and lost big because I couldn't pull out my dazzling bag of tricks from the muddle of my brain any more.

They knew that, all of them. Frank, Judge Jordan, Jack, Henry . . . the whole damned lot of them had already relegated me to the file of "poor Tal, she was once quite a gal," and didn't give a rat's ass. Well, Frank and Judge Jordan probably did, seeing as they wanted this trial over with faster than Frank's sex life, which meant pretty damned quick. Henry still cared, I had to give him that much, but he had his doubts. Jack had Alma to cope with, and I was only an old memory gone bad when I reappeared to make his life difficult.

I could feel the burn of anger start somewhere near my pubic bone and work its way up. They all knew Crystal was guilty, and I was the one who would go down the drain with her. My cheeks flamed, and I almost pulled the Mustang over to the side of the road so I couldn't hurt anyone with it.

My hands shook, I was so furious. Parnell may have taken my confidence, my pride, even my soul with him when he walked out of the courtroom in handcuffs, but I wasn't without reserves. I just hadn't wanted to dip into them until now.

I downshifted, hit the gas, and left rubber on Highway 212. I was going to give Crystal Walker whatever I still had left. I just hoped it was enough. I had to get to work, and that meant now.

My fears about June had come true. I recognized a first-class organizer and whip cracker when I saw one. She barely looked up from the desk she'd taken over in the front parlor when I walked in the front door.

"Second line will be up and running tomorrow morning. Bought you a few things to tide you over, until the order gets FedExed from Atlanta. I got you five suits, six blouses, and one simple, but sincere, feminine dress I picked up in town. Just so they don't brand you a lesbian with all those suits." She was playing it cool, but I knew she was daring me to argue with her.

"Where'd you find anything to fit me in Wynnton? I thought everything sold on Main Street started at size 16." Her reaction was going to give me great pleasure.

"That's where the white folks shop. I have connections." June stared down her nose at me. I snorted.

"I see." I couldn't wait to get a look at the outfits June had in store for me.

I tried to squelch my overactive imagination, but it was harder than making a hole in one. She'd have me looking like I stepped out of some fashion magazine if I wasn't careful.

She'd hung the dress on a hanger hooked over the partially opened door of the wardrobe. A pair of plain tan pumps peeked out of a box on my bed, along with a package of new hose, a slip, and another smaller box containing some chunky gold earrings. June left nothing to chance, I noted. I pulled the brown bag off the hanger, and had to stop myself from applauding. June had pegged me from the second she'd seen me.

Standing in the tub, I ran a dull razor over the forest on my legs, and decided I'd dig out the lipstick I'd hidden somewhere. My short hair still damp and curling over my forehead, I slipped into the beige sleeveless dress she'd found God knows where. Cut from linen, its simple lines fit my thin figure amazingly well. June should have been a fashion consultant. If she'd bought purple flowers with a lace collar, I would have killed her.

I had to force myself into the earrings, but I managed to do it. The pantyhose were sheer torture, and I considered wrapping them around June's neck, but in the end, I decided I'd fall into line and play the part to the hilt. From Miss Ena's jewelry box, I added a gold bangle bracelet and an antique pin made of gold and pearls that had always looked to me like fighting birds.

Hovering at the top of the stairs, I squared my shoulders and prayed I wouldn't fall down them in the new pumps. How June knew my shoe size was a mystery, but everything fit. Descending slowly, I tried to pretend nonchalance. But I never was good at hiding my feelings.

June was, though. She glanced up briefly. Then, as if bored by my presence, she punched the buttons on the phone, twirling the cord in one hand, tapping a pen against the desk with the other.

"Henry," I heard her say loud and clear, "she's gonna be all right."

I had arrived. And so had my briefcase. Leaning against the chair beside June's desk, it looked slightly bulging. As June continued to give Henry a blow-by-blow rundown of my reformation, I clicked it open. Just as I feared, June had filled it with a new PDA, notepads, pens, docket book, even a cell phone. I didn't want a cell phone, despite my threat to Alma to use one to call social services.

I picked it up with two fingers, as if it were a dirty baby diaper.

"What's this for?"

"Uh oh, Henry, rebellion in the ranks. Talk to you later." June slid the phone into the receiver.

"It's a modern invention, a telephone you carry with you wherever you go. Then if I need to get you, or if there's someone else who has to talk to you right away, I can call you, or even leave voice mail on it." She spoke slowly and deliberately, as if explaining how a toilet works to a child.

"I've had one before, June. I don't want one now. Hell, I can get from one end of town to the other walking on the gossip line. You need me, holler. Someone'll spread the word."

"That's precisely why you need that. I got you a digital, keeps the conversation safe from anyone eavesdropping over the lines." For the first time, June actually smiled. "Well, as safe as it can be. There's always someone out there looking for trouble."

"June, you seem to be laboring under the misconception that fancy gadgets are going to help me win this case." I tapped the phone in my hand, trying to work up a temper.

"Tal, you seem to be laboring under the misconception that playing the country lawyer is going to win this case. Don't be naive." June was as cool as a woman in control.

I had to salvage something out of all this. "None of this is going to make one jot of difference, you know that, don't you? Crystal Walker either did it or she didn't. If they can prove she did it, nothing I say or do or wear is going to make her any less guilty."

Rising, June smoothed her skirt over her hips, raised her chin, and poured her amber-colored eyes into mine. "You don't get it yet, do you? This is your last chance. Even if you lose, if you do it right, you'll be able to salvage something out of this mess you call your life. You want someone to fight with, you go give Henry some of your snotty attitude. I'll do what he tells me to, unless and until you change the locks and throw my ass onto the sidewalk. Now, you got a problem with this, you march yourself over to Henry's office and tell him."

At least she had the honesty to give it to me straight, just like I liked it. I'd suspected Henry was pulling the strings, but June sure didn't have to enjoy it so much. At least the air had been cleared with the ozone-enriched smell that came after a hard-crashing thunderstorm. I wondered how long we'd be this honest with each other. June didn't like me, that much was as plain as my purple shutters. But she'd stick by me and make sure I got it right, at least until Henry told her otherwise.

"I'll be down at the courts building," I cleared my throat, clicking the briefcase closed, cell phone inside, "if you need me."

Seating herself, June was once again the unflappable woman-in-charge. She wiggled her bottom in the chair, as if saying she'd been disturbed in the middle of an important chore, and picked up a file.

"You should read this before you beard Mr. Amos in his den. He's taken the case himself."

I'd seen enough of the morning papers that littered the booths at Becky's to know Owen Amos had been elected county prosecutor.

I whistled softly. "So I get the big man himself."

June's eyebrows lifted minimally. "Why not? It's a piece of cake, he gets all sorts of political mileage out of it, and someday, he'll use it as a cocktail story on the judge's circuit."

"June, June, you missed your calling. I don't know what you should have been, but you missed it."

"Don't be so sure." Her smile would have out-classed

that of the Mona Lisa. "And don't tell anyone you saw that before the discovery got going."

Flipping open the file, I was astounded. "Who or what do you know to get this so fast?" I stared at the transcription of Crystal's interview with the police. Normally, I'd have been raising a ruckus to get this, and gotten nowhere fast.

"Just count your blessings. Don't do any quoting from it, not yet." June turned to a list on a legal pad. "Henry said to remind you that Amos was in the army. Use it."

I couldn't stop staring at her. "Did Henry tell you to tell me what to say?"

"Don't get sarcastic with me, Tal. Like I said, I'm doing my job." She shooed at me. "Get going. I've got work to do here."

I had no idea what she had to occupy her time in my house, but clearly, she didn't think it important to illuminate me. Lugging the briefcase, I headed for the porch swing and some fast reading.

I didn't enjoy it. Crystal hadn't said the words "I killed Trey Kinsale" but she'd come mighty damned close. Still, she'd been cryptic enough to keep the police from having the classic open-and-shut case, and for that I thanked the god of the guilty ones. As spaced out as she'd been when I saw her, she'd had more smarts than most white-collar criminals I'd represented. She was cagey, changing the subject when the questions cut too close, the notation "No answer" appearing frequently beside her name often enough to fill me with hope.

I hadn't drunk from the bottle of hope in a long, long time. I'd read enough to know that Crystal had problems, but unless they could find a murder weapon with her fingerprints all over it, I had a fighting chance, and so did she.

Heading back inside, I caught June on the phone again, this time with someone she didn't want to explain to me.

"I'll call you back." Abruptly, she hung up. "So, got anything you can use?" She held out her hand for the file.

"Not yet, but nothing in it convicts her with her own words, either. By the way, what's the number for the cell phone?"

"It's taped on the back. Just leave it on. If I need to get you, it'll ring." Turning to the computer keyboard, she began to move the mouse on the pad beside it. "Remember what Henry said about Mr. Amos being in the military."

I nodded as if I would get right on it. Something niggled at me, like an old hangnail that wouldn't heal, but I was too tired to figure it out. Thinking about the history of the new county prosecutor, I headed for the Mustang. I needed food if I couldn't drink.

My hands were steady as I pulled out into the street, the huge magnolias lining it like guardians from the past. Maybe, like those green giants, my past had come back to protect me, to guide me. Instead of running from everything that had happened, from everything that had gone into the making of the person I'd become up to the age of eighteen, I was going to be forced to face that girl down and whip her into shape. But for now, I could put off the inevitable. I was about to step into my role as Crystal Walker's hard-ass, give-'em-hell defense attorney with both barrels blazing.

I felt almost cocky with false bravado as I swung into the municipal lot and parked. At 12:30, I knew court would be recessed for lunch. That was the way it had always been in Wynnton, and I was sure nothing could change that tradition. I'd been inside the municipal building to pay my real estate taxes, file my grandmother's will, and generally nose around when I'd come home.

When Owen Amos was elected prosecutor, after almost a walk-thru-with-his-eyes-closed election, I'd read about it in the papers. There'd been editorial speculation that he was going places, politically. A new Democrat. Unsullied. I'd read that far, snorted my disbelief, and hadn't gone farther than the second paragraph of the article because I hadn't been interested. Democrats with political ambitions were a dime a dozen in my experience. Now, I wished I'd paid attention.

I didn't remember Owen Amos from my days as the young hellion of Wynnton. Maybe his family had escaped before he was born. I hoped so. I was dragging enough of the past around with me during this case, I didn't need a prosecutor who fit into the puzzle I was trying to figure out for myself.

The municipal building, a sixties-style block of concrete situated next door to the graceful pre–Civil War courthouse, should have been blown to smithereens years ago. The linoleum lining the hallways hadn't been changed in thirty years and needed it desperately. I climbed the steps, trying to appear cool and unconcerned in the ninety-degree-plus heat, and made a sharp right at the end of the corridor running from the front door. The nether recesses of the hallway housed the prosecutor's office.

I didn't hesitate. Shouldering the door open, I breezed in like I knew what I was doing. The receptionist was shoveling yogurt into her face and reading a romance magazine, a lurid drawing of a half-naked man in a loincloth leaning over a raven-tressed woman in a corset and ripped bloomers. I took a good look.

"Great pecs," I noted not totally without admiration.

"Oh, it's John Pelham. He's the greatest, isn't he?" She wore her hair long with colorful plastic barrettes clipping it back from her young face. She looked barely old enough to sigh over teen magazines.

"Not bad." I tried not to chuckle. No one was that good looking unless he was gay, but I didn't want to burst her bubble. "Is Owen in? I'm Tal Jefferson, and I'd like a word with him if he has the time."

She almost dropped the yogurt in her lap. "You're Talbot Jefferson?" She stared at my neck, as if searching for an Adam's apple.

"Sure enough. Is he in?"

She looked guilty, then picked up the phone. In a voice squeaky with surprise, she told the person on the other end that I was standing at her desk, looking for a chat.

Wynnton was still small town enough that Owen Amos opened his own office door. Remarkably well-preserved for a man in his late fifties, he was tall enough to tower over me. That, in and of itself, was enough to make me stand up a little taller and take note. His closely clipped brown hair was beginning to show some solid gray, but nothing else about him looked like it was aging fast. The tie had been skewed aside, and I squinted at what looked like blue cavorting pigs on a background of pink silk. Yep, the tie was a dead giveaway. The boy had possibilities.

Not to mention a face not handsome, but all male. I jerked my eyes back to his tie.

"Sorry to barge in like this, but I thought I should introduce myself." To my surprise, I sounded reasonably confident and not at all flirty. Flirty, however, had never been in my repertoire.

I stuck out my hand, smiling what I hoped was a warm

but nonsexist smile. "Tal Jefferson. I'm afraid we haven't met before."

His hand on mine was calloused. I was surprised. "You weren't what I was expecting." He glanced at his receptionist. "For some reason, I thought Talbot Jefferson was a man."

I breathed a mental sigh of relief. My reputation hadn't preceded me into this office, which was a good sign. It meant that Owen and his gang didn't hang out with the good ole boys who had probably made me their number one topic of conversation over chitlins and beer for at least a month when I'd gotten back into town. But then again, what kind of man with politics printed with his name in the newspaper didn't eat chitlins?

"Not in this life," I chuckled. I held on to the briefcase with both hands. "Could I buy you some lunch? I'd like to discuss some preliminary motions with you. For Crystal Walker."

He looked surprised, but quickly rallied. Nice eyes, wary but not stupid. "Sure, I'm not working on anything too important right this sec. Emmalee, we'll be at Becky's."

I felt Emmalee's eyes on our backs as he held the outer door for me. His proximity was doing things for my libido that hadn't been done for a long time. He smelled like soap and clean cotton. I had to watch myself, or I'd look like a slobbering basset hound very soon. This was not a good tactic to use when I was planning my moves to bash this guy's head on the judge's bench in the courtroom.

The walk to Becky's was short enough that I didn't have to make much conversation. Mundane comments about how hot it had gotten in the past month smoothed over my alarm at my reaction to this man who was going to be my arch enemy. I'd played this game long enough to know you had to hate the prosecutor, or you couldn't win.

The usual lunchtime hubbub died like a car running out of gas. I could have sworn every eye in the place was glued on us. On me. I turned to Owen.

"A table in the back?" I was letting him know I wanted to talk, and talk seriously.

"Sure. Looks like there's one available now."

He almost put a hand in the small of my back to steer me in the right direction, but caught himself at the last moment. I wondered if I would have been pissed at such a gentlemanly gesture, and decided I wouldn't have. In fact, I'd rather wanted to feel what it was like to have his hands on me. *Bad girl, bad girl,* I chastised.

Once we had slid into the booth, Becky materialized from the kitchen. Someone must have blabbed to her at light speed that we were in her restaurant, and together.

"Chili, Owen? With a salad?" He nodded, never taking his eyes off me. She peered over the rims of her reading specs at me. "Tal?"

"I'll have a tuna sandwich. And a glass of tea. Unsweetened." Liptons soaked in Karo syrup made me ill.

"Be right back."

I had the feeling she was trying to hurry us along. I, however, was in no rush.

"Why do I get the feeling I've met you before?" Owen frowned slightly and stared at his hands, resting in a loose knot in front of him on the table.

"Don't think so. Been back in town just a bit, never did any criminal stuff around here." I cleared my throat, decided I'd let him have the story, at least my version of it.

"Dropped out of the big city firm, came home to my roots, that sort of thing. Been putzing, mostly, for about a year or so. May take me a bit to get my court legs under me again." I would play the nice guy for as long as I could, I decided. Actually, I was already up to speed, but he didn't need to know that. Let him think I was small stuff, I might slip one by him. Somehow, I doubted that.

"Same here. Been here about three years."

"I'm guessing you retired, settled down here because Fort Delaplane was your last posting." I slid the iced tea glasses from the edge of the table where Becky had dropped them. Squeezing the lemon wedge into mine, I waited for him to tell me where he'd been living before Wynnton.

"Grew up in Atlanta. Wanted to stay in the South when I got out. This seemed as good a place as any." He followed my routine with the lemon.

"Why'd you stay, though? Doesn't the army give you a year after you retire to make up your mind?" I was getting personal, but I figured he'd tell me to butt out when he was ready.

"Liked it here. Small enough, I'm busy but not too busy. Got my law degree at night school, when I was stationed at the Pentagon. This seemed a good place to use it. I was lucky to win the election."

"You do any private practice in Atlanta?" Maybe he *had* seen me before.

"No, worked for the feds for a while after I retired from the army. Prosecuting." A self-deprecating smile. Almost artful.

Little buzzers and flashing red lights were going off in my head. "Don't tell me you handled white-collar stuff."

If he answered yes, I'd wonder why he hadn't recognized me.

"Nope, did the nitty-gritty, the bank robbers, drug dealers. Nothing big time, but I learned the ropes."

I let out my breath. Now, I thought, back to the other red warning light. "Your wife, she like it here?" I guessed maybe three kids, the youngest one a surprise baby who was still in college.

"Never made it that far," he grinned. "She waved as I hit I-95, I waved back."

This was not bad, I mused, not at all bad. But if I didn't rein in my curiosity, he'd think I was out to get him into the sack. Not an insane idea, but I knew I'd have to win this pesky case first. When that happened, of course, he'd have my face on a dart board in his office, so I may as well drop all hope of a serious flirtation.

"And you?" he asked. "What about you?"

I trotted out the name of my old law firm, failing to mention I'd made partner. He whistled.

Before he could start playing twenty questions about my legal life, I jumped into Crystal. Becky slid our lunches over to us, keeping a wary eye on me as if expecting me to pull out a gun and start shooting her customers.

"Judge Jordan asked me to take on Crystal Walker. Actually, as I understand it, she requested me. I plan on giving her the best defense I can." I owed him honesty. So far, he'd been more than open with me.

His eyes crinkled in the corners as he tasted his chili. "That's what I heard. How does Crystal know you, if you haven't been in practice here?"

"Long time ago, third grade. We were in the same class."

He whistled softly. "Got a memory like an elephant, that woman. You two must have been tight."

"Nope. I'm as surprised as you that she asked for me." I lowered my sandwich.

"I'm filing for a psychiatric on her. When I saw her in

lockup, she was practically a zombie. Has she been checked out by a doctor that you know of?"

He shrugged, and in his eyes, I could see the prosecutor asserting himself. He'd been interested in me, enough for him to let down his guard a bit. But business was business.

"That's up to the sheriff. Guess you know I'll be taking this one myself."

I nodded. "That's why I decided to drop in." I took too big a bite of my sandwich and spread my fingers over my bulging lips.

Chewing fast, I got into it. "I don't think Crystal did it, but if you're going to offer a plea bargain, do it now, while I'm not vested in this case. Because once we get the ball rolling, I'm not likely to back out."

I wasn't just blowing smoke. I'd always operated like that, and if Crystal or anyone else didn't like it, they could fire me. It had never happened, at least, not yet.

"I hear she just about confessed." Owen was all business now. I'd expected it. "I wouldn't take less than murder one, anyway."

"There are ways around anything." I was obedient to June and didn't let on I'd seen the transcript of her interview. I'd noted that nowhere had it shown she'd asked for an attorney, me. A major problem was brewing here for Mr. Sexy Owen Amos. Since the Judge had told me she'd requested me, the statement was just about useless to Owen. Not one word had been transcribed about a Miranda warning. I guess Frank didn't believe in Miranda. Too bad for Owen.

I wiped my mouth with the tiny paper napkin, noticing my lipstick had already disappeared into my sandwich. Now I remembered why I'd given up on the stuff.

"Well, I just wanted you to know me when you saw me

in court tomorrow at the prelim. Been nice meeting you." I wish it had been nicer, but what the heck, I'd gotten about all the kicks I could handle for one day from a good-looking man. Jack was more like a leftover toothache than a yearning deep in my gut.

"I'll know you, for sure." His grin was a little less wolfish. He understood the game we'd been playing, which relieved my mind immensely. I hated taking out the naive and innocent. Owen Amos had been here, done this. He was no rookie, politically or legally. Maybe this case wouldn't take him down the road he wanted, but one day he'd realize I'd done him a favor when he lost. Those Dixie Democrats were a bloodthirsty lot.

I stood, reaching for the bill Becky left with the food. He made a losing grab for it.

"I invited you, remember?" I shifted my briefcase to the other hand, wished the pantyhose weren't so damned hot. "See you in court, Owen Amos."

I shook his hand again, letting him know I wasn't afraid of him, that this was the last time we'd be able to chat in a friendly manner untouched by what was to come.

His eyes looked shrewd. Yeah, he'd been here before.

"I look forward to it, Ms. Jefferson."

I could have sworn he turned to watch my ass as I clicked out of Becky's, my high heels adding a sashay I couldn't control.

7

"JUNE, I need the name of a respected psychiatrist. I don't want one of those guys who'll sell their soul to one side for the bucks."

I could feel the gears clicking into place. I had a prelim coming that I could waive. I'd thought of doing that and proceeding directly to a competency hearing, but I'd change my mind. I wanted to see how Owen handled himself in the courtroom. What I learned at the preliminary stage might help me in the final showdown, like learning if someone drew left-handed.

I flopped on the settee she'd moved into her office. Ignoring me, June continued clicking on the computer keyboard in front of her.

"You know everyone." I didn't need to ask. June was one of those women who made it her business to store names and gossip in a mental catalog. "If you don't know a psychiatrist, Henry will. Speaking of which, will Henry be finished with the autopsy by tomorrow?"

"He's finished now. Just called. He scanned his report, sent it through. It'll print out in a sec."

I was properly humbled. Kicking off the heels, I hovered over the printer. "Any surprises?"

"Henry said to tell you you were right, whatever that means."

Frowning, I tried to recall our conversation. Hard to believe I'd gone this long without a bit of Southern Comfort. I was distracted by the memory of a bottle in the kitchen, however, when the machine began to click and hum. Slowly, pages began to shoot out.

Reading the report quickly, I almost missed it. Trey Kinsale had died just the way Henry had surmised, with one barbaric detail.

"June, I need a specialist in mutilation crimes, along with that psychiatrist."

Her perfectly plucked eyebrows lifted slightly. "What on earth?" She was, momentarily, confused. "Why mutilation crimes?"

"Because. Just do it." I didn't have time to burn like a gas guzzler from the sixties. I'd have to pay for this, no way the county would spring for any kind of specialists. Crystal Walker was going to be a steady drain on Miss Ena's trust fund. Hell, I didn't have anything better to do with it.

Now, I thought, now I put the screws to my client. Crystal would have had enough time to realize jail wasn't a fun place to be any day of the week. Forcing my big feet back into the torture of high heels, I tried to think of how I'd get her to talk to me. I had to tell her about the autopsy. Maybe that would do it.

"So how was he?" June's raised eyebrows were a sure sign, I was learning quickly, that I had just about pushed her to her limits and had better hop to it. I couldn't think of any deficiencies in the past minute or so, but that didn't mean I hadn't been lacking.

"Who?" My mind was already at the jail.

"Owen, that's who. Voted for him myself, but never met the man. Sure does look good, even if he's a white guy. So, is there hope?"

"If you mean for me, no." June was a professional gossip, I realized. I'd forgotten the power of secret knowledge, the kernel of juiciness that gave you an edge over someone else.

"Don't be simple, Tal. Did he drool over you?"

I was surprised. "Me, drool? God, June, even dogs don't drool over me." I wasn't about to tell her I'd had a passing erotic fantasy or two in the space of one second of meeting him.

Her look of disgust was so blatant I had to laugh.

"Sure, I got a good look at him. We ate, we verbally sparred, we decided we'd see each other in court."

"Damn." June turned back to her typewriter.

"Why?" I was curious now, more than I should have been. If I wanted June to talk to me, I'd have to give her a proffer. I felt like I was plea bargaining with a pro.

"No reason. Just that Henry thought, well, never mind." She began clicking away at the keyboard.

I didn't want to know what Henry thought. Henry was thinking about me too damned much.

"He's into politics, I hear."

"That so?" June typed as if her life depended on it. But I knew where her steel trap mind was, and it was wide open and waiting for me to trip into it.

"Yea, at least, that's what the newspaper says."

"Man in politics, he needs a wife. Doesn't look good, folks will think he's, you know."

"Gay? Don't be silly, no one cares about things like that anymore." I chuckled at the thought that anyone would believe Owen Amos was gay.

"This is Wynnton, and he's not an interior decorator. Damn straight it matters."

"I'm here to testify, he's not. Take my word on this one."

June perked up. "So you liked him?"

That was where this was heading. Had to nip it in the bud, or I'd never hear the end of it. Had to be subtle though. Direct attacks didn't work with June or Henry.

"What're you turning out now?" I sidled over behind her chair to read over her shoulder. I figured the delaying action would soften her up for the kill.

"Request for all the evidence the prosecution's going to use at trial." June's back was as stiff as if a shotgun was rammed in her ribs. She knew I'd sidestepped her but good. Wasn't often I could, and I was enjoying the heck out of it.

"Good move." June really was great at this. I wondered again what Henry had used to bribe her to get her to work for me.

June typed away, her mouth a straight line, her eyes on the screen. She wasn't going to let me have the upper hand in this game, that much was clear.

"I'll be at the jail, if anyone wants me."

"Ummmm." Her eyes never left the monitor.

I was persona non grata at the moment. Chuckling, I knew why I was playing this game with June. Sharpening my claws, getting my game of one-upmanship going was coming back to me like rain on a hot day. Things might steam up when the drops hit the pavement, but I was going to run like hell to make sure I didn't get wet.

Driving to the jail, I figured it was time to get my air conditioning in the car fixed. It'd cost a fortune because it used Freon, but I was already spending money like it came for free. I wasn't even sure Freon existed on the legitimate market, but somewhere in Wynnton there was a good ole boy who'd stockpiled a cache. I was a mass of wrinkles, and pantyhose weren't designed for a Southern summer. Something had to give.

The jail where they'd transferred Crystal from the holding cells was next door, behind the sheriff's department. A long, low building, it was fairly innocuous. Lots of glass in the front lobby wouldn't have passed any architectural review committee today, just from a safety viewpoint, but at least it brightened up an otherwise boring interior. Brown plastic chairs lined up in front of the desk where a pimply faced kid in a tan uniform pretended to be busy.

"I'm here for Crystal Walker." I tried to avoid staring at one particular pus-topped mound on his chin.

"Who're you?" His brown eyes, bright in that thin, young face, stared back at me. He was older than he looked.

"Her lawyer." I shoved my bar card across the desk, glad I hadn't thrown it away.

"I'll put her in Room 12. Down the hall on your right, at the end." Picking up an old-fashioned mike, he pressed an intercom button. Technology hadn't yet penetrated into the Wynnton County jail.

I hurried down the hallway before someone blew the whistle, told me Crystal was at lunch or some other excuse and couldn't be brought out of the back. Sheriffs' departments loved these cute tricks, playing power trips with defense lawyers. I hustled before the kid got wise, was buzzed in.

Today was my day all around, as I barely had time to give the hot, tiny cubicle a distasteful look. Painted chickenshit yellow, the interview room was designed to rattle anyone who dared enter. I felt like I should be shoveling guano. Dropping my briefcase on the desk, I tried to sit, but the seats weren't designed for no-butts like me. I'd rather stand.

A door clanged like the mouth of hell opening to swallow another lost soul. My client appeared at the interview room door so quickly, it was as if she'd been waiting for me. I wondered if June had called over to say I was coming. The deputy shoved her inside and closed the barred door behind her. He wouldn't look at me.

"Crystal." I stared at her.

She wasn't manacled. Crystal slid into the battered wooden chair at the scarred table. Prison orange jumpsuits weren't exactly a fashion statement, but who was I to criticize? "How's it going?"

Staring at the desk, she nodded once.

Frank no longer deigned to distinguish Crystal with his personal attention. The lower-level guard locked us in the room with an oversized key. If there was a fire, Crystal and I would be toast. I didn't like the feeling one bit. Ignoring my client, my eyes honed in on the deputy who folded his arms on his chest like an Egyptian guard from a frieze, and leaned against the opened bars that constituted the only door to Room 12.

I cleared my throat. "Excuse me, deputy . . ." I tried to sound pleasant, but I was very, very hot. Too hot to be civil.

Twisting his thick neck so one eye bulged at me, he grunted.

"Yeah?"

"I'd like some privacy with my client." I was getting tired of educating everyone in this department about basic attorney–client privilege.

He grunted again. "Don't leave no prisoner unattended."

They had more manpower in the Wynnton Sheriff's Department than any one law enforcement group deserved. Not enough crime to keep them busy, I mused. Maybe things would pick up. There was always hope.

The room was as hot as hell times ten. Fighting to keep my temper, I didn't give him a chance to come up with another inane excuse.

"If you're not out of earshot in five seconds, I'll call the ACLU so fast you won't have time to hide your electric cattle prods."

His bloodshot eyes wheeled away from mine. Still hunched against the bars, he pretended he hadn't heard me. I counted, as slowly as I could, to ten. Then, I snapped.

"That's it. I'm getting a judge." Mentally praising June, I jerked the cell phone from my briefcase and began to punch in numbers.

By some quirky luck, I got the weather. As a carefully modulated computer voice told me the temperature was ninety-nine degrees Fahrenheit, I spoke rapidly.

"I need a court order this afternoon. Will the judge be available for a few minutes?"

I paused as I was told the time was 3 P.M. and the temperature was still ninety-nine degrees Fahrenheit. I'd called time and weather a lot when I was drinking just to hear another voice, even if it was mechanical.

Turning my back to Deputy Dawg, I managed another quick look at him. He slid off the bars. I hit the power-off button and focused on Crystal. I was sick of this place already, and I hadn't been in it for fifteen minutes. I felt sorry for Crystal.

I couldn't see the guard. I'd say something to Owen about Frank's lack of understanding of privilege and how he failed to communicate what he didn't comprehend to his underlings. That was going to be a fun conversation, but heck, it was the least I could do.

Sitting gingerly on the hard chair across the table from Crystal, I saw she looked even more pathetic than the first time I'd seen her in the holding cell. I had the feeling she'd be in a ball in the corner if I let her. Perched on the edge of her chair, she reminded me of a child about to get a scolding.

"We'd better get down to work." This time, I was ready with a legal pad and pen. "Saw Desiree out at Jack Bland's place. She'd like to see you, I'll try to arrange . . ."

"No!"

I was unnerved. What kind of mother didn't want to see her child?

"Look at it from her side, Crystal. She's a little girl and she needs to see her mommy." Technically, my job didn't extend to personal advice, but I had a hunch Desiree was going to be my magic genie to getting Crystal to open up.

"I don't want her havin' anything to do with this." The planes of her face had sharpened like a knife on a whetstone.

"That dog don't hunt." I tapped my pen on my legal pad.

"Remember when we was girls, Tal?" For the first time, she looked me in the eye. I'd expected desperation, an entire Greek tragedy. But she was, despite her submissive body posture, nowhere near defeat.

"Long time ago, Crystal. You weren't around much, not after third grade."

Straightening in the chair, Crystal stared at my twitching fingers as if they held the secrets of the universe.

"Know why? My daddy didn't want me around all them boys. Got my period then. Early, too early, I guess. Said they'd have me on my back, their peckers going at me like hungry birds. 'Course, he came to get me to eat lunch every day in his pickup. You know that? Every day."

Her voice was as hard as a dried river bed. All her tears had been shed a long time ago.

I shook my head. "Didn't notice much in those days, Crystal. Just a dumb kid, I guess."

I had a hunch from the way she was talking as to what went on in that pickup at noon. My stomach knotted as I tried to stop the vision in my head.

"Dumb like a fox." She snorted. "Knew way back when, you were gonna get outta this hell hole, Tal. Had that look, when you thought no one saw, like you were weighing all of us rednecks, deciding if we went in your keeper box."

I was startled at her perspicacity. "Yeah, well, I was pretty much a little snot."

She bent her legs like grasshopper stems Indian style on the chair, leaning against the wooden back as if it were electrified metal.

"What I mean is, you saw through all that crap, all the bullshit. You didn't give a rat's ass who had money, who had to chop cotton."

I was extremely uncomfortable with how much she'd

recognized in me at the ripe old age of eight. "What's this have to do with seeing Desiree?"

"She's like you, Desiree is. Sees the bastards coming a mile off. Can't have my own kid sitting in judgment of me, can I?"

I knew better than to touch that one, but I had to do it anyway.

"What does she have to judge?" Standing, I edged closer to the bars to make sure Deputy Dawg was still hiding from my threats. Also, I wanted to look anywhere but at Crystal if and when she answered.

"Shit, told you, I did it. Just want you to hold my hand when I go down. Hear tell you been in the bottom of a bottle so long, won't make you no never mind."

I tried to analyze my feelings dispassionately. Anger, yes, fury, not quite there yet, surprise that my drinking had been gossiped about on Crystal's poor side of town. No, I wasn't happy, but Crystal didn't give a shit. Why should I?

"I don't believe you." Through the haze of conjecture, my mind kicked in with the force of a semi hitting a subcompact. "Told you, I didn't want to hear your confession. I'm not a priest, in case you haven't noticed. I'm a lawyer. Your lawyer. So shut up with this crap. Anything I find in a bottle is none of your fucking business. You don't like it, get rid of me. County has to find you another attorney, and Lord knows, you've got enough grounds to have me fired."

Tension tightened the skin around Crytal's mouth. Behind the big violet-hued eyes rimmed with long, dark lashes, she'd pulled down her screen. I had the feeling she'd given me a test, and I'd halfway passed it. Not an A, but not a D, either. When she spoke, her voice was totally flat, as empty as if the reservoir of her soul had been drained.

"Don't want none of it out in the open, you know what I mean? Don't want this town knowing all about Trey Kinsale and how he done me. Got my girl to think of."

"It's a little late for that, isn't it? Hell, Crystal, he died on your property."

"Yeah, well, his wife didn't know until a few months ago. No one knew. She'll keep her mouth shut, I keep mine closed. No need for all the details," she stretched out the 'e' in details until it sounded obscene, "and folks can't gossip about what they ain't never heard."

I tried staring at the chicken-shit yellow walls, the gouges on the table top, my own long, pale fingers. I still had purple paint underneath one nail.

"If you killed him, tell me why." I'd told her the first time I saw her I didn't want to know if she was guilty or not. Now, I had to know. If I lost, she'd sure as shootin' had better be guilty, because I couldn't bear another Parnell Moses.

Crystal tapped her fingers on her orange-coated thighs, her eyes seeing somewhere other than this putrid yellow room.

"He was gonna leave me. Bam, like that. Said his wife found out, was packing his suitcases to throw on the sidewalk. Good ole Trey couldn't have that, no siree, shit, he owned the land that house was on, it was his, by God. Spent all his money a long time ago, did you know that? Little Marcy's family money kept him in green fees, so she'd get the house for sure. Trey couldn't afford to live there.

"Hell, if I'd known, I'd have squirreled some away." She fumbled in the pocket of her prison uniform. "Shit, you got any cigarettes? I'm about to go bananas in here without a smoke."

I shook my head. My eyes on hers, I pretended to believe her. "Was he supporting you?"

Crystal nodded. "Least the cocksucker could do. Then he stopped paying my electric, forgot my trailer payment. When he cut off my account at the Piggly Wiggly market, I knew we were down the toilet." She tried to smile. I couldn't imagine worrying where my food money was coming from week to week, but if I couldn't buy my bourbon, well, that might instill a mite of panic.

"How long were you with him?"

"Too fucking long." Laughing hoarsely, she sounded like a smoker on her last lung.

"Did he beat you?"

She snorted. "Hell, yes. What man doesn't?"

"Did you ever file any police reports? Take out an injunction?" I knew better, but I had to ask.

"Now why the fuck would I do that? Every time I gave him what he wanted, he'd buy me something pretty. Well, he did until he ran out of his own money and his wife took away his checkbook and credit cards."

"So if you killed him, why'd you do it? You're charged with premeditated, first degree. Was he knocking you around, you lost it, fought back? I don't believe you offed him because of some account at the Piggly Wiggly."

She hadn't had any bruises earlier, and nothing showed on her face now. If I was lucky, she had some old cracked ribs and a dozen bruises under her clothes.

"Naw, shit, I need a cigarette." Nervously, her fingers drifted toward her thin hair, then stopped in midair. I could have sworn she'd been about to pluck out some strands.

"I think it's smoke-free in this jail." I'd seen a sign in the corridor. Sure as hell a good way to keep the prisoners in an uproar. "Crystal, look it. You've gotta give me something to go on, or I'm back to square one. I don't believe you did it. You want to know why?" Leaning back myself, I crossed my ankles under the table and wished I had a glass in my hand. My butt ached from the chair, my brain hurt from thinking too much without a break.

Crystal stared at me like a cat stalking a doomed jaybird. I ignored her.

"Simple. Those nails are fake, and if you'd stabbed Kinsale as hard as it looked when I saw the body, they would have snapped off. Plus, there'd have been a regular Niagara Falls of blood. You didn't even have the smell of it on you. Believe me, Crystal, I know what blood smells like.

"And you wouldn't have done it with Desiree anywhere near. If you really wanted him dead, you'd have done it by the river, rolled him over a bank into the current. Buried him in the mud, let the fall rains cover him up with more water. Hell, it's what I'd do."

Her irises didn't have any pupils again. In the overhead glare of the ugly fluorescent lighting, they were lavender pools filling her eyes. I could have sworn she hadn't blinked in five minutes. My own eyes were itchy with tension, but I resisted the urge to rub them raw.

"So who killed him? Who are you protecting?"

A small muscle at the edge of her jaw contracted. I should have ducked, but fool that I am, I thought I'd backed her into a corner. Crystal was a better fighter than I.

"Why'd you come home, how'd you screw up, Tal?"

I didn't want to play this game. "None of your fucking business. In case you haven't noticed, you're the one wearing the cute orange jumpsuit."

"Then leave Desiree out of it. I don't want to see her. Tell Alma I'll give her custody, if she'll take her on. With that brood, one more won't matter."

For a second, I wondered how Alma and Crystal had become such close friends that Crystal would give up her daughter to her. My own opinion of Alma was tainted by her wedding ring, and I knew it.

"Why Alma? What about Desiree's father?"

The smile on Crystal's face was as potent as a dead skunk on a hot afternoon. "Her daddy don't want her. Never did."

I wondered about that. But if there was a chance Crystal had kept up the relationship with Desiree's father, and he'd gotten wind of Trey Kinsale sniffing around his woman, the code of the South would have dictated the ending. Kinsale knew the rules when a man crossed the tracks to the wrong side to dip his wick where he oughtn't.

"Who is he? Tell me."

I'd lost her. With a voice thick with the lie, she answered, "Dead."

I was getting nowhere as fast as some slick Northern lawyer in a Southern courtroom. Hauling my ass to the door, I yelled for Deputy Dawg. The preliminary hearing was my chance to go fishing, and I had nothing but dead worms for bait. I thought of Kinsale's severed ear and got angrier by the minute. Crystal knew what was going down, but she sure as shootin' didn't give a hoot in hell if I went down with her. My reputation as a drunk had put me in her league, I guess.

It wasn't until I was hiking up my skirt in the ladies's room to jerk off the panty hose that Crystal's last words sank in. She'd said Desiree's father was dead.

I assumed Henry knew how to run a paternity DNA. He could use whatever he wanted from Kinsale's corpse to see if it matched Desiree's.

If they matched, I'd know something Crystal wanted to hide. The possibility made me feel smug, very, very smug.

8

ᘒᘒᘒ

"HENRY called. He wants you at his house at six for dinner. No excuses." June was packing up for the day, her makeup as perfect as when she'd arrived this morning.

I felt like I'd been trampled by a dozen good ole boys stampeding for the beer cooler. "I've got work to do. I'll call him and renege."

"No you won't." June never raised her voice, I noticed, but its timbre changed instantly to reveal her mood. "He wants to go over the autopsy with you and discuss it before the prelim."

"Oh." I should have known they'd drag me through this by the short hairs, the two of them. "Okay, I'll be a good girl and go."

Henry probably wanted to keep me away from anything

with a long neck and an alcoholic content. "What time is it now?"

I didn't wear a watch. I'd inherited my grandmother's tiny gold pocket watch she'd worn around her neck on an eighteen-karat chain for as long as I'd known her, but it had stopped running when I came home. Time had seemed irrelevant anyway.

"Four. I need to pick up some stuff for tomorrow. The office supply place special-ordered it yesterday morning, UPS should have delivered it by now. I'll be in early, get the colored tabs ready for the exhibits."

"Oh, yeah, thanks." I still wasn't thinking of details, just the larger picture. I had a client who for some unknown reason hated me enough to want me to sit beside her as she waited for the lethal injection to start, a friend who thought I was incompetent, and an assistant who was sure I'd graduated at the bottom of my law school class. Owen Amos had been a bright spot, but maybe he'd hidden what he really thought of me. At least he'd had the courtesy to treat me like a worthy opponent. Then again, that could have been his way of practicing to be a politician. Smarmy and insincere.

"You need a watch," June noted as she headed for the front door. "Get one. I don't want you paying any fines to that old fart who calls himself a judge because you're late."

"Yessum." My sarcasm was lost on June. She floated out the door without a glance back at me.

Changing into my jeans and T-shirt, I opened the old mahogany box that held Miss Ena's jewelry. Most of it had been handed down for generations to the women in our family, and I'd worn a piece or two when she'd first passed away. But my casual life, as I liked to think of it, since returning to Wynnton hadn't called for a diamond and sapphire circle pin, or even the platinum and ruby earrings that I'd seen her wear only once. As a rule, Miss Ena didn't favor colored gemstones unless they were small and unobtrusive. The rubies were a show of poor taste, in her opinion, by some less-than-ladylike relation.

Pulling out the exquisite little watch, I held it in my palm. I had a picture of Miss Ena wearing it as a young girl, the chain longer then and looped so she could put the watch in the pocket of her dress. She'd been given the watch as a high school graduation present by her parents, back in the early part of the twentieth century. The works were probably worn to nothing, but I thought I'd see if it could be repaired before I bought something else. I'd lobbed the Rolex I'd bought in Atlanta into my toilet and flushed it when I'd quit the firm.

One jewelry store had dominated Wynnton's main street for generations. The Swinfords had been selling engagement rings and tasteful baubles since Miss Ena's parents tied the knot. I wasn't sure if they could fix the antique pocket watch, but I needed a reason to get out of the house and move my feet. I walked the five blocks downtown, hoping that Swinfords hadn't closed down shop at the same time as June.

Main Street in Wynnton would never change. Stores built after the war bore carved lintels displaying names of establishments still in business since 1865. Swinfords was one of them. The jewelry displays reposed in small boxes standing behind the plate window that had been added in the sixties. A boring array of inexpensive wrist watches and chains didn't inspire raptures that would bring in customers. All in all, Swinfords felt sad and tired. I empathized.

They hadn't locked their doors yet. I stood in front of the old oak display cases, waiting for someone to notice a customer. A middle-aged man appeared from the back room. I didn't recognize him as one of the Swinfords.

"Hi," I opened, reaching into my jeans pocket.

He stared at my hand warily, and I had the strangest feeling he was armed. I jerked the watch out of my pocket quickly.

"Do you have anyone who can work on an antique watch?" I slid it across the scratched glass.

His face was almost babylike in its roundness, with pink cheeks and a soft chin. Only the gray hair, the antiquated sideburns that had gone out of style twenty years ago, the paunch hanging over the belt, gave away his age. I found myself staring at his hands as he popped the back off Miss Ena's watch. He had young hands. Hands that had never chopped cotton. He wasn't from the wrong side of Wynnton, not with those hands.

"This is an old one," he sighed. "I'm not sure, but I'll ask my father-in-law. If anyone can get in there and make 'er run, he's your man." His grin was tenuous, as if he wasn't sure I'd like him.

I nodded, filled out a claim receipt, stuffed my half in my pocket. "When do you think he'll have a chance to give it a look?" I was remembering now, there'd been two Swinford daughters, older than I. They'd graduated from high school in the late sixties, which meant that this guy had to be, if he was one of their husbands, in his late fifties. I hadn't been in Swinfords in years, but something was niggling at the back of my mind. Some sort of scandal about one of the girls.

"I'll give you a call sometime tomorrow. Shouldn't take him long, figure out if it's reparable." He didn't have a Southern accent at all. A hint of the Midwest was still there, under the bland, no-accent-at-all.

What was it about one of the Swinfords? Someone she'd married? I couldn't remember the story, only that there'd been a flurry of gossip about the time I was a young teenager. I'd been too self-absorbed to care or even pay much attention. Wynnton gossip was always floating, like flotsam in the river that ran with muddy debris outside the edge of town.

I had the feeling he watched me until I'd walked out of his line of sight. Something was wrong, very wrong. A Swinford didn't marry a Yankee. Not even if she'd been knocked up without a ring on her finger.

Gossip brought me up on my haunches when I hit the sidewalk. It was only 4:35, and the courthouse didn't close until 5:00. Secrets about the crème de la crème of Wynnton were harder to dig up than most, and the Swinfords had been cream once upon a time.

Thanks to Miss Ena, I knew where to go to find answers about the Swinfords at the very least. Trey Kinsale was too young and nouveau for my sources, but the old goodies, the ones that couldn't hurt anyone anymore, lived in the women who worked in quiet dignity in the basement of the courthouse.

If I walked fast, I'd have at least thirty minutes with the three women in Wynnton who knew all the secrets of the dead. The rulers of all they surveyed, the three witches had come young to the job and were now old. Fuzzy-haired these days with bad permanents, they clothed themselves in print dresses they must have ordered from a catalog specializing in the anachronistic.

They'd begun their careers entering notations of deed transfers, releases, and mortgages with black fountain pens, their handwriting a showy flow of nineteenth-century correctness. Miss Anne's School for Young Ladies had taught them well. The powers that be in the state legislature had declared that all the records would go into a computer database, but no money had been set aside to convert the original transfer books, filled with similarly spidery script, to microfiche or the database.

I loved the old basement where the record room hulked and hid from all but those forced to descend the slick marble stairs to its nether recesses. The walls had been painted army green, probably in the 1940s, and the color had never been changed. Red leather book spines, stamped with gold letters denoting the year, the letter of the alphabet, and the volume number, were stacked like the bones of the dead in Roman catacombs. There was neither rhyme nor reason to their placement. Whoever hauled down a book, replaced it where it would fit back the easiest. The damned things weighed a ton, so a lot of them cluttered the floor.

But the three witches knew where everything was. Including the Swinford bodies, I was sure.

They'd been friends of Miss Ena's when I was very young and they weren't, though they were quite a bit younger than Miss Ena. As they'd become absorbed in their lives in the courthouse basement, Miss Ena had seen less and less of them. I cleared my throat at the back of one of them, leaning over a keyboard.

"Miss Hanscomb, do you remember me? Miss Ena's granddaughter, Tal." I extended my hand to the flagpole-thin woman with slightly blue hair. I'd recognized only her eyes, still the deepest blue I'd ever seen. As a child, they'd reminded me of sapphires.

I was hesitant, wondering if they'd remember me. But evidently my ignominious return to Wynnton had filtered down to the bowels of the record room.

"Of course it's you, Tal. We recorded the probate of

Miss Ena's will." I'd done the filing in the probate clerk's office, not realizing in my alcoholic fog it would find its way downstairs.

"Always knew you'd come home, we did." Nellie Hanscomb slid her paper-thin hand into mine.

I wondered at the ages of the three witches. Miss Ena had been quite a bit older than they, and I suspected she'd had a hand in getting them their jobs in the record room. Something about sweethearts who hadn't come home from the Korean War and that Southern determination to languish most tragically and with constant references to the deceased fiancés came to mind. Miss Ena must have tired of hearing the refrain and put them to work.

"Birdie, Cilla, come here. Guess who's come to visit."

She sounded as if I'd dropped in for an after-church social call. Cilla had grown into an amazing plumpness. Her hand, when I shook it, was a soft as yeast rolls set to rise on a warm window sill. She was, as I remembered, the most quiet of the three.

"Tal Jefferson, what's a pretty girl like you doing without a husband?" Birdie Mills flitted like a dying sparrow from the room behind the oak counter.

I'd never grown accustomed to the obsession Southern women have for marriage. Perhaps it gave them the only real power possible to women—the right to refuse sex, to keep a man panting at their feet. Whatever it was, I'd abhorred it since I was a child and would get comments like, "Oh, she's going to be a beauty, all right. Catch herself a fine fella afore she's outta her teens."

I stifled my long-held prejudice. "Just lucky, I guess," I purred so sadly they'd believe I was mourning my lack of marital status.

"Well, there's time yet. Maybe not for children, but . . ."

Nellie's sad tone forced me to reassess my internal mocking-meter. They'd been raised to become wives and mothers and been handed another fate. Who was I to judge?

I had to steer them away from our collective failures and to my real reason for descending to the courthouse bowels.

"I'm sure you've heard, I'm Crystal Walker's lawyer."

They nodded in unison. I risked a quick glance at their earnest faces, filled with pity, and stared at the lace collar on Cilla instead.

"What I'm looking for is a copy of Trey Kinsale's last testament. Would you have it yet?" I had no idea if it had been submitted for probate. Marcy Kinsale could take as long as she wanted before qualifying as executrix, if she'd been named to that position under her dead husband's will.

Nellie gave Cilla "the look." Cilla passed it on to Birdie. I half-expected them to start the "toil, toil" line from *Macbeth*.

"Actually, Tal, it's not public record until it's copied at the computer place and put into the system." Cilla was speaking for all three.

Glancing around the quiet room, empty of anyone else but the four of us, I slid into lessons learned at Miss Ena's knees. When you want something, and you're a woman, pour on the charm.

"I'd really appreciate it, truly I would." Lowering my eyes, I stared forlornly at my left hand, conspicuously ringless.

"Well . . ." Birdie, I could see from under my lashes, was looking distressed. "She has admitted the will to probate. It's not as if she hasn't produced it yet."

"I'll give it a quick glance, right here," I promised, spreading my fingers on the scarred oak counter. "I'm sure it has nothing to do with his death, but I need to cover all the bases."

"It won't help that poor woman." Nellie was speaking to the other two.

"And heaven knows, it'll be the talk of the town before we get it into the system." Cilla pursed her lips in a disapproving line.

I wanted to ask how the will's contents would make it onto the grapevine, but figured I'd wait for that revelation. I didn't want to appear to be too anxious, but inside, I was barely holding the leash on my curiosity.

Birdie flew into action while the other two dithered on. Flitting into the sanctum sanctorum, she emerged seconds later with the classically blue-bound bundle of papers. I tried to keep the drool in my mouth.

"It's not long, only five pages, and the last two are the witness and self-proving clauses." Birdie slid the rubber band off the packet and carefully unfolded it. "It was heading out today to the company that copies them onto the disks."

I was amazed at their ease with the computer world. Miss Ena would have considered a hard disk drive to be the devil's work. I reached for the will.

"Oh no, dear, come back with me." Again, Birdie took the lead. "This way, no one will notice you having a look-see."

I didn't wait for a second invitation. Flipping up the hinged end of the counter, I ducked onto their private turf.

"Miss Ena always expected great things of you," Nellie threw after me as I obediently followed Birdie.

I bit back the retort I wanted to make, that Miss Ena expected a lot of everyone, and none of us met her high standards.

"I hope I'll do her proud with this case." As soon as I said it, I wondered if I'd crossed the line. Crystal would be known in their circle of friends as a fallen woman. Women like her, in the true Southern tradition, were damned forevermore. The three witches would want Crystal to meet her maker for her final judgment sooner rather than later. After all, while Crystal was a great source of gossip, she was still a blot on the reputation of Southern womanhood.

"We just don't want to see Crystal go down without a good fight, you see." Nellie spread the will open on a desk and gestured for me to sit.

I managed to pull my bottom jaw back up just before she turned to me. My shock must have shown, however.

"You really need to work on a poker face, Tal," Birdie chuckled. "Everyone knows Crystal put up with a ton of rot from that drunken man, just so she could put clothes on that child's back and food in her mouth."

I swallowed, hard. I'd underestimated these three, and badly. "Is Desiree his daughter?" If anyone knew, I sensed they did.

Cilla frowned. "If she is, she doesn't favor him nor his people. And Crystal's dark-haired, was even as a girl. No, I'd say Desiree came from some other stable. But she loves that girl and did right by her. Better than her own ma did for her."

My hands turned cold, and I actually felt the blood rush to my head. I had no idea I'd been the only person involved in this case who'd been oblivious to the abuse Crystal had suffered at the hands of Trey Kinsale. Maybe that's why she'd asked for me—I was the only person left in Wynnton to be shocked.

Birdie twittered on. "Back in the old days, folks kept

quiet about such goings-on. Ladies weren't supposed to know awful things like that happened, and the men who should have done something about it were doing the same." She clamped her lips, as if afraid she'd said too much.

I wondered of whom she was speaking, but at the moment, it wasn't my problem. Crystal was.

"I keep wondering if this mess is about Desiree." I was talking to myself and the words just slipped out.

"If it is, there's nothing in the will about her." Cilla tapped the red-lined pages, pulling me back to business. "We checked, quite carefully, you may be sure. A child shouldn't suffer because of the sins of the father."

I sat. Reading quickly through the preliminary legalese, I saw pretty much the language I expected. Kinsale had left the estate in trust for his wife, who had a life tenancy with the power to invade the principle with the trustee's approval. I expected a will like this from a man with a wife who had majored at State in her M.R.S. degree.

Turning the pages, I hurried to find the name of the executor and trustee, figuring Kinsale would have named his bank. Such practices were more than chauvinistic, but still the norm in a society where the wife was still referred to as "the little woman."

I saw the name under the paragraph titled "Executor and Trustee" and thought I was having an out-of-body experience. I read the name again and decided my eyes were playing tricks on me. Cilla was watching me closely. I glanced at her face and knew I'd read it correctly.

Crystal was executrix and trustee of the estate, with authority to draw a percentage of the estate as fees for her services. In addition, she was permitted to receive reimbursement for all expenses she incurred in the faithful performance of her duties, including attorney's fees.

"Lord have mercy." I changed it from a curse in the last millisecond. The three witches wouldn't have put up with what I almost said, and I'd have been thrown out of the record room on my skinny bottom.

Crystal had a damn good motive for killing Kinsale. If his real estate was worth anywhere near what I'd thought, and I was guessing there was life insurance in the pot as well, she'd pull down exec fees in the hundreds of thousands of dollars by the time the trust terminated. Marcy may have had the cash, but Trey owned land. Crystal had authority specifically to sell it. Marcy Kinsale was still a young woman, she'd be pulling money from that trust for years to come, and Crystal, if she walked on the murder rap, would be right in there, too.

But why would she kill him at her own place and make herself the obvious target of the investigation? Was she really that stupid? Had she not known about the will? She wanted to go down the river on the murder charge, she'd told me as much. I was just along for the ride, I wasn't supposed to do her a bit of good. She couldn't serve under the will if she was convicted of murdering Trey.

"There's no proof she knew about this," I mused aloud. "Hell, Crystal can barely read."

Cilla stared at me as if I were as dumb as a cocker spaniel. "You need to learn more about your client, Tal."

With that, she reached around me and swept the will from the desk, folding it briskly and snapping the rubber band back into place.

I felt as if I had fallen into the tar pit and the birds were circling to peck out my eyes. I was doing one piss-poor job of representing my client, and the three witches knew it.

They say the wife is always the last to know. That's not true—it's the lawyer.

I totally forgot to ask about the man in Swinfords and to get the story behind the daughter he'd married.

9

CRYSTAL, why the hell didn't you tell me about the will?" I should have been feeling no pain, but I sure as shootin' was wide awake and all too aware of it. I was going to be late for dinner with Henry, but he would just have to understand.

She was looking right peaked, I had to admit. Her black hair clumped to her head in greasy strings.

"What will?" She tore at a hangnail. I cringed as she sucked the blood from her finger.

"Kinsale's will, as if you don't know. You're executor, and you'll pull down big fees if you get that far. Of course, if you're convicted of his murder, all bets are off." Warning lights went off somewhere in the fuzzy corners of my mind, but I didn't have time to stop and clear away the dust bunnies. I was good and mad and I wanted to go with it.

Her laughter was as bitter as old cucumbers. "You're joking, right? You mean Trey actually wrote a will? What the hell for? He didn't have enough cash to pay his green fees."

Hearing Crystal talk about the country club startled me. Because she'd grown up in a trailer didn't mean she couldn't know about things like golf and afternoon mint juleps, but my prejudice brought me up short. Maybe there was more of Miss Ena's snobbery in me than I'd wanted to acknowledge.

"Randolph Wells filed the will." I waited for a reaction but got none from Crystal.

"He has three months to file the first accounting, listing assets." Again, nothing but a hard, blank stare from Crystal.

"He was Trey's lawyer, I think. Trey wanted him to sell the land that house is on." Crystal pulled her finger from her mouth. Her lavender eyes were cloudy today, as if she wasn't sleeping.

I wished I could just read in a book what was going on here. There was layer upon layer to Kinsale's death, and it all left me feeling like a lost child.

"I thought that land was in Kinsale's family for generations. The Kinsales hang on to what is theirs. Always did. Lived in town, but that land was gold to them."

There was a famous story about Kinsale's great-grandfather and the KKK. The carpetbagger government had confiscated Kinsale land for nonpayment of taxes, and then had the unmitigated Yankee stupidity to try to give it to the newly freed slaves. Kinsale's ancestor and those of his similarly affronted frame of mind had made a terrifying example of the poor people who had dared to actually try to plant crops on those bits of dirt. I'd heard whispered stories as a kid of the mutilations inflicted by those men in white masks. Trey had inherited his nastier tendencies from ancestors who should have been lynched themselves.

Crystal almost laughed, but it died in the back of her throat. "Trey wanted cash. Ever hear of the Global Transport Park? Going to make Wynnton into the mecca for Southern commerce." She spoke the words as if she were the chairman of the board. I'd never heard Crystal lose her Southern accent before, and found it strangely disquieting.

"Don't read the newspapers, don't own a TV." I had to have some excuse for my ignorance.

"Find out about it." Crystal seemed interested for the first time since I'd started talking to her. "They're offering a lot of money for a big chunk of land. Trey thought he had a chance to hit the jackpot."

I needed to have a conversation with Randolph Wells.

"Crystal, if you knew all this, why didn't you tell me?"

"I didn't know about the will. But I know what land is worth. Land where investors are ready to plow the cash." Her eyes were like a leech on my face. I wanted to pull away. "Put it together, Tal."

I already had. If Crystal was executor, she'd be fully within her rights to bring the biggest return for her handling of Kinsale's assets. Selling the Kinsale land for megabucks would certainly be the wise act of a prudent trustee and executor. Crystal already knew that. I'd bet my bottom dollar on it.

"Crystal, how'd you know that you'd be able to sell that land? As executor?"

She stared at me as if I'd crawled out from under a rock.

"Just 'cause my daddy diddled me, don't mean I'm dumb."

She swept my breath away with the depth of her fury. "I never implied . . ."

"Yeah, you did. I may not have any fancy initials after my name, but I know how to read. I read lots. Trey talked to me. We talked, and he listened to me, you know? He heard what I was tellin' him. You think I done nothin' but spread my legs to earn my keep, don't you?"

I couldn't stand the force of her hatred. I also despised her accuracy. "If you feel like that, Crystal, why'd you ask for me to represent you?" I was back to square one with the questions I'd needed answered up front.

"I thought maybe you were different. You were, back when I was jerking my hair out by the roots, hoping someone would ask me what was wrong, why I bloodied my hands and head like that. You didn't look at me like I was poor white trash. You were the only one."

I could barely swallow, and my spit tasted like hemlock. Nothing I could say would take back my surprise at her quick grasp of the legal situation.

"I don't think you killed him." I tried to offer a tarnished peace bough.

She was having none of it. "It doesn't take a law degree to figure out I'd hardly kill Trey in my own backyard and expect to stay on as executor of his estate. Maybe you can get me off, even if you don't have any other prime candidate for this comfy shithole." She waved her hand to encompass the jail.

I'd already said the same to the three witches. "So who takes over your job if you get an orange jumpsuit for the rest of your life? I'm thinking out loud here. The will didn't say." My pride went down slow and hard, but I'd given it to a bottle long ago. It wouldn't hurt to remember that, I told myself.

"Is that normal?" She tapped her chewed finger against the rough canvas fabric covering her knees.

"No, not really. The fact there's no alternate executor could be considered malpractice." I hunted and pecked through my memory of the wills and estates course from years ago. "Any immediate family member can qualify, I think. But does Marcy Kinsale have the smarts to do it?"

Crystal snorted. "Marcy's IQ is below her waist."

"That's what everyone thinks about you," I pointed out harshly. "If Marcy's smarter than you think, who'd she get to front for her? Do what she wants?" I hesitated. "What does Marcy want, anyway?"

I'd avoided talking to the grieving widow. Mostly, I figured she'd hate my guts for representing Crystal, and I didn't need to waste my time with an unpleasant scene. I'd made quite an error.

"Marcy wants that big fancy house her money built on Kinsale land. She'll take His Honor Linwood Jordan as long as he's got a pecker that works. Been having a fine old time, the two of them. Can't see it myself, him all wrinkly and, well, you know how old men are."

I don't know why, but I glanced involuntarily at the open bars behind me. "You don't mean it? Not Judge Jordan . . ."

The idea of Marcy Kinsale fooling around wasn't so wild. Bored ladies of breeding had been known to take a lover or two when their husbands strayed. Revenge upon one's spouse was a time-honored Southern tradition. Some women took their full measure with a shotgun, but the upper crust generally did it between the sheets.

"Trey knew all about it. They had a knock-down-drag-out over that land. Marcy and her judge wanted to keep things the way they'd always been, their houses next door to each other, but not so close there'd be gossip."

I thought of Marcy Kinsale, sobbing at Judge Jordan's house when I'd arrived the night Crystal had been arrested.

"Jesus H. Christ," I blurted. I was so dumb I shouldn't be allowed to cross the street alone. I'd wondered, briefly, what she'd been doing there, but hadn't the imagination of a peanut to pursue it past idle curiosity.

"Guess I'd better roll my tail feathers out of here and have a talk with the not-so-grieving widow." I collected myself, rising slowly to allow the circulation to restart in my bony butt, paralyzed by the hard wooden chairs in the interview room.

Crystal unfolded herself like an opening flower and stretched with the aplomb of a yoga instructor. "You remember what I said about my kid?" she asked casually.

I felt guilty. I'd said I'd bring Desiree in for a quick visit with her mother and then forgotten it. Crystal had seemed so dead set against it. Now what did she want?

"Yeah, I remember. You don't want her here." I tried to think of something positive to say about Desiree. "Alma seems to really like her."

Smiling like she'd heard a semi-funny dirty joke, Crystal turned to the bars behind me and shouted for the guard to unlock the door. Turning back to me, she lounged against the metal barricade as if she'd learned the correct prison posture all her life. I straightened my shoulders.

"She'd better, if she wants to keep that husband of hers."

I wanted to jump into that one with both feet, but I was already swimming up shit creek. Whatever Alma had going with Jack and their marriage wasn't part of the big picture. And I desperately needed to get something on the canvas before I met Owen in court. Mrs. Kinsale and I needed to chat, whether she liked it or not.

I didn't have time to wash up or change before heading to Henry's and Grace's house. Since I was turning into a

socially responsible inhabitant of Wynnton again, I
stopped by the grocery store to buy a gift for Grace. Eying
the wine bottles in the back, I decided I'd better not tempt
Henry to give me a hard time. I settled on a wooden box of
Brie. Why the Piggly Wiggly was carrying Brie was beyond me, but I was sure Grace would know I was trying to
observe the social niceties.

A homemade pecan pie would have been more in Miss
Ena's tradition, but I didn't cook. Well, the truth was, I
knew how, but I didn't do it anymore. Miss Ena had insisted I learn all her favorite recipes, and as a girl, I'd stood
on a stool by her side as she cracked eggs and whipped
cream until I could barely keep my fingers out of it. I had
learned to make a mean angel food cake and stunning
brandied cherries to give as Christmas gifts.

Someday, I promised myself as I pulled onto Henry's
and Grace's street, I'd set up the kitchen pantry with bottles
of vanilla, almond extract, baking soda, biscuit flour, even
bitter chocolate I'd store in the freezer. I'd bake and sauté,
fry and flambé until I came close to Miss Ena's expertise.

My daydream was at best idle, at worst self-flagellatory.
Slamming the door to the Mustang, I took a second to suck
in some hot, humid air and calm down. Henry and Grace
lived in the black section of town, but the houses were the
same neat ranchers and white frames you'd find on the
other side of Wynnton where the white middle-class
planted the same grass and pruned identical azaleas. Integration may have been crammed down Wynnton's throat,
but certain things would never change. Henry could have
forced the issue, and certainly had every right, but he'd
chosen to live in comfort close to his family and Grace's.
They still worshiped at Beulah Baptist Church two blocks
over and one to the right.

Henry and I had gone to church together only once. I'd stopped going as soon as I escaped Miss Ena's clutches. Henry and I had been friends forever, but those words probably don't mean much to anyone who doesn't remember the deep South in the late sixties, early seventies.

Miss Ena's church was the first to officially let "persons of color," as it was euphemistically phrased, out of the heatstroke balcony and into the congregation on the first floor. No one with any sense sat in the balcony anyway, so the church had been safe from integration for all practical intents and purposes. Then Miss Ena invited Henry to church with us one Sunday morning.

When we were eight years old, Henry, dressed in his starched white shirt, a black pair of pants with black suspenders, and a perky black bow tie, sat beside me at the 11:00 service. Only Miss Ena would sit next to us in our pew. An hour later, as the minister stood at the front door to greet the exiting parishioners, Miss Ena, her hair silver even then and encased in a blue net hat with a satin bow at the back, took up a regal stance beside the reverend. One white-gloved hand on Henry's shoulder, the other extended to snag the dodging Christians, she would say pleasantly,

"Maylee, I'd like you to meet Tal's good friend, Henry Rolfe."

No one had the effrontery to snub Miss Ena. Every single person held Henry's small hand in some semblance of a handshake. When Miss Ena was sure she'd made her point, she turned to Henry and me and spoke in her most firm voice, the one she never raised but which carried across town with its intensity.

"Children, I'm ready for dinner if you are. Tal, would you lead the way?"

As I was standing below Henry on the first step of the front portico of the church, I marched down to the sidewalk.

I heard Miss Ena behind me.

"Henry, lend me your hand to steady myself," Miss Ena commanded as Henry turned to follow me.

"Yes, ma'am." Henry's hand in Miss Ena's birdlike fist, her feet sure and clad in three-inch high heels, back ramrod straight, Miss Ena sent a message to all Wynnton. They heard her loud and clear, all right.

I'd often wondered who had cooked up this display, Miss Ena and Henry's mother, who did alterations and tailoring? Or had Henry and I suggested it as a way to flaunt the unwritten rules of Wynnton? I don't remember Henry and me being as socially aware as I'd like to believe we were. Vaguely, I remembered Miss Ena inviting Henry to Sunday dinner. He'd had weekday suppers with us before, just as I ended up at his house, a neat, white bungalow, on many a night, seated at the Rolfe table and holding hands with Henry and his sister as their father said grace over our bowed heads. I suspected that Miss Ena used us to make a point. We were too young to care about much except Mary's fried chicken and biscuits, waiting for us when we arrived home from church.

Even though we were some thirty odd years down the road from that Sunday dinner, Henry and I were both still eight years old in each other's eyes. I felt like giggling whenever I saw Grace. She too had grown up in Wynnton, four years younger than Henry and me. The idea of Henry as a responsible husband was still strange, and he and Grace had been married ten years.

Straightening my shoulders, I tried to shake off the fatigue that gripped me. My day had been as hard as it had ever been when I was with the big firm in Atlanta. But I wasn't about to crumple under the pressure this time. Parnell Moses was the shadow at my shoulder I'd never lose. But he was keeping his mouth shut, at least for now. Amazingly, he grew more silent the farther I kept from the bottle I'd hoped would silence him forever.

Parking the Mustang, I ran a hand quickly through my hair. Grace would give it a swift appraisal and suggest a hair appointment, I'd decline, she'd roll her eyes at Henry, he'd shrug. I was looking forward to the tried and true. Too much other stuff was flying in my face today, and I have never liked batting at ghostly gnats. I rang the doorbell.

Henry opened the door so quickly I knew he'd been watching for me from the front window.

"Grace is having a cow. The steaks are like leather."

"Sorry, I had to run by the jail and see Crystal again. She's about as talkative as a cockroach, but I think she's warming up to me."

Henry snorted. "Crystal doesn't warm up to anything without an extra chromosome."

"Henry," I warned, "I don't need this sexist shit from you. Who she sleeps with is none of our business."

"Hell, it is when she kills her bed partner." Henry's eyebrows lifted suddenly as Grace came sailing through the kitchen door. I took the hint.

"Grace, I'm so sorry I'm late." I handed her the Brie. "Forgive me, I got caught up in work."

"About time," Henry muttered.

I literally bit my tongue, smiling at Grace through clenched jaws. "Can I do anything to help?"

Tall and thin as I, Grace had more style than June and three times as much in the intellect department as Henry, June, and me combined. I knew she designed something having to do with rockets, propulsion, emulsion, I had no idea what, but it was very big stuff. She did most of her work at home, then met with her bosses once a month in Houston or some other big city where they were going to make her star-cruisers. I was in awe of her. When men stood on Mars, it was going to be because of Grace Rolfe.

"Nothing, Tal. Henry insisted we put the steaks on early, they're probably impossible to eat. We can always send him out for Chinese." Wrapping her arm around my shoulder, Grace hugged me gently, as if afraid I'd break in half.

"Hey, I've got the incisors of a wolf. Show me a plate, I'll do 'em justice." Following Grace to the backyard, I noticed a few pieces in the kitchen that had made their way from Henry's mother's house. The old oak round table that had held the Rolfe family meals, all except Sunday dinner, was in the corner of the kitchen. I ran my hand over its scarred surface as I tried to float as elegantly as Grace into the backyard.

"Where's your mother these days, Henry?" I hadn't heard about Mrs. Rolfe in a while. Henry's dad had died when we were in college. Miss Ena had sent me the death notice from the newspaper. I'd sent flowers to Mrs. Rolfe, but not in time for the funeral.

"Sold the house, moved to a condo in Arizona. Says she never wants to see another humid day again as long as she lives. Plays golf, swims every morning, and is going to out-live us all."

I laughed, enjoying the picture of the stout, solid woman I remembered flailing away at a golf ball.

"We hear from Henry's cousin Lucinda that Mother Rolfe's seeing a gentleman, but she won't let on to us she has a beau." Grace smiled as she slipped T-bones onto Portuguese pottery. Even her cookouts were elegant. The forks and knives had china handles that matched the color of the dinnerware.

"So how's June doing?" Henry pretended nonchalance.

"Fine." I wasn't about to satisfy his curiosity as to how we were getting on. Let June be the tattletale.

"I hope she's keeping her mouth shut." Grace looked at me from under raised, perfectly shaped eyebrows. Her skin was the color of milk chocolate, her eyes flecked with bits of gold. I felt crumpled and unkempt in her presence, and infinitely glad Henry had found a wife who could keep him under her thumb.

"Well, not exactly," I laughed. "But I deserve it. She's a great paralegal. Why isn't she working for some big city firm, pulling down the bucks?"

Clearing his throat, Henry sighed at the same time. "June doesn't like the city. She doesn't like much, but the city was at the bottom of the wish list. What June wants, she usually gets."

"And what does June want?" This was interesting. I loved getting gossip on my secretary from her own family.

"A law degree. She should have gone straight to law school from college, but no, she had to marry that no-count, worthless . . ." Grace seethed, but in a very controlled, ladylike manner.

"Now, Grace, he wasn't that bad." Henry piled our plates with avocado salad and steaming baked potatoes. "At least he was in the military."

I had always thought Henry was an intelligent man, but any fool knew better than to argue with his wife when she was dishing dirt on a cousin's ex.

"Bad? You want to hear bad? Tal, let me tell you, this one was the cream of the bottom of the barrel . . ." Grace launched into the man's multitudinous sins as Henry shook his head. I enjoyed the drama, stuffing my face to keep myself from laughing. I hadn't had so much fun in years. Later, I wondered if they put on the show on purpose, just to amuse me. I wouldn't have put it past them.

"And then she called to say she was getting a divorce, could we offer a change of scenery. We could hardly say no, could we? I was thrilled she'd dumped the SOB, and then when she showed up here, she was so lost with nothing to do. And then Henry said . . ."

I could guess what Henry said. Tal needed a keeper.

"Henry said she'd whip me into shape in no time."

Henry had the decency to add an embarrassed laugh. "Well, not quite."

"She's really a good person, just a bit, um, particular." Grace added salad to my plate.

"No kidding." I suddenly realized how hungry I'd been. Gossip could wait for my stomach, and I ate with more relish than I had in a month of Sundays. Cooking for myself held no attraction, but when the food was as good as Grace's, I'd have been a fool not to fill up for a rainy, non-cooking day.

After we finished the dessert trifle on the porch, surrounded by cut gardenias from Grace's garden, with the smoky citronella candles attracting suicidal Japanese beetles and the growing roar of cicadas drowning out all conversation, Henry leaned over and said into my ear,

"Why don't we head for my office, Tal, and talk about the autopsy?"

Grace must have been looking for his signal, because she instantly rose, shooing us off the porch and into the house. By the office, Henry meant a back bedroom equipped with computer, printer, and scanner.

I thought I knew enough about the way Kinsale had died, but evidently Henry didn't think so.

"You know that interesting bit of trivia you mentioned about Indians and ears?" Henry was busy tapping on the keyboard.

I was checking the room out. Even in here, Grace's good taste came through. The chairs we sat in were black leather, the computer equipment a matching sable, and the curtains picked up a crisp black and white theme. How appropriate, I thought. The black town doctor/pathologist and the white once-upon-a-time lawyer discussing a truly sick crime in a black-and-white room.

"Guess what. I found his ear."

I sat down hard. "Okay. And where was it?"

"Down his throat."

Swallowing was difficult for a moment. "Okay. So, does this give any clue as to who killed Kinsale?"

"I did some research," Henry continued. "Seems there's a trend in that particular style of mutilation. It was used, just as you said at first, by some tribes upon their dead enemies. Women did the deed."

I snorted. "So let's blame mutilation murders on women? This ties it to Crystal? I can shoot that one down in seconds."

Henry was unimpressed with my disbelief. "Some of Custer's men, after the Little Big Horn, had ears removed by the women when the battle was over. I believe one account said they did it because the white man didn't listen when he was told to leave the Sioux alone and get off their land."

I raised my eyebrows. "Are you telling me for certain that a woman did this to Kinsale based upon this one mutilation?"

"Not necessarily. Just that historically, mutilation of appendages was a female act in certain situations." Henry was flipping through a folder of stuff he'd printed up. "I can tell you the killer was left-handed, that the victim was drunk as a skunk when he went to meet his maker, and that there's more history to this form of mutilation than you want to know about."

I sighed. "More happy bedtime reading, I suppose. Any more fun ideas for my free time?"

"Yeah. Watch out. I've got a bad feeling about this. Whoever killed Kinsale wasn't kidding around. Death was definitely the plan, the mutilation was just for kicks. If Crystal's innocent, then there's one sick puppy cruising the streets with those of us who know we should have been locked up long ago. Watch your back."

For a second, I thought Henry was kidding. Lawyers ended up splattered on the walls of courtrooms when unhappy ex-husbands didn't want to pay more in spousal support, not dead at the hands of homicidal maniacs.

"I mean it, Tal. Whoever did this to Kinsale meant for it to take him a while to die. Miscalculated, is my guess, about the thrust under the ribs. A little too deep. No passion, no anger, no flying-off-the-handle can explain the precise, careful puncturing of Kinsale's torso." He flipped over a photograph of the body.

I'd seen it in real life, of course, but not with Henry's red pen tracing the outline of the cuts. They formed a perfect dollar sign down the middle of Kinsale's body, like a cruel connect-the-dots puzzle for a child. An 'S' with two lines drawn through it.

"Jimminy crickets." I could barely breathe. "So this was about money."

"And who'd just lost her grocery store account paid for

by Trey Kinsale? Everyone knew he was paying her bills, and when he stopped. No secrets in Wynnton, remember?" Henry's eyebrows, I swear, could have taught Groucho Marx a thing or two. "And if it wasn't Crystal, then we're all in deep trouble."

"Shit."

"Precisely. Owen knows this. I showed him the whole file earlier today."

"Thanks a lot." I grabbed the manila holder from Henry and began flipping frantically through the stacks of papers he'd offered. "No way I can get through this tonight."

"Well, if it's any consolation, Owen said the same thing."

"All they have to do is prove Kinsale died, and that there's enough evidence to hold Crystal for trial. If I can get through tomorrow's prelim, I'll ask for a trial date down the road so I have time to get an expert onto this."

"Good luck. I heard Owen saying he'd cleared his docket so you could have a speedy trial. Something about he figured you were the sort of woman who worked fast?"

I almost laughed. I hadn't been working on Owen Amos when we'd had lunch together. If I had been, he'd have known it, loud and clear.

"He wants a quick trial so he can solidify his reputation. A politician on the way up needs a lot checkmarks in the 'win' column." I sighed.

"He's an up-and-comer, that's for sure. Won't hang around Wynnton long. Heard he was a rising star with the feds. Needed to build a civilian basis to get a name within the party." Henry rubbed the bridge of his nose where his glasses pinched. "Too bad you had to run into him now. Maybe later, when all *this*," he waved a hand over the autopsy file, "has died down, you two can . . ."

"Why did he have to choose Wynnton?" My head dropped into my hands. I had a headache building. "And you are *not* to go there. I'm not interested."

I was already tired of this case. Nothing was straightforward. In Wynnton, murder should have been simple, a clear-cut case of manslaughter, an act of passion raging in affronted Southern veins that everyone understood. Symbolism and mutilation didn't seem like Crystal's style. But then again, I was the first to confess I didn't understand the psyche of a woman abused since childhood.

My own childhood, though bereft of parents, had been an idyllic romp compared to Crystal's. I had a lot of work to do, and I needed help.

"Kiss Grace good-night for me, will you, Henry? I've got to get on home." Standing, I tucked the file under my arm. What I wanted to do was drop it in the trash basket sitting next to Henry's computer desk.

Henry stood, politely leading me to the front door. "Remember, Tal, I got a lot of this stuff off the Internet. Most of it came from reliable places, but you never quite know the reliability with anything scientific that you download."

"Thanks a lot," I tried reverting to my sarcastic self. "You drop a bombshell in my lap and tell me I'm probably up the creek without a paddle, and the information I need is suspect. Just what I love hearing at the end of a long day."

Henry smiled. "At least the playing field is level. Owen's wading through the same shit, you better believe it."

I hesitated on the front porch, feeling the warmth of the night caress my bare neck like a lover's hand. "Where do you stand in all this, Henry? Why the extra work? All you had to do, legally, is determine the time, date, and cause of death."

A dark shadow against the light pouring through the glass storm door, Henry was silent a few minutes too long.

"I stand beside the dead, Tal. I don't think Crystal did this, but if she did, she deserves what she gets. I don't care how badly Kinsale needed killing, he didn't deserve to die this way."

I had to agree, but then again, I didn't know much about Trey Kinsale as an adult.

"Maybe he did," I objected. "Sometimes people put themselves in harm's way. It's as if they're asking for the horrendous, the unthinkable, to crawl out from under the bed in the middle of the night and get 'em."

Henry let that one sit a bit, steaming away.

"Is that what happened to you, Tal?"

Jingling my car keys, I headed down the sidewalk to my escape machine. I knew better than to answer him.

10

〜〜〜

OWEN Amos was playing hard-to-get. In my salad days, I'd never have tolerated this, but I realized he had to act his part for the peanut gallery. After all, he was elected to office and the folks had to feel like he was a real hard ass when it came to murdering bitches like Crystal Walker. He was out to score points, I understood the game. The prelim was the first move, his pawn scooting across the board. I was as ready as I'd be, and I didn't even have a drink that morning. Hadn't wanted one. Wonder of wonders.

I winked at him from the corridor as I passed him, heading in the opposite direction. He started to smile, then slid back into his tough military face. I kind of liked it—all angles and cropped hair. He wore his Sears suit like a uniform, and wore it well.

I was on familiar ground in the courtroom. The small, older space was filling quickly with the gossipers and those looking for a morning's entertainment, jostling for space at the front of the gallery. I didn't expect news cameras and a live feed from the courtroom, so I was surprised when a woman grabbed me.

"Hannah Rumson. *Daily Ledger*. Can I ask you a few questions on the record?" Her hair was a gold that probably looked good on television, but didn't hold up well under fluorescent lighting. I stared at the green hues in her perky flip and tried to keep my face straight. I never talked to the press, gag order or no.

"No, I have to get to work, Miss Rumson. Please excuse me."

Her Miss Georgia Peach complexion darkened. I kept the icy smile on my face as she continued.

"Word is that Crystal Walker's going to plead guilty." She clung to my side like a stitch in a rib.

"Word's blowin' smoke." The old juices were still there. I didn't have to stoke my furnace with ninety proof to get my soul on fire for the battle to come. I set one foot on the industrial-strength courtroom carpet and focused on the counsel tables at the front.

Normally, I studied the layout of the room that would serve as a stage for the legal drama I planned to win. But the old courthouse felt as familiar to me as the red-carpeted hallways of the Fourth Circuit Court of Appeals in Richmond. I knew Crystal would be brought through the door leading into lock-up behind the judge's bench. Assuming the bailiffs would place her at the table closest to the door, I plunked down my briefcase.

The court reporter June had hired was setting up her equipment beside the box that held the witnesses. I'd already decided I'd mostly listen today, but my senses were sharpening like an old saw held to the twirling whetstone. The spectators, who must have been standing in line when the guards unlocked the doors at eight this morning, buzzed like a gaggle of high schoolers at a school assembly.

"Hi, Tal Jefferson." I held out my hand to the court reporter, a small, mousy woman with a teased bubble-cut. I wondered how long it took her in the morning to get every tiny hair in place and shellac it down.

"Winslow Hoggett. Pleased to meet you." In the South, manners are mandatory. Pleasantries before business, or everyone will think you're a Yankee.

"The pleasure's mine." The niceties observed, I cut to the chase. "I'd like a transcript of today as soon as possible, if you please."

"Sure, no problem. You're the only case on my docket. Copy to Mr. Amos?"

I hesitated, decided I'd let Owen ask me for the transcript. No rule said I had to provide it, and at least I'd find out how long it took him to swallow a small lump of pride.

"No, just an original to my office. Thanks."

She looked startled, but my attention was drawn to the bailiff, who was crooking a finger at me as if I were a barmaid. I checked behind me. I was it.

"Yes?" I sauntered very slowly over to where he stood. No sense in letting him know he has power in the courtroom, I thought.

"Your client wants a word."

I'd had June carry over a plain blue dress for Crystal to wear to court. I hoped to heaven it didn't fit. I wanted it to hang on her, to envelop her like a little girl playing dress-up in her mother's clothes.

I'd guessed correctly about the size. Leaning against the

wall of the holding cell, Crystal was drowning in the cotton size eight. Chewing her fingers, she waited until the bailiff retreated before speaking.

"You keep my kid outta this. Remember, I told you before," she warned.

I hesitated. I'd seen and heard nothing tying Desiree into any of this. What did Crystal think I was going to pull out of my magic hat? That Desiree killed her mother's lover? I froze. The image flashed before me like a vision from Murder 101. Could I have missed the possibility?

I was fifteen minutes from the first step into the morass of a criminal trial, and I was lacking some very important information.

"Did she have anything to do with Kinsale's death?" I couldn't imagine a child as young as Desiree mutilating a corpse, but perhaps that was done later by someone else.

Someone who wanted to make sure Desiree wasn't incriminated. The pale, silent child who tricked out a Barbie like a streetwalker might have hidden horrors in her young mind, but none as twisted as those carved in Kinsale's flesh. I didn't see how she was strong enough, either.

"No, and don't you even think it." Crystal's eyes took on a depth and concentration that led me to believe she cared, truly cared, for that child.

"Did Desiree like Kinsale?" I'd never thought to ask the question before, I don't know why.

"What the hell difference does it make how she felt about him? He didn't have anything to do with her. I just don't want her dragged through this, is all."

"It's a little late for that. Half the town knows you have a daughter, and the other half probably knows her daddy. Life isn't going to be easy for her, no matter what happens out there in that courtroom. So if you want to keep things simple and easy for her sake, you do like I tell you.

"You keep your mouth shut out there. Make notes of things you hear you think we need to check out. Poke me if there's a question I need to ask and I haven't." I spoke as if to a child. A panicky Crystal wasn't what I needed at this moment.

Glancing at the door, I prayed no one had overheard her. If Desiree was somehow involved, I wanted to be the first to find out how and why.

"Crystal," I started, hesitating. "It's been a while for me. The whole song and dance of a courtroom battle. But I wanted you to know, I'm not drinking. The only thing I want is for you to get a fair trial, if such a thing is possible in Wynnton." I felt vulnerable. I had no malpractice insurance, I was representing a woman charged with premeditated murder who could end up dead after a mandatory appeals process, and all I cared was that she knew I was trying my damndest.

"Yeah, well, break a leg," she muttered through the fingers in her mouth. She tried to laugh. "Not really. Got enough problems without you looking stupid on crutches."

"Gee, thanks, I think."

Owen's head showed at the doorway, and I wondered how long he'd been listening.

"Damn," I spit, hoping he was hard of hearing.

"Moment of your time, counselor?"

I squeezed Crystal's shoulder and was surprised at how cold she was. The air conditioning hadn't yet reached as far as back as the lock-up. Judge Jordan's door was still shut at the end of the corridor. I couldn't wait to ask him to take himself off the case. I was going to enjoy this.

"Don't be afraid," I whispered.

"Afraid hell, I want this done and over with. Let's get this show on the road and let my little girl get on with her life."

I didn't have time to ask her what she meant. Ducking into the courtroom, I bent my head as I listened to Owen's very properly phrased, very polite request for a transcript. He was nicely charming, in a way. The lad would go far if he played his political cards right in Wynnton.

"Sure, I'll share. You pay half." I knew he had to have it. As long as he knew I had one and he didn't, he'd always feel like he'd gotten the short end of the stick, even if he had every motion granted and I was tossed out on my ass into the street.

I didn't tell him I planned on a very short hearing. If Judge Jordan didn't recuse himself, I'd go through the motions, then I'd file a writ to get him tossed off the case. If sleeping with the widow of the dead man didn't make you a suspect, it sure as hell made you unfit to sit as a judge over the trial of the accused murderer.

However, I wanted to live in Wynnton a while longer. Being able to shop for groceries and not have to dodge spitballs would be a pleasant enough existence for the likes of me. I had to handle the request to recuse with utmost tact.

Tact is not my middle name. In fact, I don't think about the word or the concept unless I'm remembering Miss Ena. She would have handled this scenario behind closed doors, having a very private chat with the good judge's long-suffering wife. That would have been all it took. But I didn't have that luxury. I had to have my grounds out in the open and on the record. I also needed to buy myself more time. I had a lot to find out about my client before we went to trial, and it was like pulling teeth out of a turnip. My feet were already sweating in my pumps.

"By the way," I touched Owen's arm as he turned away, thinking our business was concluded. "I just want you to know, I'm going to ask Judge Jordan to take himself off this one. As soon as court convenes."

I didn't like the look on Owen's face. He didn't look properly surprised.

"He's already done it. Harlan Goode is the substitute for this court. I thought you knew."

Like hell he did. "Oh, okay, that's good. Saves time." I was ticked. All my planning disappeared in a second, but I wasn't about to let Owen see I was off-balance.

"Did he give any reason?" I'd have bet my virtue, or the memory of it, the reason wasn't the real one.

"Yes, as a matter of fact, he did. Told me he was close to the Kinsales, them being next door to each other and all. Didn't think he could avoid the appearance of impropriety." Owen looked as if he believed every word.

"How long you lived in Wynnton, Owen?" I worked hard on my poker face.

"Long enough to get elected." He was looking smug again.

"Not long enough to know the good judge was sleeping with the dead man's wife, however." On that gloating disclosure, I pranced to the counsel table and awaited my client. I hadn't needed to tell Owen that bit of good news, but it served its purpose.

He looked shaken. Hallelujah, I prayed. Now, while he was off-balance, I needed to get this trial under way.

Crystal was walking toward me, a bailiff on each side. I pulled out the chair next to mine and stared at her. She was calm enough. Good. The play was about to begin, and I was ready. Harlan Goode waited until everyone was seated and the tension in the courtroom was building to the breaking point before making his grand entrance.

I didn't know the name, and with good reason. Judge Goode was, as Miss Ena would have said, a whippersnapper. I doubted he was as old as I. Despite his old-fashioned name, Judge Goode wasn't one of Wynnton's favorite sons, at least, not any that I knew of. I'd sit back and see how he handled himself. Probably, I snorted to myself, he was the junior partner in the only other good-sized firm in town, Hawkins and McGlone, and therefore, the only lawyer in town who hadn't done legal work for the Kinsale family at one time or another.

He took charge of the hearing right off the bat, insisting on formal introductions in the courtroom. Wherever he'd learned his procedure, it had been the old school. If he wasn't a jackass, he and I would get along just fine.

June had done a good job of labeling everything we'd collected so far. I didn't need to hunt for reports as they were mentioned by witnesses. Owen was keeping it clean and simple, the same tactic I'd have chosen in his place. He paraded the first officers on the scene, the dispatcher who'd taken Crystal's 911 call, and ultimately, Henry.

I waived a reading of Henry's credentials. Henry smiled.

"Cause of death, doctor?"

Henry spoke clearly, calmly, and very precisely. "Shock. Trauma from knife wounds to sixty percent of the torso. Loss of blood. The blood loss was the precipitating factor."

"And how did Mr. Kinsale lose this blood, Dr. Rolfe?" Owen looked down at his notes.

"A series of cuts and stab wounds. Many were superficial, but one of them killed him. Nicked an artery."

"And did you discern a pattern to this violence?"

I didn't object. Henry's observations would come out eventually. What I needed to do was to make sure the jury, when we got that far, didn't see close-ups of the really gruesome wounds in bright color.

"I did. It appeared to me that the wounds formed a pattern. A pattern of a dollar symbol."

The imagery titillated the gossipmongers behind me. A swift murmur ruffled the crowd like a spring breeze.

Henry completed his description of Trey Kinsale's human remains, describing the severed ear and its placement as an after-death mutilation. More titillation for the peanut gallery. I watched Crystal out of the corner of my eyes.

I hadn't told her any of the details of the autopsy. For one thing, I'd wanted to see how she'd react. For another, I'd discovered a sacred need within myself to figure it all out before I spoke to my client about it. I told myself my actions arose from an attempt to see if Crystal had lied to me.

She was shaken, no doubt about it. Her pale face washed another shade lighter, something I thought was impossible. Closing her violet eyes, she seemed lost within herself. I waited for her to emerge.

"You didn't see it when you found him?" I scribbled on the notepad I'd centered between us.

"No," she scrawled back. Crystal was left-handed. I felt ill. Henry's report had determined the killer was left-handed.

She would have had to either do the deed herself, or poke around in his mouth to know about the severed ear. She saw it was missing, I was sure. No one with eyes could have missed that. What did she think had happened to Kinsale's appendage? She'd never asked me. She was a hell of an actress, I was a witness to that. I shoved all thoughts of her left-handedness from my mind.

Henry continued to describe the killer as left-handed, Kinsale as having been inebriated, and that was about it.

When my turn came, I didn't ask Henry a damned thing. He'd given me all the information the night before. The gory details could wait for the full-blown trial.

Owen established Kinsale's death, his relationship with Crystal, that Crystal had been cut off from Trey's financial support, and the fact that a drunken man was an easy target for a weaker woman. I couldn't argue with that. My client had no alibi to present, so I held my own counsel and let the judge certify it, which meant he'd found enough evidence for the case to go forward to a jury trial.

Let Owen chew on my silence, I thought smugly. He'll be wondering what the heck I have up my sleeve.

Owen and I whipped out our calendars. Mine was filled with white, unmarked pages. I pretended to study it, holding it close to my chest.

"I'll need time to get my experts together, Your Honor." I hadn't given him any guff, so we hadn't had a chance to lock horns. Not yet.

"How much time, Miz Jefferson?" He was trying to look stoic, but I could see the beginnings of judicial impatience. He thought Crystal was guilty and he wanted this done and over with. He was probably pulling down three times as much per hour in private practice as he was as a substitute judge.

"I need at least ninety days, your honor," Owen interrupted.

I made a quick decision. A speedy trial would help me as

well. The longer the story of Kinsale's severed ear and dollar sign symbol dragged on, the less chance I'd have to give Crystal her life back. Maybe if we were a ninety-day wonder, she'd live through the notoriety when she was acquitted.

I was living in la-la land and I knew it. "I'll go along with that," I said anyway.

Owen looked surprised. Crystal was slumped in her chair, thinking God knows what. I snapped the calendar shut, shook Owen's hand, and waited for the bailiff to escort Crystal back to lockup.

I needed to get some help on this, and fast. June was about to expand her duties, whether she knew it or not.

11

∽∽∽

MARCY Kinsale hadn't attended the preliminary hearing. I wanted to ask Owen why she'd been absent, but that would have tipped my hand. I had to be careful of that with Owen. Men with politics and prosecution on their minds were tricky. For that matter, what man wasn't?

I drove straight from court to the Kinsale place. Built in the recent past, the house was big enough to shelter half the county. As I pulled in the long driveway, lined with boxwoods that must have cost a hundred a pop, I realized I'd never been here before. The first view of the house from a distance was intriguing.

Up close, I realized Marcy had put beaucoup bucks into her showplace. How Trey had thought he'd sell it out from under her was the product of the rambling mind of an idiot male who had no concept of female pride. I vaguely remembered the old days when the Kinsales had lived on Main Street in town, a brick house from the turn of the century, large but not palatial. Their wealth had been held in acreage on the outskirts of town. Marcy must have insisted some of the land be converted from tobacco and soybeans into her little fiefdom when they built the house in which she now lived alone.

I don't know where she got pecan trees as large as the ones shading the house. Maybe this area had been a grove in the past, and she'd knocked down the rest for her palatial glory. The shining white wood siding shone in the noon sun. A huge porch sheltered both first and second floors, and the brick steps leading upward for a good ten feet to the first floor were twined with ivy. English ivy, I saw upon closer inspection. I left the Mustang in the crushed gravel driveway under the shade of one of the pecans.

Ringing the doorbell, I waited and stared at the mile upon mile of gleaming white fencing. Horses chewed aimlessly in smaller enclosures, while other paddocks held jumping rings and an obstacle course of some sort. Marcy was into the horsey set. That took even more money. For the first time, I began to feel sorry for her husband. Sleeping next to money and knowing it wasn't yours to play with as you wished would be hard for any man's ego. I sincerely doubted Trey Kinsale had ever had that much self-confidence.

The perfect family retainer cracked open the door. As black as only a Southern African-American could be when untainted by any white parentage, she guarded the space with her tiny, uniformed body. The gray dress matched the gray streaks in her hair.

"Miz Kinsale's not receivin' any visitors," she announced curtly.

I put on my best Miss Ena smile, hopefully serene, superior, and sensitive. "Please tell her Miss Jefferson would like a word."

Graying eyebrows shot up, and for a minute I thought she'd slam the door in my face. "You got your nerve," she chastened me.

"I do indeed. Please pass my message on to Mrs. Kinsale."

I was about to get the boot. But a voice slurred with too many mimosas slid out of the darkness in the hallway.

"Hell, Callie, let 'er in."

Marcy Kinsale was, as Miss Ena would have said, a comely woman. Even in her blue satin bathrobe at noon, her hair a cloud of perfectly streaked blonds and pale browns, she looked as if she'd just stepped from a shower and was merely in her dressing gown to receive an inconsiderate visitor. The Waterford glass in her hand held orange juice and something stronger, however. The something stronger had been poured a lot more liberally and a lot longer than the orange juice. My throat ached for a sip.

"Marcy, it's been a long time." I strode past the door guardian, my hand extended.

Marcy looked startled, as if she'd forgotten we'd once been in school together. She was about two years younger than I, but in a small town, you knew everyone at one time or another. I vaguely remembered she'd been elected homecoming queen when she was a sophomore and I was a senior in high school.

"Tal, you're so much . . ." she wobbled a little, put her hand out to steady herself and brushed a clump of funeral lilies languishing in an ugly vase on a spindly legged table, "taller."

"Well, I guess so," I offered by way of appeasing her. I had no idea what she wanted to say instead of her quick substitution of words. I was the same height I'd been in seventh grade.

"You're looking good, Marcy."

Callie, standing with her hands locked over her stomach, harrumphed behind me.

"Well, I've looked better. I haven't been able to play tennis or ride, or really do much of anything since . . ." She waved her hand holding the glass, sloshing its contents onto the waxed parquet floor.

"Miz Marcy, you go lie down right this instant." Callie stalked around me, ready to head her employer off at the pass.

"I'll be glad to help Mrs. Kinsale upstairs." Offering my arm like a cavalier, I weathered a stormy look from the protective Callie. She knew why I was there, and she didn't like it. I admired the wiry woman for her acuity.

"It's all right, Callie, Talbot may be a stinkin' lawyer, but she's just plain folks. Aren't you, Tal?"

I rumbled noncommitally and took the Waterford from Marcy's hand, passing it to Callie.

"Watch the hem of your robe, Marcy," I warned, leading her to the sweeping staircase. Marcy had seen *Gone with the Wind* once too often. The red carpet on the steps was too much like a hotel in Richmond for my taste, but then again, my money hadn't paid for it.

We managed the stairs with Marcy clinging to the polished bannister and me clutching her waist on the other side. She'd been on a real bender. I was almost envious.

"Marcy, maybe you'd better try the cold shower trick," I offered from my long experience with the bottle. "It won't do much for your frame of mind, but it'll give you goose bumps."

She snorted. "That'll be a first."

She wasn't as drunk as she acted. But I still wasn't sure how much credence I could put in what she'd tell me, if anything. I knew as well as anyone that lying through your liquor was standard procedure. Tripping on the edge of the oriental carpet in her bedroom, Marcy staggered onto a chaise lounge. She could have posed for Titian, with that wild hair and the voluptuous figure straining the satin robe. Losing her husband to a woman like Crystal must have been hell on earth.

I took a seat at her dressing table, trying to ignore the potent scents, all too heavy and cloying, rising from un-stoppered bottles.

"First off, let me say I'm sorry about your husband. As you know, I'm representing Crystal Walker, and if you have a few minutes, I'd appreciate talking to you about your hus-band." I just didn't have the social graces to segue into the niceties of beating around the bush.

Marcy didn't notice. "That bastard had it coming. I'm glad he's dead, I'm glad it was at the hands of that bitch, and I'll never admit I said that."

This was going to be interesting. "What makes you so sure Crystal did it?"

"Obvious, isn't it? He was dumping her. Trey was prob-ably the best thing that had ever happened to her, the cow. My bet is they were both drunk as skunks when she sliced and diced him."

I made a note that Owen had shown, or told her, about the autopsy report. "I understand your marriage was rocky for other reasons, most notably the Global Transport Park."

I'd been right, she wasn't as drunk as she pretended. "What about it?"

"Word is, you didn't want to sell this land to the development, and your husband did. Makes for some mighty interesting speculation, doesn't it?"

"Speculation, hell. Kinsale land has belonged to Kinsales since seventeen seventy-five, there was no way Trey would sell it. He was jerkin' my chain, per usual."

"And what about your, uh . . ." I stumbled, trying to come up with a pleasant way to call Marcy an adulteress, "relationship with Judge Jordan? Did Trey approve?"

Snorting through her nose like no Southern lady should, Marcy brayed like a mule. "Approve? Hell, he was glad. Trey hadn't been able to get it up in years, and I'm not talking about capital for investments, either."

Startled, I glanced around the opulent bedroom. The antiques were new, all carefully crafted to look old and expensive. Marcy must not have approved of the family pieces that came down to Trey.

For a second, I was angry at her. I treasured each old piece of wood in Miss Ena's house, whether I dusted it or not was another matter. Still, I had Miss Ena's sense of family, that the accouterments of a household held the spirits of the dead who'd pulled open those same drawers, laid forks in the sideboard drawer after every Sunday dinner.

The mental break helped me readjust my sympathetic poker face, if there was such a thing. I wondered how many other people had heard Marcy's complaints about her husband.

"I'll bet you didn't relish leaving all this, if Trey sold the land." I stared around the room, so she'd think I was admiring her taste.

"I already told you, no way he would sell." She fluffed

the robe around her ankles, hiding them from me as if I'd been staring at her like some kind of predator.

"You didn't hold a dower interest. If I remember correctly, Trey inherited this land long before you two were married. Sorry, Marcy, I'm not buying it. You couldn't stop him if you got down on your knees and begged."

She wasn't drunk, no matter how much she wanted me to believe she was. "I didn't kill the son of a bitch, and if you're so all-fired sure your client didn't kill him, then why don't you take a look at the other dirt she was screwing? That piece of shit Susan Swinford made the mistake of marrying Moran. Bet he didn't like the way Crystal clung to Trey, even after he cut her off. Couldn't give her what she really wanted, Moran couldn't."

"If it wasn't sex, what was it?"

"Honey chile, what it always is. Money. No woman should be without it. Just like a good push-up bra." She chuckled.

I could have sworn I heard the gears clicking in her head. Mine hurt. I wanted that drink melting in a wet ring on the Sheraton side table where Marcy had plunked it.

"Moran?" The long-ago gossip was still foggy. "Where've I heard that name?" He must have been the pink-faced man who'd waited on me when I took the watch in for repairs. I wished now I'd remembered to ask Cilla and Company about the Swinford gossip.

"You know, that baby-killer from Viet Nam. The one who nuked a whole village, ended up court-martialed out of the army. God Tal, his face was on every magazine and the evening news for a year." She was snorting again. I wondered if she had a physical problem.

I shook my head. "So what about him and Susan Swinford?"

"She married him, took him into the family business when he got out of Leavenworth. God knows why. He wasn't anything to look at. Personally, I think she wanted to get married so badly, he was the only thing she could catch. You know the type. . . ." She glanced at my ringless finger.

"Whatever happened to you and Jack Bland, by the way? I always thought he knocked up Alma, and that's why he married her so fast. But their first kid didn't show up for two years, so that couldn't have been it."

I fought the urge to get up and run like hell. No way I was going to discuss Jack with Marcy Kinsale, and she knew it. She'd thrown him into the mix to rattle me. *Boy howdy,* I thought, *she's a piece of work.* I almost began to feel sorry for her dead husband. Life with this bitch must have been as hard as hoeing ten acres by hand.

"You mean that guy with the sideburns, pink cheeks, he's Lieutenant Moran?" I heard in my head the flat accent, saw his wariness as I reached into my pocket to extract Miss Ena's watch.

"The one and only. God, remember the reports about what he did to those poor villagers? He and his men, they tortured half of them before they burned them alive. Just the thought of living in the same state with him gives me the creeps." She was enjoying this, I saw. "And your sweet, innocent client was boffing him before she did Trey."

"How do you know?" I pretended I couldn't care less, but inside I was mentally reviewing what I remembered about Lieutenant Moran. Not much.

"Trey told me all about it. Thought it was funny. Him having the same woman a guy like Moran screwed. Made him feel like more of a man, like he'd scored the big one, having a whore who'd put out for a mass murderer. Hell, he probably couldn't do it with Crystal, either. Can't you see the two of them sitting around in that shitty trailer, drinkin' and just chatting away the night about how many ways Moran dreamed up to torture those poor Vietnamese?"

Someone had put ice on my feet and hands. Crystal hadn't told me about Moran, and those vicious little foxes were nibbling at my confidence in her. I needed to find some old news reports about Lieutenant Moran, and fast.

Standing, I picked up Marcy's glass, wiped the wet circle off the wood with my hand, and shoved it at her.

"You'd better get good and drunk, Marcy. You can't hide up here forever, you know. Owen's going to call you to testify, and I'm going to cross-examine you. So do your drinking now for real 'cause it's going to get real rough." I almost added I spoke from experience.

She laughed, a throaty, sexy laugh she probably reserved for Judge Jordan. "You forget, I'm the grieving widow. Why, poor little ole me just can't take all that ugly stuff going on down at the courthouse."

I could have sworn she'd had acting lessons, but I knew better. That sort of style came with the genes. I leaned closer, wishing the vodka in the orange juice would jump from the glass through my pores into my central nervous system. I needed a drink, badly.

"Crystal's not taking the fall for you or anyone else, Marcy. I don't care if I have to drag you by the hair to the witness stand. You may convince Owen Amos you're all spun sugar and the heat of this trial will melt you into taffy, but I know better. You don't fool me, and I'll bet you never fooled Trey, either."

That one hit its mark. Glaring at me, she threw the Waterford at my head. Ducking, I had to chuckle. Her aim was damned good. Crystal flew everywhere.

"You missed your calling," I shouted over my shoulder as I clattered down the crimson stairs. "You should have gone to Hollywood when you got out of school."

Callie glared as I pulled the front door open.

"Leave her alone, you hear me? Miss Ena, she'd spank you good, hear you talking to Miz Kinsale like that," she scolded me.

"I'm sure she would," I agreed. Callie didn't deserve what was coming, the complete and total upset of her quietly ordered world.

I paused, my hand on the doorknob. "If things here get out of hand, you call me, you hear?" I didn't know what I'd do, but I'd do something. "And don't worry about her drinking. She's not as looped as she pretends."

"I know that," Callie spit back at me. "I been takin' care of Miz Kinsale since she wore diapers. I'll do the takin' care of 'round here."

"I believe that's true," I said, turning to put the door at my back. "I don't want to drag Mrs. Kinsale into this, but I will if I have to." My threat wasn't all that subtle, and Callie knew it.

"She took enough off that no-count husband of hers. She's earned her peace," Callie agreed warily.

"Did he ever hit her?" I watched Callie's eyes. The question was easy enough, and an answer wouldn't be disloyal to her lady.

Callie was on her guard and no fool. "Not that I ever saw. Miz Marcy woulda put him in his place right fast if he'd tried it."

One down, I reasoned. "Did they fight?"

"All married folks fight." Callie was still on firm ground here, giving me nothing I couldn't get out of anyone in town.

"Was she jealous of her husband's mistress?" I had to get down to business fast. Callie was glancing anxiously at the upstairs, as if waiting for a call from Marcy.

"Harumph. Not in this life, she warn't."

"Was Mr. Kinsale jealous of his wife and the Judge?" Callie was bound to know about that little mess.

She cackled loudly. "Now ain't that just like a lawyer? You ask the Judge how happy he was when Mr. Trey ended up dead. Ask him about how much cash he got left, after Mr. Trey got through with him. Seems to me the good Judge got more reasons than most to kill Mr. Kinsale."

I must have looked surprised. The idea of blackmail hadn't occurred to me. But then again, Trey had been short of cash for a long while. I wondered when the golden goose had dried up.

"I will. Why'd Marcy stay with him? With Trey, that is?" Marcy had the money, the looks, and the libido to walk into any room and take what she wanted. Why she stuck with Trey Kinsale was beyond me. Maybe the judge was who she wanted, but he wouldn't leave his wife. I had no idea.

Callie'd had enough of me and my questions. "Shut that door behind you on the way out. We got enough bugs in here already, one less when you're gone."

I'd been dismissed by an expert. Humbled by her finesse, I chuckled nonetheless on my way to the Mustang. She'd given me a real gem with the news about blackmail and the judge. I liked the sound of that, I liked it a lot. I wondered if Owen Amos had any idea Judge Jordan had a classic reason for getting rid of Kinsale.

But before I worked my not-so-subtle wiles on Owen, I needed to find out more about Susan Swinford's mass-murderer of a husband. I knew of only one person I could ask who would know every bit of up-to-the-minute gossip about everyone ever born in Wynnton for the past thirty years, and probably longer by osmosis.

Even as a girl, she'd hoarded gossip and traded it for favors. If my visit the other day was an indication, she'd kept her ear to the wall.

Alma Bland and I had to talk.

12

❧❧❧

I hoped June was in a willing mood the next morning. She'd spent about five thousand dollars of my trust fund setting up an office she liked, she should have been eager to do what I asked. However, I knew better than to count on it.

My last secretary in Atlanta, a blatantly gay man with more on his mind than getting my work done, had involved me in all his domestic crises. I'd played sucker to him for as long as he stayed with the firm. When he left, it was so he could have some quality time with his Great Dane. I'd waved a fond farewell and meant it. At least he'd had a life.

"June," I called out in what I hoped was a cheery way, "Got a list a mile long. Got a minute?" This was my "don't-stop-to-breathe" technique.

If I used the right tone of voice, maybe she'd fall into

step like a good soldier. Yeah, right, and I'm a sixteen-year-old virgin.

"You'd better get in here," she called from the front parlor. "There's a stack of messages a mile high, if you start on them now, maybe I'll be able to get some work done and quit answering that damned phone."

"Turn on the answering machine," I offered.

June's look could melted Antarctica in the middle of winter. "Got any other bright ideas?"

"No." I tried to sound contrite, most unsuccessfully. "But I've got better things for you to do."

That perked her up considerably. I ran through the list of snooping I wanted her to handle, and I swear, she looked like a contented woman. She was a picture of the perfect cool—makeup meticulous, classic summer sheath in a deep coral, with discreet gold earrings and, I swear, a string of pearls. Miss Ena would have approved. Hell, she'd have adopted June.

"Finding out how much Jordan paid Kinsale is going to be the tricky part. I'll see if I can get my Aunt Alice onto it."

I whistled. "Aunt Alice sounds like a stealth bomber."

"Better than that." June gave me the 'you dumbo' look again. "Aunt Alice is related to the help at the Jordans. If there's been talk around that house about how money was being spent, they'll know."

"I like a woman with connections." Judge Jordan had no idea who he was dealing with. He only thought he'd kept the blackmail a secret.

Next, I launched into Marcy's description of the man she said had been Crystal's lover before Trey. June's perfectly plucked eyebrows rose a fraction of an inch, and I knew I had her curiosity champing at the bit.

"See if you can dig up something on him, any old news

stories, maybe something national? Tell you the truth, I was a kid back then, and Miss Ena wouldn't have enlightened me about anything that scary if her life had depended on it. I need everything you can get on him before I ask Crystal what the hell was going on. A man like that, his secrets aren't pretty. They're in the public domain."

June picked up the phone and began dialing.

"Who're you calling?" I asked as if it were any of my business.

"Got to get us connected to the Internet, of course. That sort of information should be easy to retrieve."

I bowed to a superior force. All I wanted to do was scrape flakes off my shutters with a putty knife and a small butane tank of gas to heat the old, leaded paint. I hadn't thought in terms of the late twentieth century, much less the twenty-first, since I'd been wallowing in the past in Miss Ena's house.

"Go for it, girl," I cheered. Retreating to my desk, I considered calling Owen and asking him if he'd known about the blackmail, but decided it was too good a surprise to spring without being able to see how he took it. If he'd known all along, then I was dealing with a scumbag prosecutor and all bets were off. If he choked on his spit at the news, there might be some hope for the boy yet. I loved a surprise.

June hung up the phone. "All set. They'll have us up and running by tomorrow morning."

I consulted the list I'd written on a legal pad of things to do before the next time I met Owen in court.

"Oh, before I forget, I need you to talk to those experts you dragged up. The one in Greenville and the other guy, too. Here's what I want to know." I handed her my list. "I'm heading out to the Bland place. If anyone knows the talk that went down when a Swinford married Moran, it'll be Alma Bland. God help us all."

I wasn't looking forward to this, but it had to be done. June could get a detailed description of what kind of psycho used mutilation on his victim like Trey's killer had used on him from the so-called experts.

Me, I was highly doubtful there was a logical explanation for something so icky. I don't care for psychiatrists and the like, especially when they held themselves out as experts on something really sick and disgusting. I've always wondered how the hell they know what drives a sick mind unless they think the same way.

June would relish the assignment, if I knew anything at all about June. She'd probably store the information to use on her next husband. The first one got off easy with a simple divorce.

"Hey, I'm not the lawyer here. Those guys with all the initials after their friggin' names won't talk to me." June tapped her nails together, annoying me more than her brush-off.

"They'll talk to whomever writes them a check for their time. All you have to say is that you're working with me on the Walker case. Let them draw their own conclusions."

June liked that suggestion. Her face lost some of its annnoyed look. "Do I get mileage for the drive to Greenville?"

"Be my guest." What the hell, the trust fund was shrinking fast, what were a few dollars more?

"I'll call and make an appointment." She was dialing before I could shake the feeling I'd created a monster. Now, I'd have to figure out a way for June to get through the bar exam. Since Grace's revelation about June's thwarted dreams of becoming a lawyer, I'd known I was going to do something to help her. Just what, I wasn't sure about.

Before I thought too hard, I pulled my bar card from my wallet and memorized the phone number. I'd call and ask if it was possible to have law readers qualify to sit for the exam.

I was avoiding what I had to do. "Better get going."

"Yes, you'd better." June waved me toward the door. "Before I forget, stop by the store on the way back from the Bland's, we need food in that kitchen. Goin' to be pulling some long hours, what with the trial coming up fast."

"I don't do food. You do food. I do liquids."

She frowned, hands on her hips. "You better not. I'll tell Henry."

She'd given me the best thing that had happened to me all day, a reason to smile. "Please do. You take sugar with your caffeine or are you the kind who sucks your poison in the diet variety?"

I could see her stunned expression as I pulled away from the curb. One for the boss lady, I chortled. If I could keep June off balance just a tad, there might be hope for her yet.

Heading for the Bland farm, I tried to keep the Mexican jumping beans from doing their acrobatic act in the pit of my stomach by telling myself I needed to see Desiree, too. Asking Alma for information gave me extreme indigestion. June could dig up the official story about Moran, but Alma would know what everyone else believed to be gospel. That was what mattered. Truth was, there was usually a hair of truth somewhere in the heart of the gossip.

I hoped to hell Jack was gone when I pulled up to the front yard. Slamming the door to the car, I assumed I'd made my presence loudly felt so that anyone who wanted to run and hide, could—Jack being the primary target of my clumsy warning. I scuffed up the wooden steps, sounding like an angry teenager coming home after school. The big white farmhouse had a sleepy feel to it, as if it had been cursed by the wicked witch to slumber through the lives of its entombed princesses. No prince lived here.

"Hello," I called out, rapping on the wooden frame of the latched screen door. "It's Tal Jefferson. You home, Alma?"

I didn't expect open arms, but this silence was worrisome. A house with five children in the middle of a summer day should have had someone slamming around the newel post to let me in. Reluctantly, I left the porch and stood in the middle of the front yard, wondering what to do next. The grass was long dead, too many weeds, not enough water. I dug the toe of my shoe into the dirt, wondering if I'd really driven all the way out here just to check on Desiree for Crystal and to pump Alma for information about Crystal's alleged lover. I preferred the wondering to the truth.

Turning the corner of the house, I heard a faint shout and cry. Alarmed, I hurried toward it as fast as my damned high heels would let me. I had to remember to put my old sneakers in the car whenever I left the house, I cursed as I twisted an ankle avoiding a cow pie. The sounds came from behind the barn, and giving up on the heels, I kicked them off and ran bare-footed. The closer I got, the more it sounded to me like a child in distress.

My heart tripped like I'd been poked with a hot needle in its muscle. If anything happened to Desiree, I was leaving town. No way I could tell Crystal something had harmed her daughter.

Slipping as I rounded the corner of the barn, I barely stayed upright as I saw the source of my concern. A huge cattle watering tank, overflowing with water pulled from a container on metal legs above it, was filled with squealing, shouting children. Watching this Norman Rockwell scene, her arms folded against her middle, a happy, contented look on her face, was Alma.

I tried to catch my breath. "Hey there," I gasped, so grateful not to see mutilated bodies of children I didn't know what to do with myself.

Stiffening as though she'd seen a ghost, Alma simultaneously glared at me and then threw a worried look at the children.

"She didn't make bail, did she?" Alma hurried over to the watering tank, as if running interference between me and Desiree.

She was trying to make sure the children didn't see me. Easy enough to do, I'm skinny enough to hide behind a flagpole. Still, I wanted to give her some of her own medicine. Turning my back, I made sure I was standing between her and the children as I faced them. A neat piroutte, if I said so myself. All those years in ballet as a kid hadn't been a complete and total waste.

I could see the girl's blond head bouncing in the water as she splashed the other children. The self-contained, secretive look was gone, replaced by the expression of a child who was having pure, simple fun.

"No way. I came to see you, in fact. Need to tell Crystal I saw Desiree, of course, and how she's doing. Looks fine to me."

"She is," Alma snapped. "If you want to talk to me, come on up to the house. They're fine in that old watering trough. Not deep enough to drown, though there's days . . ."

"This is as good a place as any." I smiled ruefully at my muddy feet. "I thought I heard a child in trouble, so I left my shoes somewhere in the field between the house and here. Don't think I'd better walk on your floor like this."

Alma hooted. "You, Tal Jefferson, came running to help a child? That takes the cake."

I was astounded at the bitterness. "Hell, yes. I'm human, believe it or not, Alma. I'd do the same for a dog or cat, maybe even you."

That got her. This time she just about fell over laughing. "I'd go to hell before I let you help me," she hiccupped.

I was tired of this animosity. Inching closer, I kept my eyes on the children as I spoke. They hadn't noticed me yet, they were so involved in their water fight in the cow tank. Their shrieks almost drowned out Alma's soft voice. Part of me wished I could join in, become a kid again. But those days were long gone, and I hadn't much enjoyed my childhood the first time around, anyway.

"Alma, give me a break. I came out here to ask you about that Moran guy the Swinford girl married. Figured you'd know the real dirt. Hell, you probably went to the wedding."

"How'd you know?" She stared at me suspiciously.

"Just a guess. I'm asking because," I lowered my voice, "Marcy Kinsale says Moran was Crystal's lover before Trey. You know anything about it? I'm thinking, maybe he wasn't too happy to lose Crystal to another man. Given his background, violence isn't too farfetched a theory."

She started, began to say something, thought better of it. I waited, but she continued to stare at the children as if ignoring me would make me go away.

"Alma, I'm asking for help here, for Desiree's sake.

That child doesn't deserve to lose her mother to the death penalty. Think of the things the other kids will say to her."

I'd gotten to her with that one. Groaning, she shot me a look of pure loathing.

"You ever stop and think who might be that little girl's daddy?" She nodded at the cattle tank, where the squeals had gotten even more raucous.

I nodded. "Sure. But Crystal's not telling."

"Would you like your daddy to be a man who killed a whole village of innocent people? You think she'll have it rough if her mama dies for killing her last lover? You ain't seen nothin' yet, Miss Big Shot Lawyer."

The wind in my sails sucked out of me like a vacuum on a hot pickle jar. "Desiree know this?"

"You really aren't all that bright, are you, Tal?" Alma was enjoying this. "And don't you go tellin' her, either."

She looked almost gleeful. Old scores between us weren't dead and buried yet, not in Alma's yard, they weren't. Something was puzzling me about Alma and Desiree, however. Alma had a houseful of her own brood, why was she going out of her way to take in the town whore's little girl?

A friendship with her own girl that age didn't explain all of it. Maybe Alma was just a woman who couldn't stand to see a child homeless or abused, like some people pour all their energy into the animal shelter and stray cats.

"Can you tell me anything else about Moran? Anything that might help Crystal?"

"Why don't you ask him? Hey, Matthew Moran, you screwed around on the only good woman in your life, the one who gave you a home, a job, and a decent family to stand behind you, so what you got to say, Lieutenant?"

Alma had a nasty chuckle when she wanted to use it. I wondered how often Jack had heard it, and for a second, felt sorry for him.

I fought to hold my temper. This was the woman Jack Bland had chosen to love. The Jack I remembered would have seen goodness in Alma, so I struggled to do the same.

"I'd never be so cruel. I'm guessing here, and I'm sure you'll straighten me out if I'm wrong, that Crystal was his only indiscretion, that everyone involved kept it quiet, and that he's been a good boy since?"

Alma's smile curled at one corner of her mouth in what I would have sworn was a sneer. "You, never cruel? That's a good one."

The children stopped their water fight and stared at their mother. Only Desiree continued to play, tossing water with her hands over her head, showering herself even if the others had ceased their game with her. I watched her, oblivious to what the other children were doing, absorbed in her own world. She'd been a solitary child too long. Alma's children had to be good for her.

"I'd like to take Desiree to see her mother. Crystal's saying she doesn't want her in the jail, but time may be running out. Once we're in the thick of the trial, I won't have time to ferry Desiree back and forth."

"Good. She's staying here. Sooner she forgets about that piece of shit who calls herself a mother, the better off Desiree'll be."

"Look, just because Crystal didn't marry the high school star athlete doesn't mean she's a lost cause."

"That's what you think. Anyone with an ounce of sense knows that woman should have been sterilized at puberty."

I tried to be charitable. Alma's dedication to motherhood was admirable, if misplaced where Desiree was concerned.

"It's really not your decision. Crystal's still Desiree's mother, like it or not."

"As long as she lives in my house, I'm her mother." Alma's voice grew shrill. "I won't have you screwing around with my family, Tal Jefferson. You hear? They're mine!"

I was getting nowhere with Alma. Clearly, she had some sort of super-mom instinct that was kicked into high gear. Never having been a mother, I didn't understand what had her breathing fire. All I was doing was riling her up.

When it came down to it, I didn't have the heart to drag Desiree out of the gaggle of children over Alma's screams of protest. The child didn't need a scene like that, no matter how much Crystal would be helped by a visit from her. I wasn't about to jerk her out of the water. Besides, I was still in my lady-lawyer clothes.

Jerking her chain over Desiree had backfired. Whatever Alma knew, she'd never tell me now. The fact that Moran's infidelity was on the gossip circuit didn't tell the whole story. The story of the marriage lay behind it, and somehow, Susan Swinford wasn't getting the rumor-treatment.

"Guess I'll ask Matthew Moran myself. Be back later, check on Desiree." I didn't bother to say good-bye. On my way back to the Mustang, I dipped to pick up my smelly shoes. Tossing them into the back seat, I jammed my key in the ignition, so eager to get out of there I didn't notice the tractor pulling in behind me.

"Good golly, Jack," I screamed as I hit the brakes and the clutch simultaneously, barely missing the tractor with the Mustang's rear end by a fraction of an inch. "You just scared the shit out of me."

Cutting off the engine, Jack clambered down from the tractor. "Thought I saw your car in the yard when I turned the far corner of the field. Soys are ready to harvest," he added as though I were remotely interested.

"Yeah, well, you'll see me and my car leaving." I was too angry to talk to him. I might ask him when he lost his mind, before or after he married the Bitch Queen Alma. She'd married Jack so fast everyone had said she was pregnant. I'd always thought she'd lied to him. A woman like that didn't understand the definition of scruples.

Reaching into my car, he smoothly turned off the ignition. "What'd you want, Tal?"

"Nothing from you, Jack, I promise."

"Crystal wants to see Desiree? Alma saying no?"

I stopped trying to get out of there. "Yes . . ." I hesitated. I didn't want to lie to him, but this was obviously a bone of contention here in pastoral paradise. My baser self wanted to see how far it went, how deep the division stretched between the loving couple. I was such a bitch myself, but at least I knew it.

"I'll get her," he said flatly. "She needs to see her real mother. Alma'd like to think she can mother any stray cat, dog, child, or man, into loving her. But it just doesn't work that way, not always." His face was grim. "Desiree's not gonna forget about her mother just because Alma tells her to."

I hadn't expected this. "No, Jack, wait," I called as he strode off toward the cattle tank, his fists balled by his sides.

Grabbing my stained shoes, I hopped along behind him, trying to stop him. "Wait," I called again, but he waved me back with a gesture that meant business. For once in my life, I decided to sit back and wait to see what happened.

He didn't take long. Desiree, clutching his hand with a

death grip, tripped along beside him, smiling a triumphant smile.

"Desiree will be out in a minute. She just needs to put on some dry clothes," he mumbled as they practically ran past me.

I hadn't any idea how I was going to get out of this one. I glanced toward the barn, half-expecting Alma to come at me with a pitchfork or a mob of angry children. The silence from that section of the yard was ominous. I hurried after Jack and Desiree. Jack stood on the porch, his arms stiff at his sides as he guarded the front door. At least it looked to me like he was doing a guard act.

"Jack, I'm sorry, I didn't mean to start something here. Desiree doesn't need to . . ."

"Yes, she does," he snapped, as if I were nothing but a recording. I must have jumped at his tone of voice, because he seemed to come back to himself with a visible effort.

"Desiree's been asking for her mother for days now. Sure, she seems all right for a bit, plays with the other kids sometimes, but she's just a little girl. She wants her mama. Her real mama. She should see her while she can." His face grew more pinched, and the stubble on his cheeks was more pronounced. Circles marred the skin under his eyes. "Doesn't look good for Crystal, does it, Tal?"

I didn't know what to make of the Jack I was seeing now. Gone was the man wishing for the past, the boy I'd seen hiding behind a man's image and responsibilities. This man wasn't so besotted by his dimpled, earth-mother woman. A little girl had driven a wedge between them, and I was at a loss as to why either of them had permitted it. Especially since Alma had dropped the bombshell about Moran being Desiree's father.

"Not right now. But there's time for things to develop." I had a thought. "I asked Alma about Mathew Moran, the guy who married the Swinford girl. She says he's Desiree's father. Marcy Kinsale said Crystal had been his lover, so I guess it's true."

Beneath his farmer's tan, Jack turned as pale as a turnip. I waited for him to swallow whatever was working its way down his gullet. His Adam's apple bobbed a few times, and I watched it carefully. I remembered kissing that part of his neck as I'd worked my way up to his mouth. My tongue pushed against the back of my teeth, I tried to shove the memory into its black corner of things-to-forget.

"I hadn't heard that rumor," Jack finally whispered, his eyes on the tractor as he crushed his baseball cap between his hands. It'd end up looking like he'd jumped up and down on it when he was finished with mangling the poor thing. I wondered whose neck he was throttling in the guise of his cap.

"What rumors have you heard?"

He kept his eyes focused somewhere over my right shoulder.

"I heard that Linwood Jordan was Crystal's father."

If I'd had any sense, I would have sat down before I fell off the steps. "Did I hear you right?" I tried not to squeak, but I sounded pretty shocked, even for me.

He nodded. "Crystal told me. Judge Jordan was her daddy, not that creep who . . ." He swallowed again, harder this time. "She wanted to keep Desiree safe, away from anything like what happened to her when she was growing up. My bet is, Trey found out somehow about it, maybe from Crystal, and put the screws to the good judge."

Things weren't looking good for Judge Jordan. Excitement almost as good as sex tingled my tummy. Almost.

Kinsale was sticking it to His Honor over the affair with
Marcy, as well as his paternity of Crystal Walker. Yes, today was definitely looking up. Now, a little confirmation,
and I'd be a happy woman. Well, as happy as I could get.

Jack wasn't looking at me, he was seeing something far
off in his mind as he spoke. I prompted him gently.

"What kind of screws?" Jesus, I repeated to myself over
and over, don't let him clam up.

"The kind Trey needed. Money. Blackmail's my bet."

I already knew that Marcy's affair with Judge Jordan was
family knowledge in the Kinsale household. Callie had said
the blackmail involved Marcy's relationship with Linwood
Jordan. But this was bigger than big. Jordan would hardly
want Trey knowing he was the father of Trey's mistress.

I remembered Marcy's comments about Trey's inability
to perform. Yeah, right . . . Trey was winning both ways to
Sunday, and my bet was that Marcy and her older, church-
pillar, tower of the community lover didn't like it one bit.
Power was a strong aphrodisiac, and Trey Kinsale had
drunk his cup to the bottom.

"Marcy and Crystal both said Trey was tapped out, well
was dry. He was going to sell all that land he'd inherited to
the Global Transport Park folks."

Jack snorted. "When hell froze over. He probably told
Marcy and the judge that to keep them on their toes. Rile
'em up. Trey was like that, he got a kick out of pulling people's chains."

I wondered how Jack knew. He hadn't had much to do
with Trey, he'd told me earlier. Was he talking through his
hat?

"Couldn't have been much money, if the judge paid at
all. Crystal said Trey cut off her account at the Piggly Wiggly, stopped paying her electric bill. Doesn't sound like

Trey was rolling in green stuff. 'Sides, why wouldn't Crystal do the blackmailing? She's the one who needed money."

"She's not like that. You don't know squat about her, do you, Tal?" This time he focused on me, and I realized I was talking to a stranger.

"Not much. She won't let me in. For some reason, I'm her lawyer, but I'm her enemy, too."

"Maybe she's trying to protect someone. Did you ever think of that? Crystal's life started out on the bottom of the barrel, and she's about sucked all the slime off the mud she can stand. But she's the kind of woman who'll make a promise and keep it, no matter what."

I heard the cicadas in the background, a sudden symphony heralding the crescendo of heat to come later. Sweat trickled down the backs of my legs, my blouse was plastered to my neck, and I didn't want to know the answer but I had to ask. "Promises to whom?"

He ignored me, staring at his fields as if he'd just regained his sight after years of blindness.

"Did I make promises I didn't keep?" I knew what this was about. Maybe.

"You betcha." Suddenly he was all grins and wrinkles in the corner of his eyes, looking older than his years. "But it don't make a hill of beans, darlin', not any more," he drawled.

I would have pressed him further, but Desiree slammed through the screen door, her wet hair slick against her small head.

"Ready, Jack." She beamed up at him. The whole time I'd spoken to her, I'd barely gotten a response. Jack seemed to have that effect on all women, they took a shine to him that never lost its gloss. Alma was still under his spell, try as she might to fight it. How many other women had the same problem? I was seeing Jack in a harsh new light. The experience was disheartening.

I was going to have to ask Crystal how she happened to tell Jack about her parentage, but managed to keep that crucial fact from her lawyer. Now, at least I understood why I'd been summoned in the middle of the night to the Jordan residence and ordered to represent her. Jordan must have realized I had more trial experience, drunk or sober, than any country lawyer hanging around Talmadge County courthouse on any day of the week. The cachet of big city practice must have given me a certain credibility I'd not yet lost.

"Miss Jefferson will be takin' you to see your mommy, honey." Jack knelt so he was eye-to-eye with Desiree. She was a small child for her age.

"I want you to go. Mommy will want to see you, too." Her voice was hollow, all exuberance gone.

I stored that one away for future reference. Jack and Crystal? He hadn't answered my question about Moran yet, and if I were to lay bets on it, wasn't going to right now.

"We won't be gone long, Desiree, I promise." I smiled with what I hoped was confidence. Crystal had stated her wishes more than clearly about having Desiree in the county jail. But then again, clients in jail didn't get much say in anything, so why this? I reached for Desiree's hand. "Want to get in my car? We can drive with the top down."

Desiree looked at Jack with what I could only label as adoration. "You come, too, Jack," she urged.

"No, honey, your mama will want to talk with you alone. I'll be here when you get back. Now, don't get upset by the jail, promise me? Remember, we talked about this. Your mama's safe in there, no one's hurting her. That's a good thing, right?" He rose slowly from his crouch.

"Have her back by supper time, okay, Tal? But if you two ladies want to stop off for an ice cream, I promise not to tattle to Alma." He winked broadly at Desiree.

If I hadn't seen it for myself, I wouldn't have believed it. I wondered where this charmer of a father had been when he was a young hellion. Hidden beneath the surface, just dying to get out? If Desiree had looked more like Jack, I would have sworn he'd fathered her. The idea was ludicrous—he had a daughter the same age, and Alma sure as shootin' wasn't about to share Jack with anyone else, not without bloodshed. If she'd for a second suspected Crystal and Jack of hanky-panky, Crystal wouldn't have been alive to stand trial for Kinsale's killing.

"We'll be back," I promised faintly. "Put on your seat belt, Desiree," I added as Jack plunked her in the front bucket seat.

Jack did the honors, tugging it tight across her thin chest. Kissing the top of her head, he leaned down and whispered something to her. She glowed.

"Well, we'd best be on our way." I felt like the odd-girl out on a blind date. I hadn't planned on visiting Crystal with her daughter in tow, but Jack had forced my hand.

I'd ride this pony wherever it took me.

13

❧❧❧

TECHNICALLY, children weren't allowed in the jail, but I wangled Desiree in by saying I needed her to corroborate testimony with her mother. I'm sure the deputy in charge didn't understand the word *corroborate* but he didn't want to look stupid in front of a woman lawyer, so he buzzed us in.

Desiree grabbed my hand when the metal door slid sideways.

"Don't be afraid, it's only noise. We're going to an interview room, and they'll bring your mother out to us."

Her pale face was a shade whiter, if that was possible. I'd never seen a child with so little color in her. Crystal's dark hair, what was left of it, matched her dark violet eyes, her delicate skin. She could have had an exotic beauty, played up right with makeup and gentle living. There was nothing of Judge Jordan in her looks that I could tell, but I'd never seen Crystal's mother, either.

Desiree had been silent much of the way back into town, answering my questions with monosyllabic words. All the vitality she'd had talking with Jack had evaporated. If my finesse with her was any indication, it was a good thing I was childless. I wanted to dig into what she knew about the night Kinsale was found dead in her mother's shed, but if she clammed up any more, she'd double over.

Her eyes grew as big as a September moon when Crystal pulled open the door to the interview room. I'd given Desiree the chair facing the door, taking a corner to prop myself up so I could see Crystal's reaction to her daughter and to me. If she lashed out, I'd make sure Desiree got out fast. I didn't need a scene, I'd had enough for one day.

"Baby," Crystal cried, flying into the room to swoop Desiree into her arms. For the first time, I saw something other than cynicism and fear on her face. She was incapable of hiding her joy at seeing her daughter.

Jack had been right. I'd been stupid to listen to Crystal and keep Desiree from seeing her. Both of them melted together like striped taffy, one head dark, one pale, arms entwined, Desiree's legs around her mother's waist as she held her like a baby. The lump in my throat was too hard to swallow.

Crystal crooned to her daughter, stroking her hair with one hand, the other anchored around her bottom. I tried to remember ever having been held like that by Miss Ena, and knew it would never have happened. If she had been especially pleased with my report card, or something I'd played at a piano recital, she would, and very rarely at that, give me a pat on the head. For a second, I envied Crystal and her child their unabashed display of affection.

Finally, Crystal sat in the chair facing the corner where I still hid. "I thought I told you to leave Desiree out of this?" she demanded, the child curled on her lap.

"You did. This is Jack's doing. He insisted."

She looked slightly mollified. "How's he holding up?"

I thought the question odd. "The same I guess. Said he was harvesting soybeans." I didn't know what she wanted me to say.

"And how's Alma?" The question had an edge to it.

"Look, what is this? Ask Desiree, she lives there."

Desiree looked at her mother adoringly. "They're okay Mom, really. They treat me real nice. I got my own bed and some dolls, and Donna's teaching me to hold my breath and go under water in the cow tank." She sounded as if she were reciting a lesson.

"That's nice, baby. Alma being good to you?"

"Oh yes, but well, she's not you. She tries to be, but I can tell, she doesn't know how to be a good mama, not like you."

Spoken like a true daughter, I thought. My own assessment of Alma was that she'd been born to successful motherhood, just as I'd been born to fail at everything I'd ever done.

"Give her a chance, honey. If you need anything, you just tell Jack, okay?"

She nodded. "When will you get out of here, Mama? I hate that funny suit." She fingered the prison orange.

Crystal stared at me. "Can't tell you that right now, sweetheart. Ask Tal here what's going on."

As if I knew. "The trial's been set, Desiree, and right now, I'm working hard to make sure your mama can come home as soon as it's over." I didn't have the heart to tell her the chances still were pretty slim. Unless I could come up with a red-handed killer, the fact Crystal was poor, a woman, and the lover of the dead man would be enough to convict her in Talmadge County.

"Can we leave then, Mama? Please? Go somewhere new where no one knows us?"

My heart just about broke with that one. I could see Crystal was having the same problem.

"We sure can, honey. We'll shake Wynnton's dust right off our feet and keep going until we find a place where we'd like to settle down. Now, how about you start making a list for me of places you think would do? I'll bet you can find a map somewhere, and see if there's anywhere with a friendly sounding name."

If I'd wanted to prove Crystal's innocence before, I knew now I had to. I didn't care if she'd mutilated and eviscerated Kinsale, she had to live and keep that child's faith in her alive. Now I knew why Jack treated Desiree with such kindness, such dignity. He'd seen the little girl with her mother, and it was something no one forgot who'd witnessed it.

"Desiree, there's a map in the glove compartment of my car. You want to go give it a look? If you like, you can keep it. I think I have a red pen in here." I scrounged around in my purse. "Sure do, it's brand new." I handed it to her. "Right now, your mama and I have to talk lawyer talk. You think you'll be okay waiting for me in the car?"

I didn't think anyone would snatch her from the jail's parking lot. She nodded.

I glanced at Crystal, who was hugging Desiree even closer. "I promised Desiree an ice cream before we went back to Jack and Alma's. Is that okay with you?"

I don't know why I felt the need to ask permission, except that Crystal was so clearly the guiding force in this child's life, I didn't dare interfere.

"Just don't give her chocolate. It gives her hives." She

kissed Desiree's forehead. "You go on now, sweetie, I'll see you later. Tal and I need to get some work done, but she'll be right out before you can shake a lamb's tail."

Desiree started to protest, but one stern look from her mother did the trick. I'd buzzed for the guard to take her out.

"This ain't no babysittin' service," he mumbled as he listened to my request to remove Desiree and keep an eye on her while I spoke alone with Crystal.

"I'm sure if I put in a good word for you with Mr. Amos, he might find a need for a new bailiff around the court-house," I promised rashly.

He perked up immediately. Courthouse duty was a plum at his level of civil service.

"Okay," he grumbled, letting Desiree leave the room on her own. "But not for long, hear? Babysitting's not in my current job description."

I nodded, waiting until he and Desiree were out of earshot before spitting out what I had to say. Crystal sat, slumped and as defeated as I'd ever seen a client before, her forearms holding her head as she leaned against the table. I pulled my legal pad and a pen out of my briefcase and care-fully arranged them in front of me, angle correct for note-taking, pen in my hand, poised to write God-knows-what.

"Crystal, I have to ask you about Matthew Moran, the Vietnam War vet who married Susan Swinford. Marcy Kinsale's implying Moran was your, um, lover. Before Trey. That Moran didn't like it when Trey . . . took an in-terest. I don't know what all's the truth, all I want to know is, was that guy your lover before Kinsale?" I doodled on my legal pad while she hid her face in her arms.

I waited. She thought about the ramifications of what I was asking, I was sure. Finally, her head inched up from the cradle made of her elbow.

"Hell yes, Matt and me had a thing going on for a while there. Didn't matter who married him, he was still that baby-killer from Vietnam around here." Her eyes, when she looked at me at long last, brimmed with unshed tears.

"What broke you up? Trey come along?" I didn't want to imply she was a gold-digger, but I had to know.

She picked at a scab on the side of her hand. "Nothin' like that. He's a good guy. Wakes up screamin' most every night, so he doesn't sleep. Just drives around town. Him and me ran into each other one night down by the river. I was havin' myself a bad stretch, too, and we got to talkin'. I knew who he was, of course, so I never asked him about them people he was supposed to have killed."

"I hate to sound nosy, but how did Susan Swinford take to this . . . relationship?"

"Hell, she never knew about us. The woman treats him like a dog, like he's supposed to get down on his knees every day and lick her feet for takin' him into the family and givin' him a job. You know what, I don't think she ever loved him. She just wanted a husband who'd be beholden to her for the rest of his life. She never really looks at him, if you know what I mean. She got her ten minutes of fame outta marryin' him."

I whistled. "Sounds like he's one pretty pissed-off guy."

"Don't go makin' things up in that pointy little head of yours, Tal." Crystal scraped hair off her forehead, as if her head hurt and she could make it hurt less by jerking on her lanky tendrils.

"Was he ticked off when Trey came along?"

"He'd given it up long before Trey. Said he had enough guilt to last a couple of lifetimes, he didn't need to add me to the list. May be true, what they said he did when he was in Vietnam. But I never seen a killer in him. Been around enough in my time, I know the signs. All kinds of ways to kill, right, Tal?" Her smile scared me. "Don't have to stop a beatin' heart to commit murder. A body can kill a spirit, it's the same."

How did she know so much? Jack was right, I didn't understand Crystal at all.

"You're not giving me much help here, Crystal. I've got to find some way to show you didn't kill Kinsale. Don't you understand? The evidence is all circumstantial, but it's enough to buy you the farm. They'll say you cleaned up before you called the cops. That you were naked when you stabbed him, scrubbed yourself later. Hell, I don't know how they'll explain why you weren't coated in his blood and why they don't have the weapon, but Owen Amos will make it look good."

I wasn't going to give up on Moran. He and I were going to talk.

"You know what?" Crystal looked as if she wanted to laugh. "You're just spinnin' those wheels of yours, aren't you, Tal? Told you from the start, it's no good. I'm going down on this one. Hey, it's been comin' to this since I was born."

"No, it hasn't." I wasn't going to let her do this to her or to me. "You have a daughter out there who loves you. I'm it, Crystal, I'm your only hope. So don't you give up on me, not by a long shot, because I'm not giving up on you."

I waited. "Besides, your father asked me to take your case. Said you wanted me, and by damned, you'd get what you wanted."

Her muscles had turned to liquid and she looked as if she'd slide out of the wooden chair into a puddle on the floor. "Who told you?" she whispered. "About my father? Judge Jordan?"

"Was Kinsale blackmailing him about you?" I ignored her question.

She shoved herself out of the chair and went to lean against the wall. Her chewed fingers dug into it for purchase.

"Yes," she whispered. "But the money wasn't wasted, it went into lawyers and planners he paid to get the Transport Park interested in his land. Every cent."

"Did Marcy know about it? That Kinsale was blackmailing Linwood Jordan about you?"

She sighed as if her soul had been ripped out of the bottoms of her feet. "How the hell should I know what that bitch knew or didn't know? She treated Trey like he was some sort of bastard child she didn't want. Hell, I've been there, I know the scene. She played head games with him, he was just getting his own back. I wasn't sorry the Judge paid Trey to keep quiet about me. He never did nothin' for me my whole life."

I didn't want to point out that Kinsale was both an adulterer and a blackmailer, and that such activities didn't lead to the most harmonious or healthy of relationships with either his wife or her lover. This was all too gothic for me. I suddenly needed a tall, cool one in the world's worst way. But first, I had to get Desiree back to the Bland farm.

I almost asked her again about Desiree's daddy, but decided I just didn't want to know. I already needed a good, hard scrubbing in my mind to get rid of the pictures of Crystal and Trey, Judge Jordan and Crystal, Marcy and the Judge, Trey and Marcy. I wondered how far back I'd have to follow the line of Crystal's men to reach the beginning. Maybe once I found him, I'd be able to start unraveling the knot of her life. One of those threads might lead me to the right killer.

If it wasn't Crystal. It couldn't be. I wouldn't let it.

I got myself out of the jail, collected Desiree, and managed to remember to stop at the Dairy Barn to get her a soft vanilla cone. Even as I tried to chat with the taciturn child, I realized I was wrong about Crystal. I'd seen her as a victim. But she wasn't one. She was where she'd put herself. She was a big girl who knew how the world worked.

Crystal could have left Wynnton years ago, gotten on with her life. No one had forced her to stick around to be a visible symbol of a respected judge's failure to wear a condom. Moran, too, was, in a way, a victim of her need to suck in men who were worse off than she. A convicted mass murderer, he must have told her tales that would wear twenty layers of varnish off old wood. Kinsale took the cake—a destitute member of the landed gentry with a wife who was unfaithful with Crystal's biological father, a blackmailer with the gall to try to dump her.

Crystal Walker was the woman she wanted to be.

I dropped Desiree off on the front porch at Jack and Alma's. Alma gave me a dirty look as she opened the screen door and pulled Desiree inside. I noticed she didn't ask me in for a glass of iced tea, though she held one in her other hand, her right one busy latching the screen as soon as Desiree was behind her in the hallway.

I didn't try to be polite. "Have Jack call me as soon as he gets in."

Jack Bland owed me the truth about what was going on. Somehow, I figured he knew and by gosh or by golly, he'd spread it at my feet like a love offering. He may not love me or anyone but those kids of his, but he'd give me what I wanted.

He had to know. He'd taken in Desiree because of that knowledge.

14

〰〰〰

I was tired, with little to show for all my prying into the private lives of Wynnton's upright citizens. I had to work on something that would give me tangible results. June was gone when I got back to the house. Taping a note on the front door telling her that she should head for the back shed the minute she got in, I changed clothes. The old jeans and paint-spattered T-shirt retained their comfort factor after the straitjacket of wearing the clothes June had picked out for me. At least I could shed any semblance of respectability. I'd been buttoned up too long in that blasted suit and tortured by shoes that were invented by men with a twisted sense of humor.

I considered driving to the liquor store and stocking up. I don't know what kept me from doing it, false pride, real pride, or the fact I'd start and not stop at one or two cold beers. If I didn't get busy, I'd be in real trouble.

More shutters awaited their transformation to purple, but first I had to burn off years of old, lead-based paint. Grabbing the butane torch and an old putty knife, I barricaded myself in the backyard shed with the unfinished shutters.

Dark and cool, sheltered by ancient trees, the shed had been built by Miss Ena's grandfather out of oak that had weathered age, war, tornadoes, and termites. I treasured its longevity and perseverance. It was, after all, just an old shed, built on a low foundation of stacked bricks, with a crumbling pine floor. But its humble relationship to the big, elegant old house facing Woolfolk Avenue hadn't worn it down.

Smelling the pungent aroma of old wood, the mushroomy soil under the precarious floor, I strapped on my mask. Maybe burning away layers of paint would help me blaze away the feeling I was getting nowhere. I doubted it—I'd been trying to do that since returning to Wynnton. But if I didn't do something right that moment that showed progress, I'd be in the car in a flash, heading to the liquor store. Moving across the floor with great care, I shifted the shutters so I could get a better angle with the butane and pulled a match from my pocket.

Turning the knob, I lit the torch. The smell of heat burned the back of my throat. Shifting my weight, I angled myself so I'd keep out of the various holes eaten through the pine. Not as hardy as the old oak, the floor was in need of replacement, but I just hadn't gotten around to it.

Paint began to bubble beneath the persistent blue flame. Drawing the butane back, I slid the putty knife underneath, lifting the lead-based black off the old wood. Again and again I aimed the butane, heating, boiling the paint, sliding it off in a gooey mess I wiped on the floor beside me when it started to cool on the knife. My legs started cramping, but I concentrated on the rhythm of my labor.

I was like that butane torch—flaming at old wounds, the petty secrets of the lives I swore I'd left behind the first time I lit out of Wynnton the summer after high school. I jabbed with the putty knife, gouging a little too deeply into the wood beneath the last layer of paint. Without thinking, I tried to smooth over the mar with my finger, burning myself but good in the process. Sucking on my scorched finger, I tried to keep the tears from coming.

But nothing could stop them. Crumpling onto the floor, I switched off the butane and gave it up. I cried because I'd never had a chance to know my dead parents, because I'd squandered my professional life with cases that didn't matter, and the one time the case did count, I was too busy to take proper care of it, and a man lost everything. I wept into the musty old floor, wiping my nose on my arm, because I'd let down Miss Ena and all her hopes for me, because I'd lost my capacity to love with Jack Bland, and I couldn't get it back.

"Damnation," I muttered, remembering the note I'd left on the front door for June. If she found me like this, she'd have a good laugh. Hurriedly, I scrambled to my feet and wiped my eyes.

"What on earth are you caterwauling about?" June blocked the light in the doorway.

I held up my hand so she could see the red mark. "Burned myself. Hurts like hell." I took a deep, shuddering breath. "So, how was wherever?" I asked ridiculously.

"Greenville. Hot. Next time, you drive."

I silently thanked her for not asking me harder questions about the tears. If she'd seen me with an opened bottle, I'd have bet what was left of my trust fund she wouldn't have been so nice.

"Hopefully, there won't be a next time. Come on inside, I need to get this cleaned up."

With a look at me as if she wanted to make sure I wasn't staggering, she followed me into the kitchen. Running cold water over the finger helped ease the pain. I concentrated on the stream of water coming from the faucet as if it could tell me the future.

June went to the fridge and took out a pop can, sprung the lid, then did a second-take at me. "You want me to open one for you?"

I nodded. Taking the cold can from her, I pressed the sore finger to it, took a deep breath, and tried to pretend I was just fine, thank you very much.

"So what did you find out? Anything we can use?"

"Depends. There's a long history of this kind of murder and mutilation." June pulled on a pair of glasses I'd never seen before, studying a notebook. "Just like Henry said, sexual crimes tend to have the multiple stab wounds. But of course, that can be faked if the killer knows that kind of stuff. Believe it or not, some study up before they do the deed, so to speak. Real sick puppies, if you ask me."

I nodded, wishing she'd tell me something helpful with what my money had paid to get from the so-called experts that we couldn't have found on the Web.

"Next, there's a definite trend to this form of mutilation in primitive types of warfare. You know, telling your enemy when he returns to recover the dead that you not only killed his brothers, but you desecrated them. A sort of double-whammy. Happens in the Far East a lot."

"Wait a sec." I tapped the notebook from my side of the

table. "Was this ever done in Vietnam? During the war?" I thought of baby-faced, baby-killer Matthew Moran.

June looked peeved. "How'd you know? But it was our guys who did it. Of course, it wasn't ever reported, not back then. Came out later, when so many of the Vietnam vets went into counseling. Dr. Waverly said it probably happened more than anyone would believe, mutilating the Vietcong dead. Bounty was one reason—an easy way to supplement a private's salary was to earn extra bucks by turning in a couple of ears now and then."

I could believe it. I'd believe any level of human depravity at that point. "Did you find any information on Matthew Moran?"

"Piece of cake. Got it off the Web." She shoved pages at me.

"Give me a summary." I was staring at a picture of Lt. Moran in his uniform, striding out of a military-looking building. He'd put on thirty-five pounds, if not more, in the years since then. The caption said Lieutenant Moran and his defense counsel were seen leaving the fifteenth day of his court-martial. I was surprised he hadn't been confined after each day's session.

"How detailed a summary do you want?" June swished what was left of the cola in the can, pretending boredom.

"You know what I'm looking for. Did Matthew Moran have, shall I say, experience in this sort of thing?"

June smiled as if she'd just been given a four-carat diamond and a good-looking guy to go with it. "Sure enough." Her smile began to fade. "How do we leapfrog him from Vietnam to Trey Kinsale and that shed?"

"No idea." But if there was a way, I'd find it if it would help Crystal.

"Even worse, what if Crystal heard about the mutilation

from Moran, or someone else? And she was trying to make it look like someone else did the job?"

I felt sick. "Then I'm going to have to tap dance real hard to keep off the radar."

Handing me her notes, June left me with them. I heard her in the kitchen, running water. Reviewing the neatly legible handwriting, I decided June should have gone to law school and left the guy who broke her heart. I should have been the one to stay home with the guy and raise his kids.

"You need more help." Returning with a glass in one hand, June waved the other over her notebook, the photocopies. "That's one sick woman if she did it. My bet says you won't have any trouble finding a doctor who'll testify that she's nuts, completely and totally loony-bin material."

I was taken aback. But then again, June didn't have the history I did with Crystal, nor had she seen her with her daughter. "I can't do that. For one thing, Crystal would object, and I can't put on a defense she won't go along with."

I don't know how I knew, I just did, that Crystal would rather die than be labeled mentally ill.

"For another thing, I don't think she's crazy. If she did this, and I don't think she did, she had help. I need to prove she didn't do it, June. Maybe this'll get me somewhere." I tapped her notebook.

Shaking her head as if I'd lost my mind and belonged locked in the attic myself, June collected her purse, shuffled the copies into a neat pile, and tried to avoid looking at me.

"I'll put these in a file before I lock up for the night."

"That'd be fine. Leave it on my desk, please. I want to show them to Henry." I needed someone to brainstorm with before I laid out a new game plan for Owen Amos that included dropping the charges against my client. I'd decide as I went along how much Henry needed to know, but the hypothetical wouldn't do anyone any harm.

June bustled about, cleaning up.

I tossed the cans in the trash and picked up my putty knife. The tears that had threatened to undo me were somewhere under the surface, but in lurk mode only. I was safe for a few more hours of work on the shutters. June was clattering around in the front parlor, so I let myself into the shed once more.

This time I had something more constructive to think about than self-pity. Crystal's loyalty to Matthew Moran told me I needed to know more about the man himself. What had morphed the disgraced soldier with a defiant stare into the colorless, expressionless man who waited on customers in a jewelry store?

With each stroke through the softened ancient paint, my mind became clearer. By the time the fireflies were dancing on the patch of lawn I could see through the cracks in the boards, I had turned over so many mental rocks, I was exhausted.

I decided to pack it in for the night, give my tired brain a rest. Putting away my equipment, I made sure there were no hot spots on the shutters and then locked the shed. Standing in my backyard in the weeds, I breathed in the thick evening air, so heavy with moisture it should have bred rain.

I didn't think I was strong enough for the burden of Crystal Walker, but I really had no choice. She was peeling back the leaded layers of my past without even knowing it.

Showering quickly, I dressed for bed, then locked my front door against the mutilators and baby-killers of the world. Sleep still wasn't my forte. I saw one hell of a lot of Moran in my dreams.

15

❧❧❧

THE last time I'd been in Swinfords, Moran hadn't recognized me. I didn't think the preliminary hearing would have changed that, but maybe so. Perhaps Crystal had told him I was her lawyer. For all I knew, he'd been to see her in the jail. I'd have to check out her visiting list later.

The jewelry shop was empty again, despite the fact it was Saturday. Frowning at me, Moran came out of the small office behind the counter. I smiled.

"Wonder if Mr. Swinford had a chance to look at my watch? The antique?"

Now he remembered me. "What was the name, please?"

"Jefferson, Tal Jefferson." I kept my hands on the counter. I'd bet my bottom dollar he thought I was going to rob him, he looked so skittish.

He bobbed under the counter and pulled out a box. I'd bet he was checking to see if the shotgun was loaded and waiting under there.

"Yep, got it here. Just a worn mainspring, easy enough to fix. That'll be twenty dollars."

I fished in my pocket for cash, watching him set the time carefully, wind the stem, then replace it in the small manila envelope before handing it to me. I slid a twenty across the counter at the same moment and our hands touched. My only thought was that I'd touched a man who'd murdered innocent civilians in a war that shouldn't have happened. With only the greatest control, I managed to refrain from wiping my hand on my dirty jeans. I'd never wear Miss Ena's watch with the same joy, knowing he'd put his fingers in its bowels.

"I have to confess, I'm here for another reason." I waited for him to finish ringing up the sale on the old cash register.

"Oh?" He looked like he wanted to run. He knew who I was, for sure.

"I just found out about you and my client, Crystal Walker." I kept my voice low, even though I couldn't see anyone else in the store. "How long ago did you two, um, break it off?"

His pink face flushed darker red. "While ago." I could literally see the sweat pop on his shiny pate. "It wasn't what you think. We were friends. But Crystal," he lowered his voice so I had a hard time hearing him, "said we couldn't see each other anymore, that there'd be talk and she didn't want her daughter dragged into what happened to me."

I could see what Crystal meant. Everyone would have labeled this mass murderer Desiree's father even if he'd been in Leavenworth when she was conceived. Still, I found it interesting that Crystal had said Moran had broken it off. She seemed to have a bad habit of protecting ex-lovers.

"Did your wife find out?"

"No!" He blurted it out before he could lower his voice. "I couldn't do that to her." He hesitated. "She's delicate. Can't get around and do things like she used to. That's why I'm the one who takes care of the counter here nowadays. Susan's feeling poorly."

I bet she was. Without a doubt, she'd found out her husband, the man she thought she'd saved, the man she probably portrayed as a patriot to her friends who cared, had fooled around on her with the town harlot. I'd bet she was feeling poorly.

"When was the last time you saw Crystal," I pocketed the watch "before Trey was killed?"

Moran hesitated, played with other manila envelopes in the cardboard box, then half-turned as if to retire into the back room.

I put my hand on his arm to stop him and felt goosebumps race up my spine. He shook me off with practiced ease.

"Last Sunday morning, before church," he mumbled. "Had to give her back something she'd lent me."

I fought for my poker face, but I don't think I succeeded. Kinsale had been killed Sunday night, early Monday morning. "Mind if I ask what that was?" Like a knife? Like self-respect?

"Money. She gave me some cash to tide me over last month. Didn't want her worrying I wouldn't pay her back, so I ran it over to her place."

"How much?" I remembered Crystal telling me Kinsale had been supporting her, and he'd cut off her line of credit at the grocery store and failed to pay the electric bill. If she was feeling so poor, where'd she get money to lend Moran?

"Couple of hundred bucks is all." His face closed, as if he'd already said too much.

A movement in the corner of my eye caught my attention. Behind the glass screen surrounding the tiny office, a pinched face topped by sausage curls going gray was exiting through the door that went into the rear of the shop. I barely caught the reflection of her face in the glass, but I knew it was Susan Swinford Moran.

He must have had wife-radar. I wouldn't have noticed her if she hadn't moved and I was looking out for her.

"You'll have to leave." He locked up the box that had held my watch. "Now, please. I don't have anything to say to you."

It would be pressing my luck to ask what the money was for. If I wanted any more out of Matthew Moran, court-martialed first lieutenant, United States Army, I'd have to issue him a subpoena to testify.

June could get on it first thing in the morning. Right after I found out from Crystal why she was pleading poverty, then lending cash to a former boyfriend. Where she got the cash wasn't something I wanted to guess. I didn't think Crystal turned tricks, but if Kinsale had been sexually defunct and broke, as his wife alleged, maybe my client had done what she could to earn enough cash to keep herself and Desiree afloat. I thanked Moran for the watch and left, feeling his eyes on me until I rounded the corner to go home.

Back to the shutters for me. My Saturday project gave me a chance to do my best thinking. The shed was quickly turning into my refuge. I'd left Moran staring at my back as if he'd like to throw rocks at it. I didn't think the day could get much worse.

But, of course, it did.

16

I don't know how long I'd been at it, burning and scraping, twisting gelatinous gobs of black paint off the putty knife as I worried away at the pieces of Crystal's life. She'd lent money to an ex-lover, a man who was, according to Alma Bland, the father of her child.

If she was still that close to him, she'd managed to keep it a secret. And with good reason. With her daughter's reputation at stake, she was smart enough to know that any connection to Moran wouldn't make life easy for her in Wynnton. Did Crystal care for Moran the way she hadn't for Trey, or for anyone else in her life except her child? I'd seen the strength of the mother–daughter bond up close and personal, and it still made my heart ache. If only I'd had a mother who'd loved me so completely.

I'd had Miss Ena, who had cared for and guided me to the best of her proper Southern sensibilities. Her love might have been tempered by another generation's views on child rearing, but she'd done her best. Which was more than I could say for myself.

When dusk settled in with its siren call for me to pull out a bottle and the silver cup, I hauled a work light out to the shed, running it off an extension cord plugged in the kitchen. The light was too hot for me, but it was better in the long run than a drink. It attracted bugs as well, so finally, I switched it off and worked by the light of the butane torch. I only needed to see a few square inches at a time, anyway.

I had a client with a history of having been sexually abused as a child, a series of lovers, two of whom I knew to be married, and a child by someone whose name she wasn't bothering to divulge. My upstanding citizen of a client was also the illegitimate offspring of a respected judge, who just so happened to be boffing the wife of her last, and very deceased, lover.

Said lover had been blackmailing the judge, using Crystal as his lever along with the judge's affair with the disgruntled wife. The wife of the dead lover knew all about his affair with Crystal, and while the wife wanted to keep the judge as her next-door neighbor and convenient old boy toy, she clearly wasn't at all pleased at having been supplanted in her husband's affections by a piece of white trash like Crystal. One of Crystal's married lovers had been court-martialed for a massacre of innocent civilians during war time, with specific and rather remarkable attendant butchering of the corpses part of his sin.

Moran, the former Leavenworth inmate lover, sure as shootin' hadn't wanted his wife to find out about Crystal, either. Was he the father of Crystal's daughter? Had Kinsale threatened to tell Wynnton he'd sired a child, a child who already bore the sins of her mother? Could Kinsale have pushed Moran too far, too hard?

And what was Marcy Kinsale's part in the strange dance that led to her husband's death? She cut off her husband without a red cent to keep him from having the wherewithal to sell his inheritance, the land on which her money had built the lifestyle to which she was rather completely addicted and of which she was enormously proud. But her husband had found a way around her—he'd used the blackmail money from the judge to get his act together, to hire lawyers and consultants, to sell the land for a Global Transport Park.

Then there was my client, lending money to the mass-murderer. Oh yeah, I was doing just jim-dandy with this one. I was about to subpoena half the male population of Wynnton to find out who'd fathered Desiree, including Owen Amos. The idea made me laugh as I sweated away, cleaning the shutters to the bare wood. Owen was going to love that one.

My instincts kept returning to Desiree, like a tongue that has to touch a chipped tooth. My mind was sore with all the sharp edges to this case, and none of them were legal. I had to go on gut instinct here. Crystal's protectiveness of Desiree had to be at the root of Kinsale's murder. I didn't have any idea how, but I'd barrel my way through somehow.

I wasn't about to sit back and let it play out in the courtroom, as I'd done with Parnell Moses. I was going to throw mud at everyone with the slightest hint of hatred for Trey Kinsale, and hope everyone looked as dirty as my client. No jury could convict my client when I got done blowing smoke their way. I'd learned my lesson.

Or maybe, and the idea made me feel ill again, Trey had done something to Desiree that had inflamed Crystal to the point where she lost control and killed him while he slept off a binge. If that had been the case, my gut said she'd have told me just because the bastard deserved to die.

Then again, maybe not. An abused child herself, she was accustomed to holding secrets close to her vest. She'd have taught Desiree to do the same. Was that why Jack was so solicitous of the girl? Why Alma treated her like one of her own? Could they be just plain good folks who were trying to keep an abused child out of the fray surrounding her mother's arrest?

Hot, tired, and sweaty, with a brain that felt like an old pillow, I turned off the butane and set it in the corner of the shed while I re-stacked the shutters. I'd scrape up my paint chips tomorrow, when I had enough light to see what I was doing without stepping through the more rotten portions of the flooring. When I leaned over to pick up my tools to take them back to the house, I smelled the smoke.

I thought at first I'd accidentally set one of the shutters on fire. Separating them quickly, I palmed each one, but they were cool to my touch, while the smoke began to curl around me. I could see it in the darkness, like some Victorian ghost, wending its way around the edges of the shed door. I thought I'd left it ajar to let in some of the cooler night air when I'd set to work the second time around.

My first thought was that the house was on fire, and that the smoke had finally worked its way into the backyard. Reaching for the shed's door, I burned my hand on the old iron latch. When I pressed my palm against the oak, it was as hot as a griddle.

I barely had time to back up before the flames began to lick under the door with little blue tongues. I knew I was in trouble. Hurrying to the far side of the shed, I held my hands up to the wall.

It, too, was as hot as anything I'd ever felt. The flames were lurking just under the rafters of the roof when I glanced up, hoping to see the old ladder up there so I could use it to climb out through a hole in the shingles. No ladder, just smoke and encroaching fire spreading faster than butter on a July sidewalk.

I was trapped. Returning to the door, my only way out, I kicked it as hard as I could. All I did was jar my knee and jam my ankle. The bottom of my sneaker stuck to the wood like chewed gum. Breathing was getting harder, and I realized I'd better get out of there fast before I was overcome by smoke. Dropping to the floor, I tried to see through the darkness and the added layer of gray haze. The air lower on the floor was slightly better, but not enough to do me much good for long.

The shed was going up like a cardboard box tossed in a furnace. I knew my shutter work hadn't caused this fire, and someone had. Now I was going to die, and no one would ever know why. I imagined Henry thinking I'd gotten drunk and burned the place down with the butane while I was working on the shutters. They'd find the tank along with my bones, if any were left by the time the fire was through with me.

The idea of dying just now didn't appeal to me. I thought of Miss Ena's fight to stay on this planet, and how she'd succeeded for ninety-five productive years. As far as I was concerned I'd just gotten going, and I wasn't about to let someone take away my second chance to make a difference in life. Royally pissed, I wrapped my hand around my nose and mouth and tried to think.

Rolling onto my back was a mistake as soon as I did it.

My shoulder blade scraped on a rough piece of planking, and I worried for a second that I'd fall through the floor. In the next second, I knew I'd found my way out.

Sitting up, I pounded with fists, feet, elbows, knees, on the floor. Slowly, the rotten piece of pine began to splinter until, with a final loud crack, it separated from the edges still nailed to the joists. Shredding my hands on the edges, I hauled, jerked, and cursed at the stubborn wood. I'd been tip-toeing around on it for months, but now when I needed it to fall apart, it acted like green hickory.

The air that rushed through the hole I'd jammed in the floor smelled of gasoline, but there were no flames. Standing, I stomped harder, driving more bits of flooring onto the dirt floor that constituted the foundation. By now the walls were a rosy hue that would have been beautiful if I hadn't known it meant they were about to explode into flames.

My breathing labored, drenched in sweat from the heat, I wiggled my legs, then my hips, and finally my shoulders, through the hole. Since the bricks raised the floor about three feet above the ground, I had to angle myself onto the dirt. I slid through years of junk that had filtered down between the floor joists and was beyond grateful to be there.

The fire, from what I could see, had worked its way up from the bottom edge of the shed in a systematic climb. Holding my breath, I prepared to roll out between the bricks. Hesitating for a second, I wondered who might still be out there. My bet was a rag soaked in kerosene or gas conveniently had been run around the shed's bottom edge, maybe even several of them jammed into the open spaces between some of the vertical slats. Only the extreme age and weathering of the oak had kept it from shooting into fireworks when the first match had been struck. I was luckier than I should have been that I hadn't set the fire myself with the butane torch.

I couldn't hesitate long. Either I stayed where I was and fried like something stuck to the bottom of a skillet, or I took my chances. Bamboo had grown up along the back side of the shed, and there was no way I could fight my way through it at the bottom. I had to go sideways or straight into the backyard. Either way, I was exposed.

If I was going to die, I wanted to see my killer's face. Pulling myself on my elbows commando style, I inched out, ducking my head to keep the flames out of my hair. As soon as I could get purchase, I grabbed some of the longer weeds outside the foundation and pulled myself into the open air as quickly as I could.

The wire grass gave way, but the fennel that had run wild from an old herb garden left a lingering scent of licorice in the air. I wondered if it, with the acrid smoky smell burning my throat and lungs, would be the last physical sensation I'd ever have. I hated licorice.

The stars were shining through the heavy layer of smoke and flame that rose from the shed. Squinching like an inverted inch worm on my back farther from the inferno, I kept my focus on the sky. As long as I could see the heavens, I had hopes of making it there eventually. Actually, heaven was a joke with me. The sky would have to do.

"I called the fire department. Are you okay?"

In a panic, I struggled to my stomach, then my knees. I couldn't run on my back. The only problem was I couldn't see whoever was above me. If he had a weapon, he should have used it by now. But if he wanted to hurt me, why had he called the fire department? Screaming wasn't going to work. I'd never known how noisy a fire could be until now.

Besides, my throat wasn't cooperating. Coughing, I tried to work up enough spit to throw it in my assailant's face.

"Who are you?" I croaked. My throat seemed to not be able to handle breathing and talking simultaneously.

A tentative hand both tugged and patted me on the back, as if I were a puppy about to throw up on the rug.

"We'd better get away from the shed, Tal. It's going to fall fast once the flames hit the roof." The voice was controlled, calm, and trying to keep me from crumbling in a fit of what Miss Ena would have called the vapors.

I knew that voice. "Owen?"

"Saw the smoke from the front porch. Thought maybe you were back here burning trash or something. I had no idea anyone was in there." He slid an arm under me and tried to lift me to my feet. "Tal, help me here, we really need to put some distance between us and that fire."

I was never so glad to see a prosecutor in my life. Then, I saw what he meant. The heat from the flaming oak was hot enough to bake bricks.

I heard him as if he were speaking to me from the bottom of a swimming pool. Raising my head took more effort than it was worth. I gave up trying to stand, shoved his hands off me, and rolled onto my back again. Sure enough, Owen Amos's face was right there, staring down at me like I was some sort of problem he couldn't solve.

"You didn't by any chance," I coughed a racking series that tried to turn my lungs inside out, "by any chance set my shed on fire by accident?"

He looked properly horrified. I liked his nose, I realized. Not small, not big, it still had character. He was frowning, however, which made him look as fierce as a marine storming a machine-gun nest.

"What're you saying? You mean this wasn't an accident?"

I couldn't see him because he'd moved behind me. When I felt his hands under my arms this time, shifting me across the grass, I guessed he wasn't planning on killing me. At least, I hoped not. He had rather nice hands. Warm, big enough to hold me up, strong. Short nails. Nothing jabbed me.

"I like your hands," I murmured through my headache. I wanted to say more, but my throat was completely closed now, and all I could do was try to breathe without ripping out a lung by the roots.

"I'm getting you to the hospital," he muttered in my ear, holding my back to his chest.

Yes, I thought, *nice chest.* I gave up fighting the gray at the edges of my mind, and let go. Owen would take care of me or kill me, I didn't give a damn at this point. At least I'd die being held by a man. What an odd thought for me. But then again, I was feeling very odd.

I came to in the ambulance where they pumped me full of fresh oxygen. Fire trucks lined Woolfolk Avenue as they hauled hoses into my backyard. Revived by the oxygen, I tried to sit up, but an attendant held me down.

"Take it easy, ma'am. We'll get you to the hospital in about five minutes. Just hold on there."

"I don't need to go to the hospital. Where's Owen Amos?"

He looked puzzled.

"The man who called you guys. Tall, short dark hair."

"Oh, the man who hauled you out of that inferno? He's over there." The attendant gestured at a gaggle of police cars.

I pulled myself off the ambulance cot. I felt rocky, but I was breathing a hell of a lot better than I had been. "Thanks." I stood. My throat hurt like hell.

"Hey, lady, you're not supposed to do that!" The kid was young enough to be, well, not my son, but at least a lot younger than I.

"I've heard that all my life," I warned him as I scrambled out of the ambulance. "Owen!" I shouted. A croak was more like it.

He didn't hear me. With the ambulance guy in my wake trying to grab my arms, I shoved myself through the uniforms to Owen. Frank was shaking his head at something Owen was saying.

"She drinks like a fish. Probably started it herself."

The expression "seeing red" hadn't meant much to me before. But I remembered knowing I was going to die, and that I'd be blamed for it because I'd been drinking, or so it would be assumed.

"You stupid. . . ." I started to scream, anger swimming before me like some giant crimson sea. My indignation sounded more like a cranky baby who'd cried all night. "I wasn't drinking and someone tried to kill me!"

I wavered on my feet, the rush of adrenaline making me woozy.

"I know, calm down," Owen soothed, his arm around my waist as he held me upright. I don't know how he got to me so quickly. "I saw the rope tied around the latch, then looped through that old tree root that sticks up beside the shed. It was one of those heavy jobs, felt wet when I touched it. Someone wanted you stuck in there long enough to kill you.

"The damned rope would have finally burned, long after

you'd stopped breathing. No evidence the door'd been tied shut. Premeditated doesn't begin to cover it."

He turned to Frank. "Get the arson people down here and get them fast. I want whoever did this caught yesterday. You understand?"

Normally, I don't let anyone else fight my fights. But at that moment, it felt awfully nice. My legs, wobbly with fatigue and probably lack of oxygen, decided to play rubber band games on me. I sat down hard on my rump despite Owen's grabbing me harder. I think he lowered me as gently as he could, but with no padding behind, it was a spine-jarring landing.

"I'm not letting you stay here alone. You're coming with me." Squatting beside me, Owen slid his hands in mine and tugged. "On your feet, Tal. I'm taking you home."

I tried to protest, but where did I have to go? Wynnton didn't even have a Motel 6. Henry and Grace would put me up, but I didn't want to suck them into whatever monster was out there waiting for his chance to get me again. Owen didn't have a wife to worry about, so if he wanted to take a chance on having me as a house guest, I'd take him up on it. Briefly, I wondered why I thought a man had tried to burn me to death.

"Okay." I didn't want to think about it. I didn't want to think at all. The burning in my nose and throat felt like hot coals. All I wanted was cool water all over my body. I hoped Owen had a bathtub. I was going to sleep in it filled with ice cubes.

Waving aside all the uniforms, Owen let me at least save some dignity by steering me in the direction of his car. I would never have lived it down if he'd carried me like some knight in shining armor rescuing a damsel in distress. I probably would have shamed myself by putting my arms around his neck.

I owed him big time, and I wasn't at all happy about it. But survivors can't be choosers, I reasoned. Besides, this would look good for him politically—hero saves woman from fire. Yeah, Owen Amos would come out of this smelling like expensive aftershave, while I reeked of gasoline and smoke.

He drove as if he were carting a new baby home without a car seat. If he'd gone any slower, we'd have gotten there faster crawling. My eyes stung, and I shut them to try to cut off the dizziness that threatened to turn my stomach inside out.

Owen lived in one of the older houses along the river, an early-nineteenth-century cottage built by some plantation owner who wanted a place to stay near town when the missus had a yen to go shopping. Cotton money had made Wynnton a mecca for folks with money before the War of Northern Aggression. I admired the blue-and-yellow paint job, visible in the period gas lights along the sidewalk. Yes, a nice house. Nice man. I liked him. I was feeling wobbly and stupid.

He maneuvered me into the living room, propped me in a wooden chair that wasn't very comfortable, but hey, it didn't have any cushions to get smeared by the sticky black covering me.

"Be right back. I'll get you when the water's warm. Here, drink this." He handed me a glass of cold water.

I sucked it down carefully, my hands hurting like hell from crawling through the splintery hole in the floor. I'd probably burned them, too.

Owen was all business when he returned. "Got the

warm water running, found you something to put on when you get out." He held up a big T-shirt. I would be lost inside it. "Let me take a look at those hands when you get the soot off them."

"I'll bet you were a hell of a soldier," I croaked. My throat wouldn't ever be the same, it was so raw. "You give orders like a pro."

"I was," he agreed calmly. "Now into that bathtub. Want me to call your insurance agent now, or let it go until morning?"

"Insurance?" I tried not to laugh. The movement hurt my chest. "Hell, nothing of value in that shed."

"Except you," he said smoothly.

I'd been ready to hit the floor, but that just about put me over the edge. My eyes were still stinging, but I saw concern, caring, and something unidentifiable in his eyes. I wasn't accustomed to strong men, handsome like Gary Cooper had been handsome, acting gallant. Frank's hostility was easier for me to handle.

Like an idiot, I patted my hair. It felt as if half of it had been singed off. "Do you have some scissors?"

"I think so, just a sec." He returned from what looked like the kitchen at the end of the hallway and handed them to me. "Anything I can help you with?" There was a hint of doubt now in those very sexy eyes.

"Don't think so. The buttons on my shirt melted into the material. I'll just see if I can get out of it with this." I waved the scissors. "Which way to the bathroom?"

He led the way with one hand on my elbow, as if he were afraid I'd fall against a wall.

"Don't worry, I won't get the wallpaper dirty," I tried to joke as I waited for him to give me the shirt at the bathroom door.

"I'm not worried about that." He sounded intensely hurt. "I'm just so . . ."

"Sick and tired of me, and will I please shut up and get clean so you can get me out of here?" I finished for him.

"No, you idiot. For a smart woman, you don't listen, do you?" He was annoyed. "Here's a set of towels and a washcloth." He passed them from the hall closet into my arms. "Let me know if you need anything else."

"What were you about to say?" I couldn't help asking.

"I was about to say I was glad I got there when I did," he muttered. "I don't want to think about what would have happened if I hadn't."

It was only as I soaked in the claw-footed tub filled to the brim that I thought about what he'd said. I'd already smashed my way through the floor when he got there. Maybe he thought he'd pulled me from under the foundation. Either way, it didn't matter. I was awfully glad he'd been there, too.

When I finally hauled my sorry self out of the bathroom, he was waiting with an antiseptic spray and tweezers. As I curled into a ball and looked the opposite direction, he dug into my hand and extracted what was left of the shed's pine floor.

"You're being awfully nice," I croaked.

"This must hurt like hell." He aimed a light closer to my palm and squinted. "Need my glasses to do this right."

"It does. Didn't know you wore glasses."

"Contacts during the day. Took them out a while ago. Kinda smeary with smoke residue." Another splinter emerged.

"You're trying to win my vote, aren't you? Hate to tell you, I seldom vote."

"You should. It's your duty." He smiled as he dug into my flesh again.

"I don't believe in duty." If he knew anything at all about me, he'd better know that.

"I do."

"That's pretty clear. You were in the army a long time." I stared at my feet so I couldn't see what he was doing to my hands.

"Yep. I was a kid in Vietnam, had to lie to enlist. Made me what I am today."

"Is that a good thing?" My mind was floating into the exhaustion of terror and physical pain.

"Yes." No equivocation. "There's a lot that needs changing in America, and I'm the man to do it." His voice was firm. Just the facts, ma'am, just the facts.

"If you say so." I was so tired I didn't even ask him how he was so sure about his future.

Tomorrow was more than I could handle. For once, it was nice to be with a man who knew what he wanted and how he was going to get it. Jack Bland had been that way when he was mine. Not anymore. I felt my head nodding onto my shoulder, then Owen lifting me in his arms.

Later, enveloped in his T-shirt, I slept in Owen's bed. He covered me with a sheet, darkened the room without a word, closing the door behind him. I'm not sure, but I think he sat up the rest of the night in the living room, checking on me now and then.

I dreamed. Flames, smoke, sirens, Owen's hands, black paint on my fingers, my face, my melted buttons. Floating through the melee was Crystal's pinched face and the shadowy men who'd once been her lovers. And Jack Bland.

I was scared shitless by all of them.

17

〰〰〰

"TAL, someone wants you out of the way. My bet is that same someone's worried that you're going to do too good a job defending your client."

I noticed Owen didn't say which client. He knew I had only one. I was still in the T-shirt, feeling rather naked underneath in the morning light on his back porch. He'd poured us each a mug of coffee, added cream and sugar to mine even though I didn't take them, and guided me onto an old slider covered with a faded quilt.

Like an obedient puppy, I sat and took the coffee. At least my hands felt almost normal enough to hold on to the mug and not spill it. I hadn't slept well, and my temper was short at the best of times in the morning. But I'd keep my complaining to a minimum. The morning sun looked mighty nice.

"Could be someone who just doesn't like me being back in Wynnton." I'd try to be rational about this. "Maybe someone I ticked off in junior high?"

He didn't laugh.

"I need you to come up with a list of who'd tie you inside a burning building." Owen didn't sound happy. His disquiet somehow comforted me.

I thought of Parnell Moses. He hadn't had any relatives, just me, his incompetent lawyer. No, his ghost hadn't come back to try to get revenge, although I wouldn't have blamed it.

"I need to get back to my house first. There's this little matter of clothes. . . ." I gestured at the T-shirt. I didn't have much of a figure, but I was feeling self-conscious.

"I called your office and left a message for your secretary to bring you something to wear as soon as she could. I assumed she'd check on a Sunday."

June was going to love that. I had no idea if June had bought a recorder for the phone that could retrieve calls from another phone. I'd have to remember to ask her. I couldn't wait to see what she brought, if she did as Owen assumed she'd do. I'd be uncomfortable all day. If it was three-inch heels, I was in no mood.

We sipped in an easy silence, Owen pushing off the slider whenever it started to slow down. I felt like I was rocking on a tiny ship. The headache from last night was niggling at the corners of my brain, and I was still feeling prickly all over. But the worst had passed. I'd even managed to sleep in between fits of terror and flaming nightmares, no small feat.

I was feeling entirely too comfortable. Owen's jeans looked like he was born to wear them, and I was suddenly conscious of the springy hairs on his forearms. He looked big and solid and as sexy as all get-out. The crinkles in the corners of his eyes fascinated me.

"You going into the office today?" It was, after all, Sunday, but he had the fidgety, harried look of someone with something he had to get done.

"Later. Just to catch up on some paperwork while it's quiet."

Again, silence that wasn't at all tense. I wondered if this was how couples felt who'd been together a long time, and why I was thinking this way. I didn't want or need to be part of a couple. I told myself this several times as I tried to pretend I wasn't half-naked and seated next to the man who'd saved my life.

"I owe you." I'd finished my coffee.

"No, you don't."

"Yes, I do." I hurried before I started remembering I wanted to play lawyer games with him with the information I'd found. "I've got some information you should know about." I cleared my throat. "It might influence how you handle the case."

I didn't need to tell him which one.

"Did you know Judge Jordan is Crystal Walker's natural father?"

I got him with that one. He whistled softly. "Boy howdy."

"It gets better. Kinsale was blackmailing him with that little goodie. Talk about motive to kill. Don't let that gray hair fool you, the judge is one tough son of a bitch."

Setting his mug and mine on the porch floor, he turned to face me. The cicadas were beginning their morning song. *Another hot one coming,* I thought, and instantly remembered the fire.

"Where'd you hear that?" He was all business now.

I'd made no promises about confidentiality, but in a way, the information did come from my client. In a round-about way.

"That's attorney–client privilege, counselor."

"Damnation." Shoving off the slider, Owen paced the back porch.

"There's more. Marcy Kinsale was screwing the judge, too."

Owen shot me a look that said more than his words. "Double damn. And I'll just bet Kinsale knew about that little secret, too. Added it to the blackmail pot, did he?"

"That'd be a good guess."

I took heart. "Doesn't look like your detectives did too much investigating, Owen."

"They didn't." He opened the back door to the kitchen, all business. Getting to my feet, I followed him. I didn't know why, it just seemed like the right thing to do.

"This is the last time they get to work a case. They'll be lucky to get a patrol car when I'm done with them. You'll understand," his words sharp and businesslike, "I've got to get to the office. Just push the lock on the front door when you leave. I'll see you later. And I want that list from you."

Hesitating, he seemed reluctant to leave me alone. "Thanks for telling me that. It helps your client, but still, it'll keep egg off my face in the long run."

He looked for a second as if he wanted to kiss me. Something within me wanted to lean into him, rest my head against his chest and feel safe and warm. I'd never felt that way with a man. My survival instincts kicked in like adrenaline, and I pulled back. We both looked foolish, like high schoolers wearing braces who haven't figured out how to kiss.

This wasn't going to be an easy relationship, if it was going to be anything at all.

"I'll talk to you later. Stay here as long as you want." He was the first to break away. I started to wave as he left, but at the last minute figured I'd look ridiculous. Letting my hand hit my hip, I posed like a pin-up, head-cocked, eyelashes batting.

"Thanks for a bed and the bath." I cooed on purpose, hoping he'd laugh.

He did. We were on firmer footing.

"Oh, and don't worry if you see a uniform tailing you around. Someone should be here in a few minutes. I wouldn't leave you alone, but . . ."

"Shoo. I'm fine. Get to work and find out you should dismiss all charges against my client. My innocent client."

He gave me the raised-eyebrow look which said "nice try," but he didn't give me hell, either, for talking about the case. Technically, I wasn't discussing my client, but the possibility someone else had committed the crime. I was feeling rather smug and not at all sorry Owen had offered me shelter.

We had a long way to go, and if we got there together it'd be a miracle, but maybe we could give it a try. I avoided thinking of relationships as long term or anything else, but Owen was in the running.

Owen was gone, and I was left with only my thoughts. Remembering the fire still scared the bejesus out of me, so I had to keep my mind busy somehow while I waited for June to bring me something to wear. I'd found the phone and called her. She wouldn't check the office machine on a Sunday. Probably, she was in church with Henry and Grace.

My message on her home phone was to the point: bring jeans, T-shirt, underwear, and sneakers to Owen Amos's house as soon as she checked her answering service. Knowing June, she was going to have a field day in my closet before she deigned to bring me some clean togs.

If Owen did as I thought he would and set the attack dogs after the judge, all hell was about to explode in Wynnton. I wanted Crystal out of that jail and as far from Wynnton as she could get if Judge Jordan was arrested for murder. As soon as he figured out she'd been pegged as his kin, he wasn't going to make nice, I was sure of that. I had to wear clothes to visit her in the jail so I fussed and fumed for a while, waiting for June to call back to let me know she was on her way.

With Judge Jordan in the picture, I was hopeful that Crystal would get a decent crack at freedom. I doubted Jordan would be convicted. But I had the awful feeling he knew who'd told Kinsale about his fathering Crystal, and there'd be the proverbial piper to pay. Maybe Crystal was paying already, and he'd set her up to take his fall for Kinsale's murder.

I couldn't imagine the twisted thinking that went into framing your own daughter for a killing, then trying to make sure she was convicted by seeing that she had a drunken, failed attorney. I'd been idiotically blind when I thought Jordan had wanted me to represent Crystal because he respected my legal acumen.

I couldn't imagine the judge trying to kill me himself. He was the sort of man who hired out his dirty work. Snide remarks, social set-downs, were more his style. Owen would never find out who tied that rope around the latch and anchored it to the tree root. But he might find out who

Jordan had hired to kill Kinsale. The judge was too meticulous about staying clean to do the deed himself.

I was beginning to feel guilty about not telling Owen Moran and Crystal had had a "thing." My bet was on Judge Jordan wearing prison orange. I just didn't cotton to showing Owen my whole hand at once, I guess.

Logically, I knew I shouldn't hide information that would exonerate my client until trial. I tucked the T-shirt tighter under my tail and gave the swing as hard a push as I could. If I had had an investigator of my own, something that the court would never pay for when the case was going to be financed by state taxpayers, I might have been able to develop more solid leads for putting out the feelers I'd just send Owen's way. With cold, hard facts in front of him, he'd be legally and morally bound to drop the murder charge against Crystal.

My perfect scenario had her walking out of jail without having her past thrown in front of a jury, so she and Desiree could get on with their lives in quiet obscurity. This little brush with a dead lover in the shed would eventually die down in comparison to the juicy news of a busted judge. How Crystal would feel about her father's trial and the common knowledge that would result about his having sired her, I didn't know or care. As far as I was concerned, she'd be better off as the daughter of a killer than as the killer.

Moran still bothered me, but I didn't have the resources to work on him as my next candidate for Killer of the Month. I should have said something to Owen, if only to give him another good reason to release Crystal. I thought about the list Owen wanted from me, and knew why I'd left Moran out of the conversation that had sent Owen running to bust his detectives' chops.

If that weasly little bastard had tried to kill me, I'd get even. I didn't want him locked up for Trey's murder if he'd tried to off me, too. As soon as I knew about him for sure, he'd wish he'd died in Vietnam when I was through with him.

Anger as hot as the fire that had eaten my shed alive was replaced by cold, wicked doubts. What if I'd given Owen enough information for him to work up an alibi for the judge? What if he wasn't the independent, uncorrupted man I hoped? Right now, I worried, he was telling the judge to get his tail to the courthouse, and then Owen would help Jordan figure out an air-tight alibi, and . . .

Just as I'd about decided I'd probably screwed my client by telling Owen about Marcy and the judge, not to mention Crystal's paternity, and I should hand in my license to practice law and offer to take Crystal's place in prison, a car pulled up. The engine pinged for a few rattling moments out front. For a second, my stomach knotted, and hurrying into the kitchen, I glanced around for a weapon.

Paring knife in hand, I told myself it was the police protection Owen had said he'd ordered. Somehow that thought wasn't reassuring. If I was going to get whacked in the county prosecutor's house, I should at least have on underpants. Mine, however, were a lost cause. The thought bothered me more than the fear of a killer coming up the walk.

If I was going to die, I'd do it in plain view. Jerking open the front door, I held my breath and hid the knife behind my back. My hand shook.

Grace greeted me with an elegant little suitcase in one hand and a hug waiting in the other arm. I hadn't been so happy to see anyone since Owen's face last night. I dropped the knife and cursed as it bounced onto my bare foot.

"Grace, how'd you get roped into this?" I held open the front door for her.

Sweeping by me in a halo of fresh air and clean soap, Grace pulled me into a stiff hug. Stiff on my part, that is. My skin still hurt.

"Ouch," I muttered. "Splinters and a lot of heat, bad combination."

"Sorry, oh my, I didn't believe it when I heard," Grace commiserated, closing the door behind her. "Did I hurt you?"

"Naw, just a little stiff and sore, is all." And stupid. Stupid about Owen, stupid for telling him what I had, stupid for wishing it'd been him walking into the house.

"June called me, complained she was up to her eyeballs tracking down something you wanted her to find. Said you were over here, needed a change of clothes. By the way, what happened in your backyard last night? I want the full story, or Henry'll divorce me. Owen's a little old for you, isn't he?"

Leave it to June to imply I'd had a sleepover with the town prosecutor after someone had hoped to turn me into a marshmallow. "Nothing much. Someone tried to make me into toast. I was working in the shed when the fire started."

Grace's face froze. "My God, Tal, are you all right? You said you were sore, should I take you to the doctor? I can call . . ."

I gestured at the T-shirt I wore. "No need. I'm Jim Dandy, except I didn't have time to rummage around for a change of clothes. Owen insisted I come here with him, he didn't want me alone." I held up my hands. "These are the worst. Mostly splinters. You should see my clothes though—not one June would approve of. Melted buttons and all."

Seizing my hands in hers, she gave them a thorough inspection, turning them over, bending my fingers, poking here and there. I winced only once. "Thank goodness, they look clean, I don't see any incipient infection. We'll have to watch them closely, and if there're any red marks at all, I want you at the doctor's office before the day's out, you hear me?"

Leaving me, she picked up the suitcase and set it on the sofa, giving me an appraising look. "Why didn't you call us? Henry and me?"

"I didn't have time, to be honest. Owen hauled me out of there while they finished cleaning up the fire, and I crashed as soon as I could breathe a little better." I clicked open the suitcase and checked it out. Grace must have done the packing. Everything in there was sensible, not a high heel in sight. "Besides, I knew you'd insist I stay with you, and the creep who poured gasoline everywhere is still out there. Some friend I'd be if I led him to your house."

"Then why're you here?" She sounded ticked, Grace of the impeccable manners and genuine distress, over my choice. "You think Owen Amos could take better care of you than we could?"

"It's not like that, honest, I'm just," I sucked in another ragged breath, "afraid of losing more people I care about. Miss Ena's gone, and you and Henry are it when it comes to family." I managed a shaky smile. "Besides, Owen threw me in his car. I was helpless to stop him."

"When pigs fly," Grace muttered. "Go get dressed, you look awful in that get-up."

For a second, she sounded just like Miss Ena, and I almost cried with relief.

"Thanks." I picked up the suitcase to head for a bedroom.

Grace stayed put. "Tal, we need to talk. Not about the fire."

I could feel it coming. Bad news always started with those words. "What about?" I wished I had some clothes on. Being half-naked didn't inspire self-confidence in the face of disaster. I shifted from foot to foot.

"It can wait. Why don't you get dressed? It's nothing important." She must have seen my discomfort. *Damn, Grace was good,* I thought. *No wonder she was smarter than both Henry and me.*

I ducked into Owen's bedroom to pull on the blouse and slacks from the suitcase. Last night I hadn't been in any shape to notice my haven, but now that I was finally awake, I figured I should give the place a good looking-over. I felt like a sneak, but after all, he'd invited me into his home and it wasn't as if I was pawing through his dresser drawers. Trying to postpone whatever unpleasantness Grace needed to dump on me, I took a good look around.

Owen had painted the walls a dark Victorian red. A spartan single bed, an army blanket thrown over it for a bedspread, was shoved in one corner, and a plain, Salvation Army–style chest of drawers was against the other. I straightened the bed and wondered if I should change the sheets.

The floor was covered with woven grass mats, the sort you'd see in a beach house, and black blinds filled the double window that faced the front of the house. What stopped me cold was the collection hanging on the walls I hadn't noticed earlier this morning. I must have missed it because the blinds had successfully shrouded the room in darkness until the sun was at just the right angle to peek through them.

Stepping closer, I saw they were all unusual weapons. One looked like a blow dart, another an old hatchet with odd markings on the wooden handle, and two spears were above them. Owen clearly was a collector.

The wall behind the dresser was filled with guns and rifles. Some of them looked like real antiques, but others I had the feeling I'd seen more recently.

Turning, I saw that the wall with the closet door held his pictures. Some were Oriental, graceful renderings of rice paddies with clouds floating peacefully overhead. Others looked like diplomas or commendations. I realized I had no knowledge of Owen Amos beyond the fact he'd retired from the military to practice law and eventually run for prosecutor in Wynnton. Hopping over to the wall as I stuck a leg in the slacks, I peered more closely at the pictures.

He had photos of himself receiving a diploma, of the campus of some school, but mostly, black-and-whites of the Orient dominated the wall. Some were faces, old men in straw hats crouched beside the road, others young women in baggy pants kneeling in the dirt, staring sullenly away from the camera in some, in others glaring at the lens with hatred as intense as the fire that had almost killed me. Whoever the photographer, he was fascinated with the people he'd shot, and not in a good way. I was reminded of pictures of concentration camp victims after World War II.

Stepping back a bit, I realized what had been bothering me about them. All developed in a gritty, stark, black-and-white, they had a disturbing edge to them, an underlying chaotic feeling. Too much hatred in some, too much despair coming from the others, made them unsettling as artistic compositions. The malevolence they expressed was aimed at the photographer, at life, at the fate that had thrown them together for the second it took for the lens to capture their pictures. Mentally, I calculated Owen's age. If he'd been young during Vietnam, he'd be in his mid to late fifties by now, just where I'd have put him.

Quickly, I buttoned my blouse.

"You okay in there?" Grace called.

"Yep, sure thing. Sorry, I'll be ready to roll in a minute." I had to get out of that room. The knowledge that it had felt safe last night was disturbing. I couldn't have slept in there again if Owen had promised me the best sex east of the Mississippi.

Grace was waiting for me at the front door. "Come on, we'll talk while I drive you home."

She didn't look upset, just determined. I slid into her Lexus, aching more than I had last night. Pulling away from Owen's house, she cleared her throat nervously. I'd never known Grace to be nervous. I began worrying again.

"It's not Henry, is it? He's not sick with something drastic, is he?" I couldn't imagine what else would set Grace on edge.

She shook her head. "I had a visit the other day from none other than Marcy Kinsale."

If Grace had opened the passenger door and shoved me out, I couldn't have been more surprised. "I didn't know you hobnobbed with Marcy."

"I don't. I don't know the woman from a hole in the ground." Grace sounded angry.

"Don't stop now. I'm dying of curiosity. Was she tipsy?"

"No. Crazy maybe, but not loaded. At least, I think not. She paid me a little visit, she said, because she felt she should warn me. So the same thing didn't happen to me that happened to her."

I squawked, "You mean someone's going to kill Henry?"

"Probably me, if he doesn't learn to put his dirty clothes in the hamper. Noooo," Grace drawled, imitating Marcy's thick accent perfectly. "She lost her husband to that thievin', murderin' bitch Crystal Walker, and by damned, she didn't want to see another good woman lose a husband to the likes of trash like Tal Jefferson."

I almost laughed aloud, decided better of it. "Wow, what did you say?"

"I told her to mind her own business and get it out of the gutter. A cliché, true, but I haven't had any experience dealing with catty women like Marcy. Took me by surprise, that's for sure."

"Why did she do it?" I was talking more to myself than to Grace. I was afraid to ask Grace if she'd given Marcy's accusation any credence. She'd smack me silly for even thinking it for an instant.

"My bet is she's worried about you getting your client freed. Everyone knows you and Henry go way back, that whatever he finds out in this case, he tells you. Most pathologists play it close to the vest, giving the prosecution the good stuff. You've got the upper hand with Henry, and Marcy knows it. Besides, Henry's neutral. He just wants the truth."

"Thank God." I gave her a smile. "For one honest man and the woman he was smart enough to marry."

"You can say that again. Why she thought I'd fall for that load of bull is beyond me. Does she think I fell off the cotton wagon yesterday? Clear as glass what she's trying to do."

"She sure underestimated you."

Grace snorted. "Won't be the first time nor the last it's happened. Girlfriend, the real reason I'm telling you this, is I think you need to be careful. Especially after the fire.

You should have seen Marcy playing it like a pro, the wronged woman warning the other wronged woman.

"It was all I could do not to laugh at her." Her perfectly manicured nails tapped the steering wheel. "I hate a dumb woman, and Marcy ranks right up there with the dumbest of the dumb."

I did laugh. "Guess she's not so stupid, she managed to outlive Trey. Bet he wanted to do her in more than once." I became serious. "Don't tell Henry about this, okay? He'll be pissed as all getout. Marcy Kinsale's grasping at straws. If Crystal's acquitted, they'll look a lot more closely at her, and she knows it."

Grace waved a hand at me, keeping her eyes on the road. "I don't want the gory details. Henry's job and yours aren't part of what I do. I make satellites stay up there where they belong. Piece of cake compared to the shit you two get into."

"We've been getting into shit since we were kids. I promise I won't drag you into it, but Henry's your problem."

"That he is." Grace was smiling along with me, I was relieved to note. "Tal, I never believed her. Not for a second."

"I knew that. I'm just sorry you're getting dragged into all this. . . ." I hesitated, because Crystal's tragedy of a life deserved more than a dismissive categorization. "This trouble I seem to drag around like a dead skunk tied to my tail. I swear, after this case is finished, I'm never practicing law again."

"That'll be the day. You'll get her off, and then you'll have clients lined up and down the sidewalk, waiting to hire you. And June'll be happier than a tick on a dog."

"That'd be a sight for sore eyes. June happy, that is."

She laughed. "What I wanted to say, before the rumor

mill gets going full tilt, is that I know that you and Henry have shared things growing up that'll always belong to just the two of you. But Henry and I have a solid marriage. I wanted you to know that."

"Never thought otherwise." I swallowed hard. "Thanks, Grace. For bringing me the clothes." I fidgeted with a piece of hair that'd dropped into my eyes. I wasn't good with women as friends. Maybe that's why I'd gone into the law, where men were more likely to be my colleagues and perhaps more. "And for not giving Marcy Kinsale any satisfaction. The woman's nuts."

"She may well be. Be careful, Tal. I got the feeling she's on the edge. You know the type, loaded to the gills with Valium but it hasn't kicked in yet?"

If Marcy knew about her husband's blackmail of her lover and why, I bet she was on edge. She would have lost her house and all that went with it if Trey sold it out from under her. Even worse, she'd have lost her lover. I'd bet my bottom dollar the judge wouldn't keep her as his mistress once her husband played out his hand. Maybe the blackmail had been the last card, and Marcy had decided it was time for Trey to fold his hand and go home permanently.

Still, why the mutilation? Why had his ear been severed? Because he wouldn't listen to her?

Or because he'd heard too much and used it to his advantage and not hers? Trey had had his ear to the gossip-beat of Wynnton through Crystal, collecting the dirtiest of the dirty he could find. And his wife had been right in the thick of some of the filthiest of all, fooling around with the very married judge who lived next door.

Marcy Kinsale and her lover had more to lose than Crystal. I wondered who else had more to lose than my client, and why.

18

~~~~~

GRACE dropped me off at Miss Ena's house, where I crawled into bed and spent the rest of the day sleeping. The shock had worn off and left me feeling more drained than a bender. By the time I dragged myself downstairs on Monday morning, I could have sworn June was glad to see me.

"Guess what I got?" She waved a file at me as I cruised in as if nothing had happened Saturday night. The acrid smell of smoke had penetrated the house, and for a second, I hesitated. If the house had been destroyed, I think I would have lost all hope.

"What?" I caught a glimpse of myself in the old mirror in the front hall. I looked like death. Gaunt cheeks. Purple under my eyes. Pinched mouth.

She gave me a hard look, opened her mouth to say

something about the ratty jeans I was wearing, then shut it. The look in my eyes must have told her to keep her opinions to herself this morning.

"I've called your insurance company," she noted as she flipped a couple of files on top of one another. "They can't do anything until the arson investigation is finished."

"Was it insured? The shed?"

"Yep. Your grandmother insured all outbuildings, and you just kept paying the premiums."

"Well, what do you know. Not that I need a new shed, but if they pay me for it, I can use the money, that's for sure." To hire my own investigator. A real pro I wouldn't have to finance through the trust fund. I started to perk up.

"What've you got there?" I asked. June was looking much too pleased with herself.

"The records from the subpoena for Trey Kinsale's bank account." A wink slipped its way toward me.

"I didn't ask for a subpoena." I stopped. I'd signed a lot of stuff all at once for June, barely glancing at it. "Guess I did, huh?"

She grinned from ear to ear. "It's a dirty job, but someone's gotta do it." She was pleased as punch with herself. Today she wore big gold hoop earrings that sparkled against her lovely dark skin. I was betting they were real gold.

"June, when are you going to apply to the bar for approval to read law? You're going to have to get it over with, so you can go into practice with me. I don't think anyone else would have you," I added just to keep her ego from flying through the roof.

"I talked to Henry about it a few days ago, made a call Friday." She looked happier than the woman who'd walked through my door not so long ago. "You need a partner if you're gonna make any money at this. I can't even find your escrow account books."

"There aren't any. So keep talking, tell me about the bank records." I looked at pages and pages of photocopied bank statements.

"That's gonna change." She frowned to let me know I was going to get whipped into shape if it was the last thing she ever did.

I ignored her. Seconds passed. She waited, I pretended I was studying the financial records, not having the slightest idea what I was looking for.

"Okay, you win. Buy an accounting program for the office. So what's all this mean?" I held up the file.

Wellll," she drawled, savoring the moment. "Trey Kinsale wasn't broke by a long shot. His fancy wife may have cut him off without a penny to keep him from getting the site plans drawn to sell the land, but he had bucks. Lots and lots of bucks, which it appears," she smiled again from ear to ear, "went to a consultant, a zoning expert, and tax accountants in Atlanta. He was paying them by the hour, and from the looks of it, in full."

I whistled. "So why'd Crystal tell me he was broke? I'd assumed, from what Crystal said, that every penny went to getting the land ready for the Transport Park. How come he had any left over?"

"Just taking a wild guess here, but she didn't want you to know where he got the money?"

"Or she didn't know he had two dimes to rub together. He may have taunted Marcy with selling the Kinsale properties, but he didn't tell her everything. Just enough to get her goat, is my guess. So he kept both of them in the dark. Wife and mistress."

I pulled up a chair next to June's desk and propped my

feet on it. Talking the case out with June felt good. I almost forgot about the fire. But not quite. Rubbing my hands over my face, I felt the rough spots where Owen had removed the splinters from my palms. They ached. What if someone tried the same trick in the house, and June was an innocent victim? I owed her a warning at the very least. I examined my torn palms.

June looked up from the computer monitor as if expecting me to ask her to pass the box of hankies on the corner of her desk.

"You haven't asked how much he paid everyone—developers, tax lawyers, architects, zoning lawyers, the whole shootin' match—involved in the actual development plans."

"So how much?"

She mentioned a figure that just about toppled me off my chair. "Lord have mercy, where'd he get that kind of cash?"

"Follow the money, isn't that some kind of rule somewhere?" June twinkled with her success.

"Or follow the trail of bodies." I was still a little shaky. "You need to know, Owen says the fire last night wasn't just arson. Whoever did it, tied the latch on the shed door so I couldn't get out. You take care, you hear me? Owen said he'd have a uniform trailing me around, but I want you to watch it."

For a second, she looked shaken. "I thought it was just an accident; you were in there when it went up. That you couldn't, I mean, weren't in any shape . . ."

"No, I hadn't been drinking. And yes, someone tried to kill me. Cute, innocent little ole me." Making light of my brush with death wasn't making me feel any better, but maybe it would help June.

Shrugging with the nonchalance of a woman who'd already made up her mind, June sniffed. "I was married to a bully. Takes a lot to make me back down."

She'd never spoken to me before about her personal life. Today was a day for a lot of firsts. I felt better knowing she was forewarned.

I thought a minute about her question about the money. "Just checking here, but you did ask for a subpoena for Judge Jordan's accounts? What if Trey had tapped the judge to the bottom of the barrel? I mean, what if the judge was going to have to sell to Trey? All that land next to his . . ."

June frowned. "I did. But so far, our substitute judge hasn't signed it."

"Figures. The good ole boys begin circling the wagons right about now." I fanned the pages of financial records.

"You have any idea how much went for just drafting the contract to sell the land to the Transport Park people?" June held up a sheet of legal pad covered with numbers.

I shook my head.

"My rough figure right now is in the range of four hundred thousand dollars." She smiled as if she'd caught me red-handed in the closet with a liquor bottle.

For the second time in minutes, I had to catch myself before I toppled over. "You've got to be adding it up wrong. That on top of what he paid the tax consultant, the other guys?"

June looked affronted. "I don't make mistakes with numbers. Now men, that's something else." She smiled to let me know she understood we were breaking ground today. "I'm not even finished with the records. And if I had the judge's, it'd be a lot easier. I'll bet every red cent of that money went into getting that land sold."

I thought about Jordan and the big, old house, the lots on his land sold off to tract home developers encroaching on the stately old mansion. I'd thought it strange, but a sign of the times. Now I knew why he needed the money. Trey hadn't been after chump change.

"No takers here. I'll bet the judge doesn't have a dime to his name except what he earns as salary. Wonder if his wife knew?"

June harrumphed. "From what I hear, his wife's a nitwit."

I had a thought. "What if she just found out about all that money going into Kinsale's pocket with blackmail stamped on every bill? Maybe she just learned her husband of forty some-odd years had fathered a child who was now sleeping with the blackmailer? Pretty heavy stuff, huh?"

The front doorbell, an old-fashioned affair that twisted instead of rang, whirred like a dying cicada.

"Good luck," June threw over her shoulder at me as she turned to answer the front door. "I don't see a sixty-some-odd-year-old woman doing in Kinsale with a knife."

While I'd been engrossed in following the trail of possibilities, June returned, trailed by Jack Bland.

"Guess what the cat dragged in," she remarked, eyebrows flying up as she made sure I knew she disapproved.

"Hey there, Tal. Got a minute?" He wore clean jeans and a shirt that hadn't seen much wear, an unusual feat for a farmer. Freshly shaved, he looked as uncomfortable as I felt.

"I don't have a cat," I snapped. June had better learn to lay off Jack Bland. Some memories are sacred, and Jack was one of them. "Come on into my office, Jack. We can talk there."

"Yeah, right," June muttered under her breath as I rose to lead Jack across the hall to my private domain.

He wasn't looking too good. Lines I hadn't seen before creased the corners of his mouth, and the circles under his eyes said he wasn't sleeping well. I shut the glass doors that led from my office to the hallway, and tried to pretend I wasn't staring at him. Attributing my queasy stomach to last night's adventures, I knotted my hands over my tummy. Frowning, he stared at them.

"Want something to drink, Jack?" Southerners always offer food or drink if it's an awkward situation.

He started, as if he'd been hit by a flying staple. His mind had been somewhere else when I spoke.

"I meant a soda. My days of bourbon-sipping are over for now, it seems. June keeps the ice box stocked with root beer."

Dragging himself over to stand by the tall windows that faced Woolfolk Avenue, he shook his head. "No, thanks. What I have to say won't take long, then I'll get out of your hair. Oh, before I start, I'm sorry to hear about your troubles. Alma told me."

"My oh my, the grapevine flourishes this morning. Bet the word is out that I was drunk and set the fire myself, right?"

He had the good grace to turn a shade darker under his farmer's tan. "I didn't believe her."

"Good. Because it was arson, and I almost didn't make it out alive." I wanted him to know I hadn't been drunk. What Jack thought of me still mattered, no matter how often and how much I told myself it didn't.

He was silent a minute, staring at the street. I felt the tension in him vibrating my way, like a client on the stand who was about to lose his temper and blow up the case in both our faces.

"Jack, if there's a legal problem I can help you with," I started.

"It's not that. I have to talk to you about Desiree."

I thought the worst immediately. "She's not hurt, is she?" There were a million ways for a kid like her to get stuck, crushed, or broken on a farm.

"No, nothing like that," he hurried on, rushing his words together as if he couldn't catch his breath. "I have to tell you she's my daughter."

After the first shock, something in me wasn't surprised. I'd thought that from the first moment I considered the possibility, in fact. Crystal had tried to steer me away from Jack, but I didn't blame her. Breathing deeply, I considered the ramifications. For my client. Alma wasn't the one I had to look out for.

"Okay," I sighed. "So why did you think I needed to know this? Crystal's made it clear she isn't about to blab." I was talking, I could hear the words spilling out of my mouth. I even sounded calm.

But all the while I was thinking that Jack had a daughter by Alma the same age as Desiree. He'd been sleeping with both his wife and his mistress at the same time. I couldn't reconcile the image with the Jack Bland I'd once loved. That Jack had been a Boy Scout, true to the end. Of course, once he married Alma, all bets were off. That alone should have told me a lot about him.

"Because Trey Kinsale tried to extort money from me to keep it a secret. Said he'd tell Alma if I didn't pay him to keep quiet." He sounded like he'd just admitted he'd committed murder.

His wet hair was still slicked back from a shower. I remembered how it'd felt once in my hands.

I hadn't realized I was holding my breath. Slowly, it escaped from me like from a leaky balloon. "Did you? Pay him?"

"No. I'd already told Alma about her. She's known since Desiree was born. I wanted Crystal to give her to me so she could grow up with her half-sisters and half-brother." He was in anguish. This nine-year-old wound hadn't healed yet.

"Guess that took the wind out of his sails." I was beginning to dislike Trey Kinsale more than I already did.

I'd been trying to avoid emotions for the past two years. They only caused problems, like my drinking. Disappointment I could deal with. But Kinsale had been evil, and I was getting angry at a dead man. The way I was beginning to see it, he'd earned what he got, and whoever sliced and diced him deserved a medal.

"I suppose. But I knew Crystal told him so he could use it against me. I can't forgive her for that. She won't let me be Desiree's daddy, but she'd let Kinsale sleep over at her place while Desiree was there." His neck bright red, he was angrier than I'd ever seen him before.

I got a sick feeling that had nothing to do with too much smoke in my throat. Jack and Crystal weren't supposed to fit together in any universe I inhabited.

"How'd you hook up with Crystal?" I didn't want him to confess to killing Kinsale. I wouldn't know how to handle something like that without a bender that could last years.

Shrugging, he finally faced me. I went from his tortured eyes to his worn Wal-Mart boots. He was my first love, the only man who'd really hurt me. I still couldn't see why he'd married Alma, and yet I was supposed to understand his fathering a child by Crystal Walker?

This was way beyond me, and I needed to understand the hows and whys of it if I was going to have a chance to keep my sanity. I kept my eyes on his boots while he spoke.

"She needed a friend. I'd see her around, it was just after her daddy died. I thought she'd get out of town, what with her mama being in the ground already. But she didn't. She was working at the Hop n' Shop nights, always seemed to be there when I'd stop in to gas up the truck. We got to talking." A faint smile stopped the words. "Mostly about you. How you were some big shot now, how we always knew you'd be the one to make good."

Nine years ago I'd been on top of my game. While I'd been playing at being the successful lawyer, the man I'd once loved was committing adultery with the one woman I'd never dream he'd find attractive. I crushed my short nails into my palms to keep myself from screaming at him.

"And? How did Alma find out?"

"I told her," he said quietly. "Then she said she was pregnant, and I couldn't leave her or she'd kill herself and the baby." He was back to looking whipped. "I was between a rock and a hard place, but Crystal told me she'd be fine. She wanted to keep the baby we were having, that she didn't want anything else from me but the baby. No money, nothing. I couldn't leave it like that."

"I'll bet that didn't make Alma's day."

"Not much, it didn't." He finally sat, as if his knees had given out. He looked so tired, I was almost sorry for him. But I knew he had more to say, and it wasn't going to be anything I wanted to hear. My hands throbbed, I was clutching them so tightly.

He continued only after staring at me for so long, I realized he wasn't seeing me, he was seeing through me. "I want to keep Desiree, raise her. I told Crystal I'd keep her as long as she was locked up, and she wasn't happy about it. Said Alma would take it out on Desiree. I want you to tell Crystal that Desiree's doing just fine. She's like one of the other kids, fits right in. Alma's no problem."

"Okay, and then Crystal will want to know why. Why Alma's not a problem, that is."

"Because I told her I'd leave her, take all the kids, move someplace she'd never find me, if she didn't do right by Desiree."

I whistled. He was a tougher man than I'd thought at first. "Would you? Leave her?"

He was farming on land that had been in his family for generations. Land that had meant more to him than I had. Land that held him as I hadn't been able.

He was grim. "Yes. I stay because of the kids, and Desiree's one of mine just as much as the others. I love them more than I can tell you, Tal. Alma's a good mother, but if she treated Desiree wrong, I'd get her out of our lives so fast she'd never know what hit her."

I had a million questions, but just one I had to have answered right then. "Did you marry Alma because you wanted kids, and I didn't?"

He stared again through the window beside him, showing me his profile. He had the Bland nose, aquiline, dominating his face in a way that had made him look older when he was sixteen. Now he just looked hawkish.

"She told me she was pregnant. I got drunk one night after you said you were leaving, and she was there, I don't know how she found me. I was out by the river, had a six pack, my second or third best as I remember, and she looked sorta fuzzy and soft, and her hair was all silver in the moonlight." His voice went hard.

"Then she said I'd knocked her up, and well, you were going, and I wanted kids. Lots of kids. So I married her. Turned out she wasn't pregnant after all."

I knew it wouldn't have worked between us, not ever. Still, I felt sorry for myself, for him. "Why're you telling me all this now, Jack?"

"Because you're asking questions all over town. I know Crystal won't tell you I'm Desiree's daddy, she's afraid I'll sue for custody. She wouldn't even put my name on Desiree's birth certificate. I always gave her money for Desiree, every month. But she'd never tell my own daughter who I was, wouldn't let me keep her for a few days, nothing to show I was her daddy." He sounded bitter, and I didn't blame him. Not many men tried to do the right thing in the same circumstances.

"I didn't kill Kinsale and make it look like Crystal did it, just to get Desiree. I swear to you. I'd never do that to Crystal. She's the mother of my child."

I must have looked guilty because I'd been thinking that exact thought. "I never said that."

"Crystal's had a hard enough row to hoe all these years. But she loves Desiree, even if she doesn't want me around her. Well, those days are over now. Even if she gets out of jail, I'm going to make sure I see Desiree regularly, that she's a part of my life. Tell Crystal that, will you? Alma's doing right by the girl, she'll keep on. That's all I wanted Crystal to know."

I nodded, not daring to speak. I was the narrator in this melodrama, the Greek actor sitting in the proscenium, reciting my lines as they were told to me. "Why don't you tell her yourself? Visiting hours are on Sunday."

He shook his head. "Alma made her ground rules clear. I don't see Crystal, and Desiree can stay. Can't say as I blame her, and I'll play it her way for now. At least until Crystal's legal problems are straightened out."

Standing, he seemed to notice his dirty boots for the first time. "Sorry if I messed up your floors." That wasn't what he meant, and we both knew it.

I shook my head. "Don't worry about it."

Moving as if his feet hurt him, he edged to the closed door. Hand on the knob, he stopped. I stayed behind my desk. I didn't recognize the man he'd become. He wasn't the simple farmer I'd thought I'd once loved.

"I'm sorry, Tal, things turned out this way."

Shrugging, I picked up a file and opened it. It held Kinsale's autopsy photos. Quickly, I glanced away.

"I'm not."

Face frozen, he slid out the door like a ghost from the past disappearing in the morning light.

19

⚬⚭⚬

I stood at the window for a long time, watching the cars
on Woolfolk, wondering if Jack had been afraid Crystal
had told me about Desiree and if he'd tried to kill me because he didn't want anyone to know. Me, especially.
When I lived, he figured out he'd better start damage control, and that meant an anguished confession.

If that was how he'd played it, he was a consummate
actor.

I thought I'd known him like I knew myself, but I'd
been wrong. Still, I couldn't imagine Jack trying to burn
me alive. The man who'd just left my office didn't have it
in him to demand his rights to a daughter he clearly loved,
much less harm me. Because I knew now he'd loved me.
That alone put him on the bottom of my list. Hands

stuffed in my pockets, I tried to think of what I should do next.

Talk to more people, get them issued subpoenas for the trial if they were helpful, figure out the money trail as June had suggested. My head ached so badly, I wanted to weep.

"June, is there any aspirin around?" She'd rearranged everything in the house so I couldn't find it. The aspirin had disappeared from the freezer not long after June had showed up.

"In the bathroom, where it belongs."

I heard her clump upstairs. When she opened the doors to my office, she held a glass of water, too.

"Thanks." I jiggled the pills in the palm of my hand.

I knew she'd been listening at the door when Jack and I talked. She wouldn't understand why I couldn't, wouldn't, believe Jack had killed Trey. I'd ask Alma if she'd known about Crystal, of course, but in my own way, in my own time, just to corroborate Jack's story. This was a leap June couldn't force me to make.

I kept coming back to Moran, paying blackmail to Trey to keep quiet over Crystal. Moran, who'd had to borrow money from his old lover to pay off Crystal's current one. Bet he'd let her know he didn't appreciate her spilling the beans to Trey. I made a note to talk to Crystal about him again.

"I talked to Owen Amos this morning. Told him about Crystal's being Judge Jordan's kid, him and Marcy Kinsale sleeping together." I needed to go over it with June.

June rolled her eyes. "Why'd you go and do that?

"So he'd investigate more deeply than he's done so far. He doesn't like surprises in the courtroom any more than any prosecutor; he'll want to cover his ass. Any exculpatory evidence is required by the rules to be turned over to me."

"And if he doesn't find anything to help Crystal? If he decides it's just gossip?" June had her 'I'm trying to learn patience, Lord, but she's more than I can handle' look on her face.

"He won't. Find just gossip. The money trail you turned up will show up on his desk, too, if it hasn't already. My bet is, he'll run it to ground. Save us some legwork."

"Hope you haven't shot yourself in the foot." June looked dubious.

"Me, too. But he did save my life. You know those ex-Army types. Duty, honor, all that stuff. Besides not wanting to look like an ass when I cross-examine Judge Jordan, he'll need some ammo to shoot me down. At least, I'm counting on him trying to find some. And sharing, like a good proseutor should when it turns out it helps Crystal."

"And that'll get you . . . what?"

"The truth," I confessed. "The truth, and nothing but. If all these circles intersect at Crystal, there's nothing much I can do about it but throw enough mud that the jury won't be able to see through it."

"Then you're not going for the truth."

"Yeah, I am. But if it won't help Crystal, I'll take what I can get." I sounded desperate even to myself.

"Just don't count on that Owen Amos, is all I'm saying," June countered. "Didn't you ever think it funny that he came here to run for prosecutor? Most army folk go back to where they came from, once they retire. Where's Mr. Amos from, is what I'd like to know. Where a man once had roots says a lot about him."

I hadn't thought about that. "Don't know. He's never said. Fought in Vietnam, from some stuff he has in his house." I remembered the disturbing photographs.

"Those aren't roots. Who're his people?"

"Why?"

"I've seen how you look at him, how your voice changes when you talk to him. You're on the make, and you'd better be darned careful what you tell him."

"You're wrong," I protested. "On the make? Me? For the love of God, that's ridiculous."

"Yeah, well, what's this nonsense about him digging up the truth that'll help Crystal? Think about it, Tal, you're not a dumb woman, though sometimes I have my doubts. What the heck was he doing here last night, if he didn't want to see what you'd spill next when he turned on the charm?"

Now I was going to be sick for real. Sitting down hard, I gulped the glass of water to keep the bile from rising.

"And then he carts you home to his little love nest, right? And in gratitude, you give him everything you've been saving to play during trial."

"That's not true," I protested. "I didn't tell him to get on his good side. I didn't tell him about Moran and Crystal."

June snorted most indelicately.

"I really think he'll track down more information and see he just can't make his case hold water. They don't have any of Trey's blood on Crystal, and it's going to be hard to work around that. He's probably praying right now he can come up with another killer, so he can cut her loose."

"Lord, give me strength," June shook her head. "I don't care what you think of Mr. Big and Handsome, I'm going to check into him. Gotta know your enemy. That's what I've been reading about trial lawyers, and last I heard, you're one."

I couldn't help groaning. She was right. "So maybe I've been a little easy on him. That doesn't mean I've told him anything that'll hurt Crystal. Everything I said will help her."

"I'm still going to check him out, find out what kind of rep he had in the army. My ex, the sonofabitch, was the same sort of creep in or out of a uniform."

"Didn't know your husband . . ." I began.

"Not any more. Long gone, and good riddance. What I'm saying is, you need to know more about Owen Amos. Just makes sense. Before you go giving away our entire defense."

I liked the way she said "our." June and me. Not Owen Amos and me.

"Okay, my libido got in the way. How do we track down who served where and when in the army, or do you think that's classified information?"

June shrugged. "Easy enough to find out if it is or not. I'll call the Pentagon."

"I know he served in Vietnam, let's see where else."

June shrugged. "Ask him yourself. He might tell you. We'll compare answers. If I can get any from the Pentagon, that is."

I wondered if Owen would figure out why I was fishing into the pond of his history. Mine was a pretty ugly open book, all he had to do was ask anyone in town about me. He probably had, which was why he'd been so nice to me. Desperate woman that I am, I was an easy mark. My hair hurt my scalp. I didn't like thinking like this.

I hadn't even told June about the faces in the photos lining his bedroom wall. The darkly disturbing, abjectly terrified faces of a war long over but still alive in Owen Amos's bedroom.

"And I'd rather he didn't know I was asking about his military record. Keep it quiet." I was feeling as tired as a two-hour marathoner.

I knew what I had to do next. I pulled out a legal pad and

pen and started making a list. Nothing like feeling like a fool to get me back to work. I'd have Owen Amos figured out before trial, now I had to work on my smoke and mirrors. Blind him with them, that was my goal. Thank God and June for jerking me back on track.

"Did you find out if Trey actually signed a letter of intent or a contract, or whatever, with those Global Transport people? We know he spent a ton of money on getting the plans drawn up, but did he actually make the deal?"

"I'll ask." June made a note. "Think if he had, it was what pushed whoever did it over the edge?"

"Who knows? It's only money, but hell, money's power. And power is what it's all about." I should know, I'd played power games once upon a time with the best of them.

"Okay." June sounded doubtful. "What about that psychiatrist I have lined up to interview Crystal?"

"You handle it. Tell Crystal it's to make me happy and she'd better be straight with the guy. I don't care if she wants to go down without a fight, I'm getting this report from the doctor or I'll have her butt in a sling. If Henry vouches for the guy, he's honest. I'll talk to him after he's seen Crystal."

I gathered my car keys, threw the cell phone in the briefcase. "Call me if you run into any trouble getting him into the jail."

I had to start over, and that didn't mean in Crystal's blood-soaked shed. If I needed to understand what made Owen Amos tick before I took him on in court, I needed to understand Trey Kinsale even more. All I knew was that he was an ambitious, greedy, amoral slimeball. There had to be more to him.

"I'll be at the Kinsale place."

Trey had been bled like he'd bled those he'd black-

mailed. Marcy Kinsale may have been more than just the
catalyst in getting her husband drained dry like a slaugh-
tered pig. Like a tilt-a-wheel, Crystal's former and current
lovers and their respective spouses spun around in my
aching head. Marcy might not want to talk about Trey, but
I was going to give it a whirl.

I hadn't known what I was getting into with Parnell
Moses, either. I'd been court-appointed, doing my civic
duty by taking on a few freebies now and then. The firm expected everyone to take losers like Parnell and keep up the
regular workload as well. Since I already worked 120 hours
a week, I hadn't had much time to prepare his case, to investigate the chance he might actually have been innocent.

I'd cost him his life.

I did a lot of thinking while driving to the Kinsale
house. About why I wanted Owen Amos to like me. About
jerking myself up by the short hairs to pay attention to
what needed tending, which was my client's case and not
my private life.

I felt so fried anyway, I wasn't bothered by the lack of
AC in the Mustang. I just wanted to get out there and start
from square one. Who was Trey Kinsale, and, from the
clutch of all the people who hated his guts, who meshed
opportunity with revenge?

The house Marcy's money built on Kinsale land looked
pristine in the hot sun, shining like a new penny. Marcy
must have had the painters out, it was so bright. I should
have thought of the estate as Marcy's, I suppose, since the
house was truly lovely. I could understand why she'd fight
tooth and nail to keep it as it was. She'd made a bargain
with the devil to buy a lifestyle she thought she deserved,
but the devil hadn't kept his end of it.

Good enough reason for murder in my book. Of course

Owen and any other male with an ounce of testosterone would think she was too lovely, too willowy, too gentle to kill her husband and cut off his ear. But I knew just how good an actress she could be. I'd see how long she could keep it up when the fire got a lot hotter under her perfect little feet.

I turned into the long drive, wondering what I was going to do, say. Any which way I played it, Crystal was a pariah in Wynnton, an expendable member of the community, the bad girl who was getting what she deserved. Throwing the blame onto Trey might work for about two seconds, but in the end, Crystal was just too easy to take down. I wished I'd sucked down those aspirins before I'd left the office.

The closer I got to Marcy Kinsale, the angrier I got. Crystal had done a lot of blabbing to Trey, but who knew what he'd promised her? A way out of Wynnton? I knew how Crystal would feel about a carrot as tasty as that. Hell, I'd given up the only man I'd loved to escape.

Crystal wouldn't have been able to resist Trey Kinsale's promises to ride into the sunset with her, no way. Not with a pocketful of money and the chance to thumb her nose at the respectable folks of Wynnton. Now *that* would have been the way I'd have flipped the bird at all those hypocrites from the other side of the tracks, if I were Crystal.

I didn't recognize the car parked in the Kinsale driveway when I pulled up to the front door. A battered minivan, it hadn't been expensive when it was new about ten years earlier. Parking beside it, I rummaged through the opened window in the glove compartment. My conscience didn't bother me one bit. I checked the registration.

Well, well, I thought, *two birds with one stone.* I didn't bother with the doorbell or the knocker, I just let myself right in and stood for a moment in the quiet foyer, a vase of fresh gardenias scenting the room as if it were heaven.

I could hear the voices of two women upstairs.

Callie appeared from the back of the house. "Thought I heard the door open. What you doin', not ringing the doorbell like decent folks, Miz Tal?"

"Didn't want to bother you, Callie. Saw Mrs. Moran's car out front, wanted to catch her before she left." Running up the staircase, I pretended I'd been invited there. Callie watched me from the bottom, not sure if I was welcome or not.

I wasn't. Susan Swinford Moran swiveled to stare at me like she'd just seen the gates of hell open up to swallow her whole.

I waved. "Hey there, Susan, long time no see. Marcy, you're looking better these days."

Marcy wasn't about to kiss me a greeting. She looked like she'd prefer to serve me arsenic rather than the vodka and tonics she and Susan were inhaling. "How'd you get in here, Tal?"

"Through the front door. My goodness, what luck. Just the two ladies I wanted to see today." I took a seat on a silk-covered wing chair, crossing my legs and grinning like Goober.

Marcy was receiving guests today in the second-floor sun room. Painted a bright golden, it shone like a jeweler's case filled with baubles. The chairs were upholstered in watercolor patterns, bright flowers bloomed in pots in every corner. I'd never been as happy as this room felt. The tension I'd stepped into came not from the surroundings, but from the two women facing each other in identical love seats.

Susan's gray sausage curls were still stacked on her head like some aging homecoming queen. Her forties had thinned her to the angles of a narrow box, while her fifties had creased deep lines on the side of her mouth. Too much pale makeup caked the crevices of her skin, while her fingers holding the glass were stained yellow with nicotine. If I hadn't known better, I'd have thought she was an old barfly falling fast on the way down.

Marcy wasn't playing the widow drowning her grief today. Her eyes focused on me sharply. "You're not wanted here, Tal. I'll have to ask you to leave."

"Not yet, Marcy." I uncrossed my legs and smiled at them both as I leaned forward. "I'll bet you two were just comparing notes, weren't you?"

The startled expression on both their faces told me I'd guessed correctly. "Wondering where all that money went, huh?"

I got them with that one.

"What money?" Marcy asked casually. "I'm sure we don't have the vaguest idea what you're talking about."

"I'll bet you do." I leaned forward, watching their hands holding the glasses with the vodka tonics. If I could keep myself from snatching one and slugging it down, I'd consider myself halfway on the road to the good life. Trying to hide the deep breath I desperately needed, I threw out the only move I could make. God help me if I'd guessed wrong.

"Susan, I'll bet you recently found out about the money your husband was paying Trey Kinsale. Blackmail's such an ugly word, isn't it? What'd he tell you, the truth finally? Or was it another lie and you needed to catch him in it?"

"You little bitch." Marcy's drawl made the words sound

even worse. Of course, I'd been cursed by those with better vocabularies in the past, so this one rolled off me without leaving a mark.

"If you wanted to play lawyer, you should have crawled back under whatever rock you crawled out from when you came back to Wynnton." Susan's voice was throaty with too many cigarettes and, I'd bet, too many vodka tonics.

"You heard me talking to your husband in the jewelry store the other day, didn't you? Get what you needed to stick it to him?"

She shrugged. "I'd had my suspicions."

I turned to Marcy. "When did you find out Linwood Jordan was paying Trey?"

"Just before he died. Linwood told me Trey was blackmailing him over our affair. I told him I didn't give a damn who knew we were sleeping together, it was classier than Trey and that piece of shit in her trailer." Marcy was smiling as if she hadn't a care in the world.

"The good judge's wife may have cared." I was still trying to piece it all together. "And you both just figured out it was Crystal who told Trey everything. About her affair with your husband and your lover." I nodded at Susan, then Marcy.

They didn't look one bit nonplussed.

"Well, let's not forget your old boyfriend, Tal. That Bland boy you had the hots for all through high school didn't earn his Sunday School award by keeping the Ten Commandments. We all knew he was takin' a walk at night to meet your client. Everyone knew but poor Alma."

I laughed at the notion of "poor Alma"—the woman knew everything that went on in Wynnton before the people it involved had any idea.

"True. So you two just figured out what Kinsale did with the money? Or did you know all along, Marcy? Is that why you had to get rid of him?"

I thought Susan was beginning to sweat, and it wasn't because the air conditioning had stopped blowing frigid air. Dressed in a pale green shirt and black skirt, she reminded me of a dying plant. Marcy was all brittle fury, trying to keep her sang-froid but losing the battle.

"I'll ring for Callie to show you out, Tal. I'm sure you have nothing better to do with your time than torment me and my guest, but I'm afraid your day's entertainment is over now." She reached for a silver bell on the coffee table between the two love seats.

"Was it the contract to sell the land, Marcy, or his affair with Crystal that really ticked you off?" I turned to Susan.

"I'll bet you didn't care about the hanky-panky your husband had with her, did you? What irked the hell out of you was the money he paid Trey to keep quiet about his affair with my client. So you two both won big time when Crystal was arrested for his murder. Let me count the ways." I rose and paced the room, flicking my fingers down as I spoke.

"First, Marcy gets rid of an unfaithful husband. Of course, Marcy had more to lose. Trey was going to sell the land out from under the life she'd carefully built in this beautiful house. Then he was going to leave her. Your husband wasn't going to leave you, was he, Susan? But how would it look, after all you'd done for him, when it came out he'd not only found another woman to love him, he'd been spending your family money to keep it quiet?"

Susan and Marcy stared at each other, then me. I was glad I wasn't in an old oak shed at that moment.

"Did you do it together? Was it easier that way? Who

planned it?" I leaned against the wall, waiting for one of them to break and tell me the truth.

But that only happens in the movies. They both rose as one and left me standing alone in the sun room. I must admit, I was as surprised as hell. Looking out the window, I saw Susan get into her battered minivan, Marcy into her Mercedes, and leave.

Callie appeared. "You stayin' long?"

"Guess not." I tried to sound nonchalant. "Tell Mrs. Kinsale I'll let her know when I figure it out."

"You doing too much figurin', Miz Tal. You figure all you want, you ain't about to end up with two plus two equals four. I swear, for a woman with Miss Ena's blood in her veins, you're dumb as a turnip."

I wasn't accustomed to such a succinct appraisal of my mental acuity, but I had to agree with her. "That about says it all, Callie. Mind tellin' me why you think I'm so damned dumb?"

"You got no call to curse at me, Miz Tal. You can't see what's plain as the fact the sun's shinin' today."

I was properly humbled. "What fact's that, Callie?"

"Them two just figured it out themselves. Miz Moran, she thought Miz Marcy done killed her husband, she come out here to thank her. Miz Marcy thought Miz Moran done it, they're up here just hootin'. No way either of them coulda done Mr. Kinsale that way. Women don't kill like that."

I agreed, but I wasn't about to give up. "Either of them could have done it, Callie. Or hired help to do it."

"That's a lie, and you know it." Callie's dark eyes were bright with anger. "Leave us alone now, you hear? Miz Marcy may not be the best woman in God's land, but she bore that man's carryings-on. When he tossed her over like a piece of old bread, she about died. She loved him, and don't you forget it. Still loves him, even if he tried to kill that love every way he knew how."

I collected my briefcase and my keys. Now I knew all about Trey Kinsale, what type of man he was. He treated love like a soiled shirt.

"Love's the best reason of all to kill, Callie."

20

❧❧❧

I had a lot of thinking to do as I drove back to town. Jack's face kept popping into my head, I'd shove it aside, then there he was, back again just like a mosquito who won't give up.

Was Jack somehow involved with Kinsale's death? I didn't like to think so, but it would make sense. Crystal couldn't leave Wynnton without Trey and his money, ergo, with Trey out of the picture, Desiree stayed put where Jack could keep an eye on her. I'd never seen such fatherly depths of devotion before, having been fatherless since my parents died when I was a baby.

Any man willing to leave his wife and take their children with him to force her to accept his illegitimate offspring wasn't taking fatherhood lightly. I just didn't know if he was capable of killing Kinsale and framing Crystal to take the fall to get what he wanted. What if Crystal knew he'd killed Trey, and she was protecting him to save Desiree?

That made more sense than anything else. Jack had paid her support money, Crystal saw what kind of father he was, what kind he wanted to be. Without her, Desiree could move in with the Blands as a foster child, get a clean start on a more normal life in Wynnton than she'd had so far as the bastard daughter of the town whore.

I hated the fact that I couldn't figure out Jack Bland anymore. Had he worried about Desiree growing up with Trey Kinsale as her stepfather when Crystal and Trey took off with the Global Transport cash? Had that suspicion exploded into a frenzy of killing and mutilation? My stomach in knots, I knew I wouldn't put it past him to do something like that, not if he thought he was saving his child from a monster.

In a way, I felt sorry for Alma. She'd used the oldest trick in the book to land the man she wanted, but she didn't really have him. Crystal had proven that, not me. I shook off the image of Jack slicing off Trey's ear, and focused on the two people I hoped were better suspects.

No matter what Callie said about Marcy Kinsale and Susan Moran, they both had even better reasons. A woman with revenge in her blood could do a hell of a lot of damage. I'd felt it coursing through my cold-blooded veins now and then, so I knew from first-hand experience. A wronged wife could mutilate without thinking twice.

Or find someone who could. Wynnton residents who felt like living dangerously sometimes crossed the river to the Stickley side of the county, where drugs, illegal gambling, and moonshine reigned. Men who dealt in broken laws could be paid to do anything an outraged woman wanted if she had enough money and he felt like a long vacation, anyway.

Hot, tired, and as frustrated as a woman in bed with a five-minute lover, I was in no mood for June's raised eyebrows and pursed lips. The minute I walked through the door, she let me know she thought I was out goofing off while she was doing all the work.

"Got the psychiatrist set up for tomorrow at two. He says he expects you to be there."

I knew it was June who expected me to be there. "I said I'd talk to him after he saw Crystal." I wasn't in any mood for temperamental secretaries.

"I'm not the one who doesn't want to practice law here. In case you missed this minor point, you're the only one with a valid license. For now. He wants to talk to you about the evidence in the case. Obviously, it affects his interview with her."

She looked as if she were about to snap the pencil in her hand in half. I knew it was my neck she was holding between her forefinger and her thumb.

The psychiatrist was correct, of course. June and I both knew it. I just didn't want to hear what he was going to say. If I'd been a betting woman, I wouldn't take the odds that he'd label Crystal an abused, emotionally wrecked woman capable of anything, especially murder.

Flopping on the settee in her office, I kicked off my shoes and reached for a file to use as a fan. The Mustang and I had cooked coming back from the Kinsale place. One of these days I'd treat myself to a retro fit on the air conditioning system and kiss Freon good-bye. Fanning my face with the manila folder, I tried to cool down.

"Any word from Owen about the judge?" He was still the best bet as far as I was concerned. Holding on to Lin-

wood Jordan as the murderer was better than pinning it on
Jack, or even Marcy and Susan.

I still wasn't ready to placate June.

"Only that he'd like to meet with you, too." Her face
said she thought Owen knew when he had a good thing going and I was dumber than shit for not seeing how he was
using me.

"Did he say when?"

She consulted a message pad. "If you'd read your messages, you'd know these things."

I wanted to offer June an olive branch, but I'm not very
good at that sort of thing. As I'd grown older, Miss Ena and
I had been like box turtles fighting it out from inside our
shells. We'd stick our necks out and clack away for a bit,
then go hide again.

"You want to come? If it's good news, you should be
there." I played with the folder, waving it like an exotic fan.

This was going to be a very long day, and I hadn't had
enough sleep. I couldn't remember eating lunch or breakfast.

"Tonight. He said he'd pick you up here, if you don't
mind. And no thank you, you can meet Owen Amos any-
time you want. You two can play lovey-dovey without me."
She was still in a huff.

"I'm not interested!" I shouted to her back.

One good bit of news, that was all I wanted, needed. If
Owen had come up with something concrete against the
judge, I wanted to trust in his fairness to drop the charges
against Crystal. If he did, I didn't have to go to trial. Didn't
have to find out just how rusty I was. Didn't have to worry
about making mistakes that could cost Crystal her life.

My reasons, when I got right down to it, were pretty
selfish. The charges could be brought up again in the fu-

ture, but when and if anyone else was indicted, the chances of that happening were slim and none.

I wished I could pray. I'd be praying like crazy that Linwood Jordan had found a way out of all his troubles that would put him in Crystal's place in the jail.

"Anything else?" I wanted to nap, to slip into my bed with a cool glass in one hand and a cold washcloth for my forehead in the other. I don't think well when I'm tired, and especially when things aren't going my way.

"I tried to find out about Owen's military record. It's not available to the general public, but I called the state Democratic Party headquarters. He ran as a Democrat in the election, and I figured they'd have his résumé on hand."

I whistled. "Smart woman. I never would have thought of that."

She looked barely mollified. "Well, who knows if what they have is the truth. You'd think they'd check the backgrounds of their candidates, but that's a joke. If the press doesn't do it, it usually won't get done."

"June, you're truly brilliant. Who do you know?"

She practically preened. "Guy I used to date, worked for the *Times Dispatch*. He did some checking on the official party résumé. Says Owen retired after thirty years in the army, that he rose through the ranks, went to Officer's Candidate School, all that boring stuff."

"When was he in Vietnam?"

"The résumé says he volunteered to go toward the end of the war, when he was seventeen. That's it, no hero stuff."

"And did your friend say otherwise?"

She shook her head. "He didn't know what, where, when, or how, but all he could find out was that there was some kind of trouble. In Vietnam. But Owen got clear of it, and stayed on in the army for the duration."

I thought of his bedroom, almost a military weapons museum. In his late fifties, he still looked every inch the soldier.

"Must not have been very serious. Lots of stuff went on in Vietnam no one cares about now."

"Nothing that'll stop his political climb up the right ladder. My friend says our Mr. Amos is going to find himself with all kinds of money when he finishes paying his political dues here. Money to buy TV ads, hire a campaign advisor, that sort of thing."

"Heard he was going that direction. Good for him. Man's spent enough time giving service to this country in the army, he deserves to go places."

"Unless he screws up big time here, he is." June smiled with the look of a woman who'd pulled off a coup.

Today she wore chunky silver earrings with big stones that looked like amethysts. "Sure you're not interested? Might be interesting, you playing the political game as the adoring wife. Making the rubber chicken circuit."

I snorted. "Not hardly. Forget it. No politician wants a wife who likes her liquor."

June shrugged, tapping her pencil on a notebook. "The better news is that I called the Global Transport people. Of course, they thought I was someone else." She was looking awfully smug again. "No one bothered to inform them Mr. Kinsale was deceased." Now it was the prim and proper act.

"I can't wait. Who exactly did they assume you were?"

"Mr. Kinsale's lawyer's secretary. I never said a word, except I was calling for my boss about the contract. I swear. I just didn't say who my boss was." Again, the coy look.

"Plausible deniability won't hold water if this is bad news." I sat upright.

"Depends on how you look at it. Kinsale hadn't signed any contracts to sell the land, not yet. The GTP legal department was in the process of sending them to Mr. Kinsale's attorney, however."

"Oh boy. I'll bet this is good."

"Sure is. Our esteemed and most honorable Harlan Goode was going to get the contracts to review."

My substitute judge. How interesting. The Judicial Ethics and Review Commission would like to hear about this, and I was just the girl to ask for an investigation. With the contracts unsigned, Marcy still had a chance to stop everything. With the estate in limbo until Crystal was cleared, Crystal couldn't sign the contracts as executrix or trustee of Trey's estate.

"My oh my." My little brain was clicking away. "I think we may just have a fighting chance."

I was going to have to drop this in Owen's lap tonight. The bigger the pile of possibilities, the more he'd hound his investigators to do the job right. Crystal was going to be a free woman soon.

I returned the file to June's desk. "Told you, you've got what it takes." I was finally in a better mood. "Still think you want to hang around here and read law?"

Chin in the air, June let me know I wasn't quite forgiven. "I'm doing some thinkin' on it. Henry says you graduated at the top of your class at Duke."

I nodded. "That and a buck fifty will buy you a cup of coffee."

"Henry also says you got into some kind of trouble, that's why you came running back to Wynnton."

"Well, Henry could have put it more delicately, but that's about it."

It was time to level with June if we were going to have a

chance to work this out together. I liked her brassiness, her
competence, and most of all, I liked the way she pressed
me to get my act together. Relentlessly. I swallowed hard
and dove into the deep.

"Truth is, I lost a case I shouldn't have. Court-
appointed. His name was Parnell Moses." I could feel the
lump in my throat. "I got to know him a lot better during
the appeal process. He finally gave up, about three years
down the road. Said he wouldn't be the first innocent black
man the state had executed, he may as well go on and get it
over with. He hated living in prison.

"I didn't prepare for his case at the trial level, not like I
should have. He was a freebie, there was no money to do
the legwork, hire the right people, and I was so arrogant, I
thought my courtroom brilliance would dazzle your run-
of-the-mill jurors, and he'd walk. I blew it."

June sat silently, her hands quiet, staring at me as if seeing me for the first time. "Was he guilty?"

"As a matter of fact, I don't think he was. He wasn't one
of those some-other-dude-did-it clients. If I'd done it right,
he'd have walked. End of case."

"That why you took on Crystal Walker? Atone for your
past sins?" She was watching me carefully.

Nodding my head, I had to acknowledge the truth even
to myself. "I have to do this one right, or it's all over."

Standing, June began to organize files and papers on her
desk. "Then we'll do it right."

I was more grateful for her than I would ever be able to
let her know. Some things took time, and this was going to
be one of them.

I needed to change out of the clothes Grace had brought
me at Owen's. I needed to eat something, and more than
that, I needed to think.

"I'll be upstairs if you want me. Got to try to wash this smell out of my hair again." I wrinkled my nose at the acrid stink that clung to me despite my ablutions at Owen's. "If I can't get it out, I'll have to shave my head."

"Try some lemon juice. Think there's a lemon in the kitchen." June disappeared, reappearing to hand me a lemon already sliced in half.

"Thanks." My hand touched hers. "For everything."

"That's why I'm here." Our eyes met. This partnership wasn't going to be an easy one, but then nothing I ever did in life was easy. We'd work it out.

Upstairs, I stripped to hop into the shower. As I crumpled my clothes to toss them in the hamper, I remembered dressing in them in Owen's bedroom.

The unease I'd felt in that blood-red room probably had arisen from the unexpected collection of gruesome memorabilia. I'd seen Owen only as a lawyer, one who was determined to win the game we were playing with each other. Nothing about him was threatening, no more so than any prosecutor with an agenda. All prosecutors had agendas.

He'd been solicitous, kind, and furious at what had happened in the shed. Without factoring in the attraction I felt for him, I still had no doubts he'd find whoever had tried to kill me in the end. Whoever it was, he or she had killed Trey Kinsale, or was trying to protect whoever had. As a citizen, I was impressed with his zeal.

In the old shower, a trickle was the best it could do just when I needed a torrent. I scrubbed my hair and let thoughts ramble around in my head without trying to connect the dots. Moran kept marching front and center—a young Moran with a stiff expression on his face as he dodged cameras and hecklers.

Owen had served there, too. But he was younger than

Moran, had risen through the ranks. A ton of guys of that generation did their duty when the draft crooked her finger and whistled, and pulled them into Vietnam. There was no way they'd been stationed there at the same time.

And if they had, so what?

A big "what" came back to me. What if Moran was hiding more than he'd been court-martialed for, more than a fling with Crystal? And if Trey had found out, it must have been good. Good enough for Moran to borrow money from Crystal.

My bet was, Crystal had felt guilty about giving up the really juicy goods on Moran, so she'd lent him hush money. She had nothing to lose in the long run, with Trey paying her bills. Then the money dried up and Trey was dead. In her shed.

Made sense. The one man I knew who'd killed before, and killed en masse with gruesome cruelty, slaughtering helpless women and children, might find a sort of poetic justice in giving Trey Kinsale the same treatment—where Crystal would be sure to find him and recognize the message it carried for her.

Pulling on a clean pair of shorts and a T-shirt, I hurried downstairs. June was on the phone when I pulled down the yellow pages from the shelf behind her.

"Please tell Dr. Draper the fax has been sent with the files he requested." She made some noncommittal "ums" and "yes" noises. "Miss Jefferson will be only too happy to meet him at the jail a half an hour early to review the file with him personally."

I hurried into my office and shut the door. My hands shook as I punched the numbers.

"Hello, Swinfords Jewelers. May I help you?"

"Can you tell me one more thing, Lieutenant Moran?" Silence answered my question. I plunged on.

"Did you enjoy mutilating bodies in the army?"

"No! Leave me alone, or I'll swear out a warrant, for harassment," he threatened.

My gut said he was lying.

"You did something awful in Vietnam." State the obvious, Tal, sheesh, I'd get original one day, I hoped.

My hands shook. I was calling him out, but like a gunfighter with too much whiskey in his system, I wasn't on top of my game. If I succeeded, I'd offered myself as a juicy bit of bait he couldn't pass up. Time to dangle the hook a little lower and give it some action.

"Something you weren't tried for."

"That was a long time ago. I don't talk about it with anyone, not even my wife." He sounded as if he were at the bottom of a deep well, speaking through a chute of water and years.

"Did you ever talk about it with Crystal Walker?"

"I don't want to discuss this over the phone." Like gravel falling down his gullet, his words stuck in his throat. "It's none of your business, anyway."

"I'll be there in five minutes. Don't think I'm going away, Lieutenant Moran. If I don't find you, I'll have to speak to your wife." I was playing dirty and I knew it. What's more, I didn't care.

"My wife knows about the money I paid Kinsale. You already know that." His voice was lifeless, as if he'd died long ago in Vietnam and the shell that was left wasn't really Matthew Moran.

"She doesn't know why you killed Trey Kinsale, I'd be willing to bet."

I let the silence stretch to razor thinness.

"I'll meet you in the alley behind the shop. Five minutes. That's all I can give you."

I hung up without saying good-bye and prayed I wasn't making a mistake. A big mistake. All along, I'd thought Kinsale's death was tied up in Crystal's string of old lovers. I think Crystal believed the same thing, and that was why she didn't want me doing too much digging, because it would lead to her door in the end. Something she'd said or done had pushed the killer over the edge, and she knew it. Was I grasping at shredding silk to chase after this chimera with Moran?

I didn't have a choice. I'd let Parnell Moses down because I hadn't tracked down every bit of information that should have been examined. I wasn't going to make the same mistake with Crystal's defense.

Jerking open my office door, I ran smack-dab into June. Her eyes were as big as pumpkins.

"That true? Lieutenant Moran did some awful thing he wanted kept secret?"

I nodded. "That's the bait. I'll see if he takes it." If she was going to eavesdrop, she should get it right. "It could mean nothing."

Shaking her head, June plunked both hands squarely on her hips. "No such thing as a good secret, not where Crystal is concerned."

"Got that right."

"Something else is going on here. I can smell it."

Her flowery perfume settled around her like a sweet-smelling veil. She was protected from the really nasty stink, but I wasn't.

I had to face Moran with an air of confidence and hope

he let slip whatever it was that he wanted to keep under wraps.

I wouldn't be able to live with myself if I failed a client a second time. And I needed help.

Only one person could tell me what I needed to know.

21

⤬⤬⤬

THEY weren't happy about my demand to see Crystal during mess hours, but they finally hauled her to the pukey room with the ancient plastic chairs. I was so keyed up, I was bouncing off the walls.

"What now?" she barked, slumping against the wall. She, too, deigned to sit. "Can't you get it through that thick head of yours, I don't want you to do anything to help me? For Christ's sake, let it go. Stand there while I plead guilty, and let's get this show on the road."

"Shut up and listen to me. Matthew Moran's hiding something else, isn't he? Something besides you, because what the hell, his wife knows about your liaison. . . ."

"And? What's your point?" She dragged a strand of dark hair into the corner of her mouth and sucked on it. Her fingers looked like bones wrapped with pale skin.

"I told him I knew what it was. The thing he doesn't want anyone to know. The beans he spilled, so to speak, to the one woman he felt comfortable with. The one woman who never judged him by his past. The one who . . ."

"Cut the crap. I get your point. You're blowing smoke." Slinking around the edge of the wall, she drew so close I could smell her body odor. Deodorant wasn't standard issue in prison.

One bony finger poked me in the middle of my chest. I knocked her hand aside.

"Get this through your do-gooder skull, you lush. You leave Matthew Moran alone. He has nothing to do with Kinsale. Nothing." Her voice screeched into the higher registers on the last word.

The residual headache that still throbbed behind my eyeballs notched up several points on the pain meter.

"You didn't love him. I don't think you've ever loved anyone but Desiree."

"Keep her out of this," Crystal screamed. "Or I'll . . ." Her voice broke off as she looked wildly around the room.

She was looking for something to bash my head in with. I managed to kick the chair out of the way before she got her hands on it, and in the same move, tripped her. Thumping on the floor, she flailed as I leaned on her shoulders to keep her down. She was tiny but as strong as anyone I'd ever known.

"I don't believe you. What's going to happen when I tell your old lover I know the secret you've been keeping? What's he going to do to you in here? He can't get to you."

"You stupid shit," she moaned. "You really think I care what happens to me?"

"Desiree." Of course.

"She's safe with her father. He won't let anyone hurt her."

I knew Jack would do what he could to protect any child of his. It was just that I didn't have any idea what he'd be up against. Or what I was facing, for that matter.

"How the hell can you say that? Didn't you notice that Trey Kinsale was missing body parts? And he was a hell of a lot stronger than Jack Bland." Tears streamed down her face so fast they hit the floor like rain.

"Tell me what Moran did. I'll see that he's held accountable. Mr. Amos will do what he can, I know him well enough to know he's a decent guy, he'll . . ." I broke off as her eyes grew wild and she landed a fist on my chin. She hit me hard enough my head rattled.

Oh good, the headache was working its way to migraine status. Releasing her, I backed off and headed for the door.

"Okay, you won't help me, I'll go into this blind. You'll be responsible if he does anything to Desiree." I'd played the hand and now I'd find out if my bluff worked.

My cell phone, thrown deep in my pocket at the last minute in case I needed to call the police when I met Moran, trilled its cheery ringer. I wanted to toss it in the hall, but it wasn't going to shut up. It was easier to answer it.

"Yeah," I snarled. "Jefferson here."

"Good thing I caught you." Owen sounded much too jovial, as if he were trying hard to be charming. "Where are you now? I thought we were getting together, but June said you went out quickly. Don't see you here where I am, thought maybe you were standing me up."

Hauling in the hot, fetid air of the interview room, I worked to steady my voice. Crystal was circling me like a wounded tiger with murder in her eyes. The way she looked now, I could believe she'd sliced Trey Kinsale to ribbons.

"Visiting my client."

"When you could be with me? I'm crushed."

I forced a laugh. He was trying much too hard. "Owen, cut it out. I'll call you when I'm free."

"You do that." His voice had gone flat. "If and when that ever happens."

The cell phone filled with dead air. Sliding it back into my pocket, I was stunned by how quickly he'd turned from flirtatious into downright surly.

"Yeah, I will, Owen," I muttered as I turned to call for the guard to release me from the locked room.

Crystal had balled up into a corner. Her hair swept over her face as she hid it in her hands. Afraid to get closer, I kept one eye on the corridor and the other on her.

"Can't you just give me a hint? I'm flying blind here, and if I crash-land, you're going down with me." Guilt worked on some people, not on others. I waited to find out which one Crystal was.

"I know Moran killed Trey. Just tell me why. It'll give Frank a reason to pick him up, question him at the very least. Maybe I can get you out on bond pending a release hearing if they file charges."

I was dreaming if I thought for one second that my client was going to help herself. Crystal blended into the ugly interview walls as if she belonged there.

"No, no, no," she moaned like a mantra.

I didn't like the sound of it one bit. For a second, I thought of asking Frank to send one of his men with me to meet Moran, but that would have been like asking the rat to stick his head in the trap while the cat held the mechanism open for him to insert it.

"You don't know what you're doing here. You'll kill my daughter."

"Not if Moran's behind bars, he won't." I ignored her use of the personal pronoun referring to me.

I got no answer. Leaving her sobbing on the floor, I felt like a first-class jerk and an even bigger fool of a lawyer. Our no-confidence issues were front and center with no answer in sight. It was too late to start over with the attorney–client relationship gig.

As I was hurrying to my parked Mustang, the damned cell phone trilled again. It was trying to drive nails into my head and succeeding.

"What?" I snarled once again.

"June here. Susan Moran just called, left a message that she knew you were meeting her husband, that she's called Mr. Amos to stop you. Something about a prosecutor would get your attention when he locked you up, and you'd leave her husband alone."

I couldn't believe Susan wanted to save her husband's ass. Somehow, her own was on the line here.

"Oh, goody gumdrops. Did she happen to know where I'm meeting her hubby?"

"Nope. She was fishing, though. Played dumb about it. By the way, where the heck *are* you meeting him?"

"Downtown," I sighed. "At the store." There were a lot of things I should have pieced together before now and still hadn't.

I guess at Susan Swinford Moran's stage of life, any man was better than none. I didn't agree with that particular bit of wisdom, but I knew many women who did.

"Okay, well, I'll holler if there's any good news."

June wasn't buying the cheery act. "Your no-good client give you any help?"

"Shit, no. Why should she? She's convinced Moran'll hurt her kid."

"Then it's a good thing Mrs. Moran called Mr. Amos."

"Not if Owen gets to Moran before me. I don't want him throwing the son of a bitch in jail before I get him to talk. I *have* to find out what he told Crystal that she gave to Kinsale. It's the only way I can prove motive, that Crystal didn't have it and Moran did."

"Be careful, you sorry excuse for a lawyer. Don't you know you're supposed to wear expensive suits and carry a Gucci briefcase while you let everyone else do the dirty work?"

"Naw, that's no fun. I hate suits, you know that. Gotta run. See if you can stall Owen."

She hung up first. I drove downtown like a bat out of hell.

I pulled into the alley, a narrow dirt strip designed for the local garbage pick-up and that was all. Wynnton had risen out of the ashes of Sherman's swath of destruction across the South willy-nilly and as fast as the town fathers could rebuild. I didn't see Moran's minivan anywhere, and figured he must walk to work. Commuter traffic never had been, never would be, a problem in Wynnton.

I parked the Mustang behind Swinfords' back door and waited. He must have been keeping an eye out for me because he squeezed through the space between the door and the car before I could back up to give him more room. The Lieutenant Moran in *Newsweek* had been a lot thinner.

"I don't ever want to see you again," he hissed at me. "There's nothing more I can tell you." His face glistened as his beady eyes darted from one end of the alley to the other.

"Probably not." I climbed over the door of the Mustang.

"I just want you to know that I know your secret, too. It's going to be a pleasure taking you down. What kind of slime lets a woman with a kid take a fall for him? Ooops, I forgot, it's been well documented that you lost your conscience in Vietnam."

I felt cheap, playing him like this. But if he didn't tell me what Crystal was willing to die for to keep secret, she was going to the white gurney in the death house.

Glancing nervously inside Swinfords, Moran slunk as far inside the half-opened door as he could and keep an eye on me. Then he laughed. I'd never heard such an awful sound.

"I'm sick of the whole fuckin' thing. Sick of keeping his secret, sick of you, sick of Crystal, sick of my wife, sick of this town," he chanted. "You think you're so smart, you tell Owen Amos you know all about him."

I bit my tongue before I spit out an incredulous "Owen?" Instead, I tried a cool, low-key, "He knows I know."

"So you're no better than me, you bitch."

I didn't know what to say, so I shrugged. He was probably right.

My heart pounded and the headache kicked it into another gear. What could Owen have to do with Matthew Moran?

"I couldn't believe it when he fell into town, like a golden apple off a tree. Didn't have any way of paying Kinsale the kind of money he wanted, until Owen decided he wanted to get elected prosecutor. And more. Got to give it to him, he's making all the right moves to get to the statehouse. Higher, even, I hear."

Owen, Owen, what did you get yourself into? I held my breath, afraid of what Moran was about to spill.

"I thought you said Crystal gave you money when you asked her." The tremble in my voice was more than nerves. I suddenly felt very chilled in the steamy shadows thrown by the storefronts on Main Street into the alley where Moran and I met like drug dealers counting our cash.

"I only did that once. Just before Kinsale died. When Owen said he was through paying me." He never used the word *blackmail*.

"Let me get this right. You were paying blackmail to Kinsale to keep him quiet about your affair with Crystal. Owen Amos was on the other end of the stick, paying you to keep quiet about his little secret. Is that about the extent of it?"

I hoped I sounded more confident than I felt, because I still didn't know what Owen had to do with Moran's secret or why he was paying him to keep quiet. Whatever it was, it wasn't good. I wanted to throw up. How could Owen be involved in this mess?

"Just about." Sneering, he looked as if he could easily slice certain body parts off me. "The only reason he didn't get caught in the court-martial was that he hid out when the shit hit the fan, then shot himself in the foot so he'd be med-evaced to Saigon. Everyone else took a fall when I did, except Owen. I kept my mouth shut, so did my men. We took care of our own." He sounded inordinately proud.

"Refresh my memory. You're saying Owen Amos took part in the massacre that you ordered?" I wish I'd read more of the history of Lieutenant Moran that June had downloaded.

"Some candy-assed news reporter had to be there. Caught a ride with us the day we hit that village full of gooks." He practically shone with disgust. "We were doing the job we got paid to do, and the brass took us off at the knees to make it look like we were the bad guys. Shit, we got paid fifty bucks an ear. Know who paid us? The fucking United States government, your tax dollars and mine at work. Owen was one of the best at getting the ears off." He laughed as if he'd heard the funniest joke on the planet.

Every inch of me hurt. "You told Crystal that Owen was under your command, and that he mutilated dead Vietcong, didn't you?"

"Not just the VC, honey. Anyone with slanty eyes we could nail." A quick nod of the head, and his eyes sought the interior of Swinfords again. He was probably keeping an eye out for his eavesdropping wife.

I gagged and bit it back. My fingers ached, I was squeezing them behind my back so tightly.

"Owen was never brought up on charges, so when he showed up in Wynnton, you figured you had a cash cow. Only you made the mistake of telling Crystal, didn't you? And she just never could keep a secret from Trey Kinsale."

"Guess so. Crystal's got to learn to keep her mouth shut, but hey, she won't be around much longer to worry about it. Way I hear it, she's begging to get it over with."

Money. June had been right. Follow the money. Trey had put the squeeze on Owen Amos, too. Stars exploded behind my eyeballs. I needed to get out of there as fast as I could, but Moran was still running at the mouth. For a man who'd kept a secret a long time, he sure wasn't good at keeping it now.

Crystal, either. Trey Kinsale had used her to get what he wanted from the men who'd talked to her as if she weren't smart enough to understand what they were saying. I guess she had her revenge on all of them, but in the end, Kinsale had taken her down with him. She was sitting in jail for his murder, and in a way, she was responsible.

"I needed money, and shit, he owed me for not ratting him out. The rest of the guys in the platoon faded into the woodwork, like I did. Just my good luck Owen popped up here in Wynnton, ambitious as all get-out."

"He didn't take off." I would have. I had.

"Where was he going to run? I know his game plan, hell, the whole county does. All I had to do was call the Democrats and let them know one of their rising stars had a, shall I say, unpleasant past. There's bound to be something in his military file, even if he didn't end up in Leavenworth. If not, I'd be glad to talk to any reporter who might be interested. For the good of our community, of course."

Moran was one hell of a lot smarter than I'd given him credit for. Or dumber, I wasn't sure which.

"So you killed Trey because he was milking your cash cow, that it?"

Eyes toward the interior of the jewelry shop, he wasn't listening to me. Moran was blabbing away, not paying attention to a word I said, as if he were trying to convince me he wasn't such a bad guy after all. I'd bet my bottom dollar he'd done the same with Crystal. She probably hadn't wanted to hear this any more than I did.

"Hell, I'd have left him alone, kept my mouth shut if it hadn't been for that pig Kinsale. I took care of my men. We stuck together, no matter how bad it got. I got my pride."

Drawing himself up, he looked as if he were trying to shuck away the poundage of shame. I wanted to run as far away from him as I could get, but it was too late for that. This time, I was stuck. Wynnton was the end of the road for me.

Anger flushed my skin, sent rivulets of sweat trickling between my breasts. I'd never be able to respect Owen

Amos again, no matter how long ago his mistakes, and I was the poorer for it. I wanted my damned Jefferson pride to take a long ride, but I was stuck with it. Pride wouldn't let me be friends, much less anything more intimate, with a man who'd done what Owen had done. I didn't want to think about it.

I tore out of the alley as if all the ghosts of the Vietnamese killed by Moran and Owen Amos were after me. Blowing through a stop sign, I tried my cell. I had to call Frank and get him to arrest Moran, pull in Owen. Owen knew Moran had killed Kinsale, and that made him an accessory after the fact.

I couldn't see straight enough to drive and hit the tiny numbers on the phone. Pulling to the curb, I glared at the world through eyes that weren't focusing very well as I tried to dial the sheriff's office once more. No bars on the battery signal. I'd forgotten to charge it.

I fussed and fumed enough during the short ride home to turn myself into one ugly-tempered woman with a blooming headache that was taking on gigantic proportions.

Why did the man I wanted to get interested in and the one I'd once loved have to turn into such losers? Maybe, I reasoned not for the first time, because a loser attracts other losers.

22

〜〜〜

I'D given myself a king-sized headache by the time I parked and went inside to face June.

"I'll be upstairs," I muttered as I grabbed the newel post to keep my balance. I hadn't had one of these crushing head-killers in a long time. "I don't want to talk to anyone else today. Tell whoever wants me that I'm out of town. Tell 'em I've died. I don't care."

June wasn't at her desk. I was too ill to check anywhere else for her, but I knew she'd have come running to ask questions once she heard me. Prying open one eye, I checked her computer. Turned off. Everything put away on her desk.

She'd gone to keep the appointment I'd blown off with the psychiatrist, I hoped. I couldn't remember what day I was supposed to meet him. That was my last cogent thought as I crawled up the stairs to my bed.

Matthew Moran had gotten away with murder this long, he could stay out of lockup for a few hours more. Besides, he wasn't going anywhere that Susan Swinford Moran couldn't find him. I had to take something for the headache before I ripped my head off and kicked it out the window. The bastard would have to wait to get what he deserved, but he'd get it. Oh yeah, I'd make sure he found out that women weren't as stupid as he thought Crystal and Susan were.

Stripping down to my underwear, I popped in a pill I'd had prescribed the first time one of the headcrushers had hit me, and stretched across Miss Ena's bed, trying not to think. Pulling the blinds, dragging a pillow over my face, I concentrated on breathing. Every in-and-out of my lungs took an effort. I wanted to hold my breath until I passed out.

Not thinking wasn't working. My brain was firing in overdrive.

State investigators would have to get down to Wynnton. If my common sense had been working, I would have tracked down a number and called it right then. All I wanted at that moment was for the powerful little pill to kick in. I wept with pain, with frustration, with my inability to do what needed doing.

What I wouldn't do was get a drink. I didn't need a drink if I could get through the next minute without one. The minute after that would be easier, and so on until I would be free.

I thought of cool mountains, silvered streams, fresh breezes, anything to block out the image of twisted, mutilated bodies that had accompanied the *Newsweek* article on Moran's court-martial. Then I visualized ears, all of them the same, all cut from one man, Trey Kinsale. Owen looked on and laughed.

I had refused to make the connection until I was alone in a darkened room and I had to face it or take a drink.

I don't know when the prescription kicked in, but there was finally darkness. When I struggled out from beneath the pillow I'd placed over my face, I was dreaming I was being suffocated by an earless Kinsale backed up by equally mutilated Vietcong in black pajamas.

Soaked in sweat, I felt like I had a hangover. At least my mind was working clearly enough to remember I was supposed to eat something when I took the medication. I couldn't remember eating today. Afraid to turn on the lights in case they triggered another onslaught, I figured I'd find the kitchen in the dark. I knew my way around the house drunk, I could certainly find the refrigerator in the dark.

Edging my way into the hallway, I couldn't see a light blazing anywhere. June must have returned and shut off all the lamps. Bless her.

Inching back to my bedroom, I pulled on the shorts and T-shirt I'd thrown at the foot of the bed. I'd get something in my stomach, then I'd worry about Owen. Moran was off the radar and already convicted, as far as I was concerned.

I had to call Frank Bonnet. He'd give me a hard time, but he'd do something about Owen. Frank was a native of Wynnton like me; he would put pressure on Owen to resign his job. One thing about Southerners, we may be disgusted with our own miscreants, but they're ours, born and bred. The outsiders can damn well take their dirty linen to some other creek.

I didn't think Owen would run—for whatever reason, he believed his secret was safe with Moran, and that Crystal

was on her way to death row. My head was a dull throbbing
sore, allowing me to walk upright and think limited
thoughts. Yes, definite progress on the physical side. The
emotional remained twisted into a knot.

I didn't bother with shoes. I tried to remember what
June had stocked in the fridge as I padded downstairs with
extreme care and limped along the narrow hallway leading
to the kitchen in the back. The old ice box, as I still thought
of it, was tucked between the end of the drainboard and the
cabinets on the wall facing the backyard. Pulling the handle, I stared into darkness. No hum of its old motor, no
blast of semi-cold air. The fridge had been off a while.

Befuddled, I considered the possibility of a blown fuse.
Still wondering when it had gone out, I heard a noise that
sent me into a mild panic. The back door was opening very
slowly, as if whoever was using it didn't want to be heard.
I started to call out, hoping it was June returning to check
on me, but I didn't. My internal alarm system clanged
loudly enough to work its way into my foggy mind.

I wished I had a flashlight. I wished I owned a flashlight
with working batteries. I wished I were upstairs asleep, so
I didn't have to find out who was breaking into my house.
Because of the fire in the shed, June would have made sure
the house was securely locked in the back. I trusted her. I
didn't know if I'd locked the front door, but it didn't matter
now. Whoever was creeping in was using the kitchen door.

I suddenly remembered the police Owen had said would
be watching me and the house. I hadn't seen one, not all
day. Sliding my fingers around the first thing I could feel,
the butter dish, I clutched it in my fist as I tried to hold my
breath. Whoever was at the back door was inside the
kitchen, moving swiftly around the table set up at that end
of the big room. I could make out a dark shadow, moving

so quietly I never would have heard him if I hadn't been standing there when the door opened.

Normally, that door squeaked on its ancient hinges. Whoever this was, he'd been professional enough to lubricate them before he broke in. I was terrified. The ordinary redneck burglar I could handle. But a professional was beyond my experience. If this was the shed-burner, I was in trouble.

I'd underestimated Matthew Moran. He'd killed women in Vietnam, what was one more in Wynnton? He couldn't frame me for murder and get away with it, as he had Crystal. I didn't have anyone I loved enough to die to protect and he knew it. For a terrifying moment, I knew what he'd do—he'd make it look like I'd had too much to drink and fallen down the stairs and snapped my neck.

Or I'd passed out smoking in bed. It didn't matter that I don't smoke, no one would look closely enough because Owen would make sure I was shuffled into the dead case files. Moran had the perfect protection system going, a prosecutor who'd protect him because he couldn't afford to wake up one morning and see Moran on the national news, talking about old war crimes.

Moran outweighed me by at least sixty pounds and I was too weak from the headache to put up much of a fight.

My only weapon was my knowledge of the old house and its peculiarities. I didn't want to learn the hard way how out-of-shape I was, but I was going to have to make a run for it. Pressing my back to the end of the cabinet next to the drainboard, I could see the room if I turned my head sideways. I was also protected from the ambient night slivering through the kitchen window positioned high above the sink and curtained with an old striped curtain that did little to block light.

Clutching the butter dish to my stomach, I tried to quell the shaking controlling me. I barely breathed, certain Moran would hear each exhalation. My eyes discerned each shade of gray and pale silver of the night as thoroughly as a cat's, I was so hyper.

The dark shape crept swiftly into the hallway. I waited until I heard a footstep on the first tread going upstairs before I made my break for it. I wasn't as agile as the dark figure—I crashed a hip into a chair and cried out as I realized what I'd done.

The back door was open. I didn't give a damn what he heard now, I opened my mouth to scream my fool head off. My throat constricted, I couldn't breathe, and little more than a hissy-fit of a squeak came out, but I thought I was yelling to beat the band. Thundering down the back porch, I raced for the side yard where I could cut my way to Woolfolk Avenue before he caught me. At least, that was my last conscious thought as my chin hit the lawn and dirt rammed up my nostrils.

I couldn't breathe. I tried to roll over, but the weight on my back was too heavy. My face smashed into the grass, I knew I was in trouble. Serious trouble.

"Thought you had me, didn't you? Heard you talking to Moran in the alley. Wasn't hard, half the world told me where you'd gone. Knew you'd figure it out, smart girl like you." Owen didn't sound like himself, but I knew who it was. This wasn't a prescription-induced nightmare, not with his knees in the small of my back.

"You were inside the store. That's why Moran kept looking back." I tasted dirt and grass.

"He didn't know I was there. Just like you didn't until just now." His low laugh hummed with the thrill of a man who was enjoying every minute. "Thought he was so smart, meeting you without his wife catching him,'cause she was looking hard. Told her you were meeting her husband in a bar, and she bought it. Hightailed out of there to catch you two." His laughter wasn't pleasant.

"I saw you just now, you cocksucker. Saw you coming through the door."

"Just luck. And yours has run out."

"There's no such thing as luck." I twisted to try to throw him off me. Failed. Parnell Moses hadn't believed in luck, either.

He sounded like Owen, but not like Owen. I was fighting the panic that threatened to kill me before he did. Consciously, I willed myself to relax, forcing my muscles to go limp.

He didn't expect that. Thinking I'd lost consciousness, he jerked my head up by the hair. I was beyond pain, lost in the knowledge I was going to die and I couldn't do anything about it.

"I liked you," he hissed in my ear. "You've got balls, Tal Jefferson. If you hadn't gone digging in my dirt, Trey Kinsale would have had company in hell when Crystal bought the big one. Figured you'd do a bad job of representing her, which is why I didn't worry about you. No one cares about her; shit, no one cared about Trey. Two worthless lives for mine."

"Isn't that egotistical overkill?"

I don't know where my voice came from. The words had been in my brain, they just worked their way out without my thinking. If I kept on talking and he continued to answer, he wasn't slitting my throat.

He had the gall to laugh louder. The neighbors were half an acre away. "That's the way it works. Survival of the fittest."

"You're scum. Worse than Kinsale. Not even half as good as Crystal. At least she loves her kid." I spit grass out of my mouth.

His laugh was less spontaneous this time. "You have no idea what kind of bastard Kinsale was. Seems my good friend Lieutenant Moran told his piece of ass on the side, Miss Crystal Fucking Walker, that I'd served under him in Vietnam, even showed her a picture of us together, holding a string of bounty ears. The little bitch told Kinsale so he could put the screws to me, too. Moran was bad enough, but him, I'd handle. Eventually, just like I did all the others. It's taken thirty years, but Moran's the only one left from the platoon."

I was going to be sick. "How'd you get away with it?" Egotist that he was, he'd love to talk about himself, at least I was betting so.

"A car crash here, heart attack there. All very mundane deaths. Kinsale wasn't worth the time or effort. Besides, he acted like a gook. Stupid. Deserved to die like one." He spit beside me.

I flinched. His weight on my back was crushing, and my spine screamed in pain.

"Why didn't you kill Moran a long time ago? Then Kinsale would have had nothing to back up his blackmail."

"Thought about it. But it wouldn't have worked to my advantage. Think about the headlines—Baby Killer Convicted of Vietnam Massacre Murdered. The press would have been all over it. Sooner or later, someone would have put us together. I'm a very patient man."

His weight shifted on me, and I wished now that he'd just get it over with. I was beyond pain and into agony.

"He'd have died before I moved up another notch on the ladder. You know about ambition, don't you? Sure you do.

Then you fucked up. Until then, I'll bet you climbed on heads all the way to the top. We're more alike than you realize." He sniggered like a schoolyard bully. "Can't tell me you wouldn't have done the same, in my place.

"Crystal was my wild card—but as long as her kid was within my reach, I had her shut down. She'd have died and she still will, keeping her frickin' mouth shut for the first time in her pathetic life."

My breath ripped in my throat in sobs. I refused to die crying. Swallowing hard, I kept the words coming.

"It would have come out one day, someone would have seen your picture and talked to the press. It was a matter of time, is all." Talking about the future was depressing. Mine wasn't going to last through the night.

His cackles filled my ears until they hurt.

"I made sure it didn't come out. None of them are left but Moran. I was waiting for the right time, is all. But the bastard doesn't do anything but sit in that hovel of a jewelry store and go home to that bitch of his. He doesn't even drive a car. But his time was coming. I just couldn't get him out of the way too close to Kinsale."

"Why kill Kinsale? Why not just keep on paying him?"

"For a smart woman, you can be stupider than shit. You tell me why."

At least he was still talking, and so was I. I tried to think.

"You couldn't control him. Moran hung onto his shame, enough that he wasn't bleeding you dry. You paid him peanuts compared to Kinsale, right? Kinsale was a bloodsucker who wanted more. And you needed to make sure he never talked again about what he'd learned from Crystal."

"Bingo! The litte lady has all the right numbers!"

"So what about me? Why were you . . ." I couldn't say "flirting." "Why were you so civil with me?"

"Come on, Tal, don't be naive. You told me more than my own investigators. I could keep tabs on you so easily, I should have put you on retainer. Thought I'd drop the charges against Crystal, didn't you? That I'd see the case your way." The chuckle wasn't charming.

I couldn't take in everything he was saying. He'd killed more than Kinsale and he'd been keeping tabs on me?

"Why frame Crystal? Why do that to her? For God's sake man, you've sworn to uphold the law." I was throwing away words.

He didn't give a shit what I said. Gloating was giving him a hard-on. Ego and politics, perfect bedfellows. Minus the insanity and murderous tendencies, Owen would have been the perfect candidate for higher public office.

"She knew too fucking much. Told her I'd make sure her kid died if she said another word about me to anyone. You in particular. You, I couldn't control, not completely. Like Kinsale. Didn't want you dead too soon, though. Had to make it look good. Shame you got yourself out of that shed.

"Figured you'd go on a bender one of these days, I could get rid of you easy enough. Then everyone involved in this sorry mess would be out of my hair, and I could get on with my life, run for congressman next. I'm a shoo-in, the Dems tell me. The right man at the right time, me being a veteran and all."

"And Moran? He'd let you get that far?"

"I'd have paid him for a while longer. Like I said, I had him under control. Money made him happy. Shit, he's not getting any sex with Crystal locked up. His time was coming, just not right this second."

Money. Money for Moran to buy his way out of Wynnton now that he didn't have to pay off Kinsale. I'll bet

Moran would have kept putting it to Owen as long as Owen was willing to pay. The fat slob hadn't known his days were running out.

"Sorry I went on the wagon. This would have been easier drunk."

His knee in the small of my back was excruciating. Pain, facing death, discussing my drinking, wasn't putting me in the best frame of mind. I grunted.

"You'll trip up. One of these days, you'll make a mistake and it'll be over for you."

I tried to tell myself it was true. But deep down, I knew that men like Owen Amos didn't get caught; they lived to a ripe old age, while innocent men like Parnell Moses died for sins they didn't commit.

He'd relaxed his grip on my hair a bit. Sucking in as much air as I could, I let loose with a scream I thought would be heard on Main Street. Growling, he twisted my head sideways like a pro. I could hear tendons in my neck cracking. I didn't want to think about my neck bones and what was happening to them.

"It'll look like you got drunk and fell down the back porch steps. Easy. Just like the fire in the shed. If you hadn't gotten through the floor, I would have had you dead to rights then. Pick up the pieces of rope that didn't burn, and *voilá,* accidental death."

The false camaraderie was gone. This was the trained killer, the boy who'd cut ears for trophies.

"Why'd you stuff Kinsale's ear down his throat?" I was losing consciousness.

"Because the bastard wouldn't listen to me. Wanted more money than God. Told him he'd gotten greedy. Like the gooks. Give 'em a candy bar, they wanted your boots. Got to teach 'em a lesson, all the gooks who don't listen.

You gotta listen, Tal, remember that when you get to hell."

My ears hurt with words. My mind swirled with images of dead Vietnamese without their ears, with how I'd look dead and lying at the foot of my back steps, grass in my mouth, eyes vacant.

Red, then orange, the pinpricks of light burst behind my eyeballs. I wondered, vaguely, if I was going to see that light everyone talks about at the end, but the light that was coming at me was hot and brighter than any afterlife could be.

I heard voices shouting from somewhere close to me. Owen cursed. I saw boots out of the corner of one eye. The gurgle that came out of my throat wasn't loud enough to sound like a dying kitten.

"Tal!"

The voice drifted from far, far away. A loud crack, like a two-by-four smashing into the hood of a car, another one that splintered my ear drums, screaming sounds that I didn't recognize. The pressure on my back lightened for a second and instinctively, I tried to roll over to claw at Owen with my hands, which he no longer pinned to my side with his knees.

Only I couldn't move. My legs, jammed tighter to the ground than my back had been, froze where they were. He'd broken my back, I'd never walk again, I sobbed.

Warmth, hot, and sticky dripped over my legs like syrup. If I could feel, maybe I wasn't paralyzed. Once more, I dug my fingers into the grass and tried to haul myself away from Owen, away from the death that had loosened its grip for one second.

"Got him, he ain't movin' again!" The cry was surreal.

"Tal, hold still, let me see where he's hurt you." Henry knelt beside me, his hands stroking my head, his voice worried, frightened. "Just hang on, we'll get you out from under him."

The weight on my legs shifted and I reached for Henry, though I feared he was a dream.

"What's going on?" I rasped.

"Frank shot him. The bastard's dead." Henry wiped my forehead with his hand, his fingers trailing down my neck where I could feel him pressing them against the artery. "Stay calm, Frank's called for an ambulance."

"Are my legs broken?" I couldn't imagine why they wouldn't move.

"No, Frank hit him dead center. Knocked him backwards." Henry was trying to sound clinical.

"She's free," Frank grunted. "I'll hit the lights on the cruiser."

I didn't want to look around and see Owen. "Is he dead?"

"Oh yeah." Frank kneeled on my other side. "She hurt, Henry? All that blood his, or some of it hers? Need a tourniquet?"

"I'm okay," I rattled deep in my throat. The words may not have been clear to Frank and Henry, but I heard them loud and clear. "I'm okay."

I'd never been so happy to see anyone in my life. If I could have, I'd have kissed Frank and Henry right there and then.

Fortunately, I couldn't. I lost consciousness, fainting for the first time in my life.

23

I called Frank, left a message telling him what you'd said about seeing Moran, and then I went over to Henry's. Told him the same thing when he got home with Grace. Henry decided it couldn't keep until morning."

June was appropriately cocky as she strutted around the front parlor, Henry, Grace, and I her captive audience. Crystal had already collected Desiree from Jack's. I had no idea where she was going, or if she was going anywhere, or what she'd do with Trey's estate. My head and neck hurt too much to care about much beside being alive.

"That was dumber than dirt, Tal. Sheesh, Moran could have been the killer, just like you thought. Then what? You really didn't think he'd try to kill you?" June wasn't going to let up on me for one second.

"Well, he didn't," I snapped. "How was I to know Owen was out for blood?"

Grace intervened.

"Henry said he'd track down Frank and haul him over to talk to Moran, arrest him if he could. Finally found Frank around midnight as he was coming on duty. He'd been fishing down at the reservoir all day, no one radioed him June's message about catching up with you and Matthew Moran. Guess Owen intercepted it." Grace straightened the lamp beside my chair and moved the phone closer. "Frank said he'd need to talk to you first. That's why he and Henry went to your house so late."

"So Owen knew he had to work fast to get rid of me when June told him I was meeting Moran. Then he heard Moran tell me everything. Stupid move, if I say so myself." If I ever held my head up straight again, it'd be a miracle. I thought the tendons were permanently twisted.

"You can say that again." June wasn't cutting me a razor's edge of slack.

Henry gave me a calculating look. "It'd help if you wore that cervical collar the doctor prescribed."

"No, thank you. And look like the whiplashed lawyer? That'd help business for sure."

June laughed. I glared at her.

"So he was hanging around the shed after he set fire to it, just to make sure no one came to the rescue, huh? My mistake for getting out. Guess he figured it would be obvious I'd escaped the fire, he may as well play hero and wait for another chance."

"That about sums it up." Grace rose, patting Henry on the head. "And that's enough for one evening. We need to leave Tal alone so she can rest. On your feet, my love."

Henry groaned but obeyed.

"Call if you need anything, Tal. You hear me?" Grace leaned over to brush her face against mine. "Anything at all."

"Oh, I'm hanging around until she starts taking her mean pills again. Shouldn't take long, she's addicted." June looked as if she dared me to contradict her.

"Me?" I screeched. "Mean? What the hell?"

June turned to Henry and Grace. "See? She's feeling better already."

Laughing, Henry and Grace left the two of us alone. Grace was right, I was exhausted. I'd spent the night at the hospital for "observation," which meant they didn't let me sleep. June had handled the paperwork to get Crystal sprung by noon, but I'd stayed conscious in case she needed me. The pain killers the doctor had prescribed were lying in June's purse. I didn't like the idea of addiction to them, and right now, I wanted to be clear-headed and cogent.

"Tell me about Moran."

"Moran's talking a blue streak. Frank says they can't shut him up. Everything Owen was afraid would come out, has. He knew Owen had killed Kinsale, by the way he did it. Said it was a message for him, to remind him to keep his mouth shut or get sliced and diced. He didn't mind, not as long as he didn't have to fork over the money Owen paid him to Kinsale to keep quiet about Crystal."

"Bet Susan leaves him. Be the best thing she ever did."

I hoped she had a good divorce lawyer, because Moran was going to prison for being an accessory after the fact.

"No kidding. Woman sticks by a man, he ought to have something worth sticking for. Can't say that about Kinsale or Moran."

"Divorced women aren't exactly presidents of the Junior League in Wynnton," I reminded her.

"Who gives a rat's patooty about the Junior League," she laughed.

"Not me, that's for sure." Though Miss Ena had been president once. "Thanks for convincing Henry it was an emergency last night, that he get Frank and that they find me."

"Knew you were in trouble big time. You're welcome."

June steered me into the hall to go upstairs to my bed. My bed, where I planned to spend the next year hiding from the world and June. Especially June, who was getting bossier by the second.

"Does this mean I have to thank Frank Bonnet for saving my life?" I was grumbling all the way up the stairs, June's arm around my waist to steady me.

"Wouldn't hurt a bit. You might say you owe the man."

"All right. But nothing too smarmy."

"I didn't say that." June held me tighter.

"I'm pretty shitty with men," I pulled out of nowhere. "You were right, I was sucking up to Owen big time."

"No kidding," June snorted.

"I really did think he'd see that Kinsale had too many enemies to pin it on Crystal without more investigating." I was almost asleep on my feet.

"If he'd been the man you thought he was, he would have."

"You ever make a mistake, about a man?" I was crossing into personal history here, unknown territory for June and me. "Besides your husband?"

"What woman hasn't?" She laughed. "Best thing to do, forget him. Move on. I have."

I straightened up a little taller, moved a little faster up the steps. "You're so right. Just the ticket. At least this mistake didn't cost me my life."

"Thank God for that."

I was genuinely moved. "June?"

"Yes."

"Thanks for being my friend."

Pulling back the old quilt on Miss Ena's bed, she propped up the pillows and settled me in as if I were a child taking a nap. I snuggled down, feeling better than I had in years.

She was in the doorway before she answered.

"Thanks for being mine."

Yes, I thought, *this was going to be an interesting few years until June passed the bar exam.* Then watch out world, Jefferson and Atkins was going to take on the big boys. Nothing would get in our way.

Except, maybe, life. Good thing, I mused sleepily. I liked living a whole lot.